The Children of Grad

Maria Miniailo

translated by Michael Pursglove and Natalia Pniushkova

First published in 2022 by Waterloo Press
95 Wick Hall
Furze Hill
Hove. UK. BN3 1NG

Printed in Times New Roman 11pt by One Digital
Unit 7 Woodingdean Business Park, Sea View Way, Brighton BN2 6NX

Originally published as *Deti Grada* by Maria Minialio
(Kyiv: Summit-knyha [Summit-Books], 2019).

Front cover image: Drawings by children of the Donbass region, Ukraine.
©Museum of Civilian Voices, Founded by the Rinat Akmetov Foundation
<https://civilvoicesmuseum.org/en/about>

Cover image design by Naomi Foyle
Author photo © Anna Belokur-Verkhovskaia

A CIP record for this book is available from the British Library

ISBN: 978-1-915241-03-0

Acknowledgements

The joint translators owe a debt of gratitude to Dmytro Drozdovskyi who first suggested that a translation of this novel be made for an Anglophone readership, and to Naomi Foyle of Waterloo Press, who not only edited the text meticulously and sensitively, but also designed the cover.

Translator's Note

A Word on Proper Nouns:

Grad: an archaic Slavonic word for town or city. Also the Russian and Ukrainian for "hail".
Rusichka: a pejorative term for a Russian woman.

Most Russian given names have at least one alternative affectionate form. Below are the names by which characters in the novel are first referred, followed by variant forms which are used subsequently. These include three formal given names: Svyatoslav, Efim and Mikhail.

Akim: Akimusha.
Fima: Fimka; Efim.
Marusia: Masha; Mashenka. All are affectionate forms of Maria.
Misha: Mikhail.
Sasha: Sashka. Affectionate forms of Aleksandr.
Slavik: Slavka; Slava; Svyatoslav; Slavushka.
Sveta: Svetka. Affectionate forms of Svetlana.
Tanya: Tanyusha. Affectionate forms of Tatyana.
Vera: Verochka.
Viktor: Vitka; Vitya; Vitek; Vitenka.

Dedicated to all the children who grew up early ...

Contents

Part I

Grey Willow Boarding School

Prologue

The Grey Willow Boarding School, which was located in the town of M., lived up to its name in everything. It was grey and faceless from the outside and less-than-stellar in matters of education. The old building was covered with cracks and partially with grapevines climbing up and around it, angrily peeping in at sleeping children at night through the windows. The narrow end of the school was painted blue in order to add imaginary freshness to the appearance of the building. 'Old Lady Willow', as the local inhabitants called the school, did not, however, appreciate the efforts of the painters; it was crumbling and peeling, five floors with narrow grey corridors, barred windows in the basement and a huge courtyard, containing a playground and football goals, and also a caretaker's house: a one-story wooden building.

The town of M. was groomed and good-natured but had long lagged behind the frantic rhythm of its fellows. Bold entertainment, colorful kiosks and posters, big plans and dreams of a happy future bypassed the town, leaving it to vegetate in the shadow of the past. Frankly, it had nothing to brag about. There was a House of Culture in the city-centre where children's amateur performances and a pensioners' choir took place; a cinema which showed old French movies, where the film kept breaking all the time; a central store and, of course, a small cafe. Still, people fell in love and parted here, attended weddings and got dogs. Oh yes! There was also a church in the city, and its bells rang every Sunday for its parishioners to attend the morning service, where Father Vladimir, an always cheerful man, would teach them about certain things.

The Grey Willow Boarding School had been in the town from time immemorial. It had existed even before the arrival of Soviet power, which had at first wanted to demolish an overly 'bourgeois' building, but then changed its mind. Nobody knew what had been in there before the change of regime, or who owned this once magnificent building, and those who did know had long since died. The Soviets established an orphanage for the children of enemies of the people here, which turned into an ordinary boarding school during the Khrushchev thaw, and had housed everyone ever since: orphans, troubled children, children from disadvantaged families.

Eleven-year-old Vitka, who was nicknamed 'Brave', was one of the inhabitants of 'Old Lady Willow'. It was the caretaker Nikichna who jokingly called Vitka 'Brave' after an incident that happened a couple of years before this story begins, when the boy was terribly frightened by her one-eyed, lame and shaggy cat Licorice. Upon first seeing the 'fluffy monster', the boy screamed and fled headlong. This is how the nickname 'Brave' stuck with Vitka, although he was no longer afraid of Licorice and even sometimes stroked the animal.

Vitya was a short, brown-eyed, jug-eared boy. He was not an orphan but was rather 'from a dysfunctional family of the third category'. The headmistress of the boarding school had developed by herself a classification for children from disadvantaged families: the first category was the most problematic and implied parents with bad habits. Vitka's category was the most bearable; he was one of the 'unnecessary' children, whose parents worked hard for long hours and were simply unable to keep an eye on their child. Such couples themselves brought the children to 'Old Lady Willow'. If at all possible, they paid money for their offsprings' stay and sometimes took them home on holidays or on rare weekends. The boy had already been living in the boarding school for four years and didn't miss his parents much, because during his stay here he had been more-or-less weaned off them, and the few memories that were associated with his life before the school were greatly dimmed.

By the time this story starts in earnest, Vitka should have been in the fifth grade, but as some students had been adopted and others had returned to their parents or other family members, there were only two children his age in the whole boarding school, himself and Akim, a Tatar orphan. It was an utter luxury to give lessons to only two boys, so after the fourth grade the children immediately entered the sixth, being now called 'ignorant' and 'idle'. This made Vitya upset; he tried with all his might to catch up with the missed year, but he lacked the strength to learn everything, so all he could do was listen to the insults in silence. Oksana Gennadievna, a teacher of the Russian language, was especially caustic in her statements. She was a short, shapeless young girl and the children called her 'the Rusichka' behind her back. For she was a violent and deeply unpleasant person and deserved to be called a hysterical woman. Neither her face nor her soul was nice. Oksana Gennadievna had a pageboy haircut and a habit of biting her chapped lips and giggling for no reason. She felt angry at life and took special delight in venting her dissatisfaction on children who were more afraid of the Rusichka than death! Oksana Gennadievna loved to make fun of the problems of her students, whether it was about their crooked teeth or their parents' drinking. Oksana Gennadievna would gloat: 'Vitya, it is no surprise that your parents handed you over to us. What's the good of you?' Sometimes she treated the children to blows and put the ones who cried in a corner and made others laugh at them.

Sometimes at night, after the teachers fell asleep, Vitya would quietly leave the room, open the rickety balcony door between the two blocks of bedrooms and stand for a long time in the wind, peering into the impenetrable blackness of the night. He thought about travels and unknown lands, about the fabulous cities that he dreamed of seeing. He just needed to wait a little, some six or eight years, and then he would be free from her, free forever!

A couple of dozen more boys and girls, like Vitya, were also students of the Rusichka. Other children attended Verochka Evgenievna's classes ... But Vitya was not lucky, so for forty-five minutes twice a week he painfully endured the insults and humiliations that were constantly falling onto his head. It seemed to the children that Oksana Gennadievna was the embodiment of 'Old Lady Willow' herself, faceless and grey. But there was one thing that the Rusichka was afraid of. Whenever storm clouds covered the sky, foreshadowing imminent rain, Oksana Gennadievna rushed to her room at full speed, pressed herself into a corner and waited ... Hail. The Russian language teacher was afraid of hail more than anything, which caused her many problems even though it was an infrequent visitor in local latitudes. The sound of ice chips drumming on the ground made her tremble; she cried then and did not leave her room all day. At such moments, the kids jumped out into the street, collected handfuls of hail and threw it into the Rusichka's window. The children laughed and danced, knowing that they would not see her face and the sarcastic expression on it for another day. Vitya even imagined that the hated teacher was now pressing her shapeless body under the bed and asking them to stop. He trilled with laughter and rejoiced with everyone else.

1.

On a dank November morning, when I was seven, my parents silently gathered my things and a few toys (wooden blocks, a grey teddy bear, a spinning top and a dozen tin soldiers) and took me to my new home.

'You will find it nice there,' my mother murmured, neatly folding my shirts and pants. 'There are many kids of your age, and the food will be better than what we have ... Oh yes, and there is heating in winter!' Then my father tied an old woolen scarf around my neck, laced my shoes and off we went to meet my new life. God bless my parents – they were good people. They worked hard to give me a teddy bear or a bar of chocolate for Christmas. Therefore, they had neither time nor strength for me. Their easy decision to put a child into a boarding school was no savagery as far as the inhabitants of the town of M. were concerned. Many couples did this if they had difficulties with finances, like my parents. Once a year they paid in money or state vouchers for their children to have a meal and a soft bed every night, and they remained convinced that nothing bad could happen to him or her. And if it did, well, sorry, this is how fate was. They had done everything they could to make the future of their child if not befitting, then at least bearable.

Thus, in the early morning of November 15th we left our home and headed towards 'Old Lady Willow'. I remember well how penetrating the autumn wind was. I remember the smell of rotting leaves, a damp, pungent smell that clogged my nostrils. I walked through puddles, feeling the cold water sneaking through the light shoes to my toes. My dad said that he and my mum did not have money to buy warm shoes; this is why last year I had spent almost the whole winter at home, watching with envy the neighbourhood boys building snowmen and playing snowballs. We walked further and further, my father carrying my modest child's belongings and my mother holding my hand. They walked very fast, and I often had to start running to keep up with them. Mother was rushing us all the time as if she wanted to hand me over as soon as possible to this new, wonderful world, where it was always warm and the inhabitants were well-fed. While we were walking, I thought about how maybe in the new world I would be given a new warm pair of shoes and in the coming winter would be able to run in the yard and roll in the snow. I also wanted a striped T-shirt with the emblem of an anchor on the chest, like the one that Sergei from the tenth apartment had, and a box of multi-colored chewing gum. My father said that Sergei's brother was a 'chelnok', a shuttle trader, as we called such entrepreneurs, so it was obvious where the kid got such T-shirts from, as well as other imported rags and things. I knew that when I grew up, I would become a shuttle too – my cupboard would be packed with boxes of chewing gum, and I would be able to switch T-shirts every day! I just had to grow up as soon as possible.

As we approached the gates of Grey Willow Boarding School, the pale sun turned the world to gold and a grey building, my future 'home', appeared before our eyes. I think I will always remember my first impression of 'Old Lady Willow' ... The building seemed huge to me then! A giant, looming overhead. I had never seen anything like it before! I felt scared. I started trembling and clung to my mother, wrapping my arms around her. She pushed me away, and shouted at me, telling me to behave myself, I had to make a good impression. I cried. I did not want this new, magnificent world at all, however magical it was. I did not want many kids and new shoes. I wanted to go home. I was crying hard but my parents didn't react to my moaning; my dad just patted me slightly on the shoulder: 'You are a man after all. Dry your eyes.'

A couple of minutes after we approached the gates of 'Old Lady Willow', an old caretaker, Lyudmila Nikitovna, or simply Nikichna, came out, a hunchbacked woman with sallow skin and a good-natured face.

'Hadmistress ordered to leading you through the black entrance. They're repairing a cornice in the front. Before you knowing it, falling right at your noddle!' the old woman said in odd broken Russian and burst out laughing. She stroked me on the head, calling me 'a nice little fellow', and led us in, closing the creaky gates of the orphanage.

'This is a good place. Don't be sad.' The caretaker smiled, noticing my tear-stained face. 'The kids are just small crooks, there's usually beetroot with spuds and noodles soup, no bedbugs, all clean. The hadmistress often hauls the nannies over the coals because of dirt. It's good here, kid,' said the old woman, moving quickly along the long corridor. Having passed what seemed to me like a hundred doors, we finally reached the headmistress's office.

'Leave your belongings here, Styopka will carry them to your bedroom later,' Nikichna said, leaving us alone.

Klara Fyodorovna, who had held the post of headmistress of the boarding school for thirty years, was a small, dry woman with dyed red hair and shifting blue eyes. She spoke quietly and slowly, and her speech was extraordinary, I had never before heard anyone speak so beautifully (as it turned out later, this is what speaking correctly sounded like). I liked this unusual woman; she smiled mildly, looking at me with a certain compassion. After discussing all the important organizational and financial issues with my parents, Klara Fyodorovna firmly shook my father's hand, and we all went out into the corridor; my things were no longer there.

I said goodbye to my parents at the large wooden doors of the main entrance. Nikichna said that the workers had gone to have a bite to eat, so nothing would fall on our heads. The doors were antique, with intricate carvings.

'They knew how to build then, they definitely did,' Klara Fyodorovna sighed, noticing my interest in the doors. I did not know when 'then' was, but I liked the mysterious meaning of her words. Mum and Dad hugged me, asking me to behave and not to cause too much trouble for the teachers. I closed my lips tightly, trying not to cry, but my eyes were still wet.

'Will you take me back soon?' I asked, pressing my forehead into my mother's belly. My parents didn't answer but hugged me once again and disappeared behind the huge carved doors, which, perhaps, still remembered the touch of some honourable visitor from the past.

So, I was seven years old when my parents gave me up for permanent residence to 'Old Lady Willow', a boarding school for orphans, troubled children and children from disadvantaged homes, headed by a thin, red-haired woman.

2.

I had a hard time during the first year. The older boys often hurt us little ones. They poured icy water over us in the middle of the night, stuffed paper into our mouths, and threw our clothes down the toilet. It was painfully insulting, because we could not resist them, and that is why the only thing left was to endure the torment. The truth is this lasted for only a year, until I settled in and got used to the new rules. Having learned to hit back, albeit uncertainly, I managed to inspire respect for myself, and the older boys reduced their bullying to nothing, only giving me a kick occasionally. But this also stopped when Slavik joined the school, a year and a half after I did.

Slavik was several years older than me. He was a tall, skinny boy with disproportionately long arms and legs, large feet and a straight nose. His skin was pale, and under his right eye there was a small birthmark shaped like an exploding star. When he appeared at 'Old Lady Willow', the older boys happily rubbed their hands, anticipating future abuse of the ridiculous Slavka. However, they did not know that this funny and skinny boy had been given Code No. 15 by Klara Fyodorovna, which meant 'exuberant and unbalanced, with violent tendencies'. On his first night, when Slavik was awakened by icy water being poured over him, he demonstrated firsthand the meaning of Code No. 15. The older ones did not touch him anymore, fearing for their already bent noses. I admired the newcomer! That is why, having heard in the toilet three fifteen-year-old boys conspiring to 'teach an upstart a lesson', I immediately ran to Slavik to warn him.

'How do you know?' asked Slavik, spitting on the floor.

'I heard it in the toilet,' I answered timidly.

'Eavesdropping, right?' He gave me a dismissive look.

'I heard it ... accidentally ...' I mumbled, upset that Slavka did not appreciate my efforts to 'save' him.

'Oh, come on!' Suddenly he broke into a smile. 'You did the right thing by coming to me. Now I owe you, kid. What's your name?'

'Vitya.'

'Well, Vitka, together we'll put things in order here!' Slavik exclaimed, patting me on the shoulder.

The older ones' plan failed miserably the night they came to 'teach the newcomer a lesson'. Slavka was not in bed. Instead, under the covers lay a pile of clothes and newspapers, which was hit by not only hands and feet, but also by knuckledusters. When the boys realised that Slavka was not there, it was too late. Having approached silently from behind, he suddenly bestowed hefty blows on all of them with a bronze bust of Alexander the Great, which he had borrowed from the study of the history teacher. It took Slavik no more than thirty seconds to bring the offenders down. The others froze in their beds. Nobody moved, afraid to provoke Slavka's anger. Only I watched with a strange mixture of horror and delight. Having finished with the uninvited guests, Slavik cast a quick glance at me.

'I need help, Vitka,' He handed me the blood-covered bust. 'Can you wash it and return it to the history teacher's study?' he asked me, and without hesitating for a moment, I jumped out of bed, pulled on a sweater and crept down the corridor towards the toilet to 'wash off' the traces of the crime. When the job was done and I returned to the room the boys were no longer on the floor. Slavik had dragged them away from our block and he himself was sitting with his feet on the bed.

'Have you taken it back?' he asked. I nodded silently.

'Well done! You are a true friend, Vitka!' Slavik smiled, hugging me by the shoulders. From that very night, we became best friends. Slavik protected me, and I gladly took part in all his adventures.

According to Klara Fyodorovna's classification, Slavik was 'from a category I dysfunctional family'. His mother drank shamelessly, his father's whereabouts were unknown, and his stepfather was so cruel that he often beat the boy simply out of boredom. There were rumours that the man ran some nasty businesses in Tsyganka, a rough district of the town of M., once quite prosperous, with a large rubber factory. Now Tsyganka was impoverished and served as a refuge for the lower strata of society: pushers, thieves, beggars and alcoholics. Slavik's stepfather often hung around there, though what he was doing was a mystery both for Slavik and for his mother, a woman who, despite being young, was already ruined by drinking.

Since Slavik was left to his own devices, he often ran away from home (which his mother barely noticed), fare-dodged on the tram and jumped off on the outskirts of Tsyganka. He spent hours wandering around the abandoned factory, sniffing glue with locals, throwing stones at the windows and stealing jam rolls. This went on until the boy was involuntarily sent to boarding school, and his mother's parental rights were terminated. The woman cried bitterly, begging them not to take away her 'treasure', but the very next day she seemed to have forgotten that she had a son and his name was Slava. She thought no more about it and continued to drink.

All this and many other things Slavik told me when we were walking around the yard of 'Old Lady Willow'. I was the only one who knew the real-life story of the category 15 boy. To the others, Slavik said that his father was the captain of a whaling ship and was sailing somewhere in the Norwegian Sea, and his mother, a kind, holy woman, was treating malaria victims with the Red Cross in Africa. She was a nurse, a well-read and intelligent woman. So Slavik told the boarding school's inhabitants and everyone believed him and admired him. Only I knew the truth, because Slavik needed to tell it to someone, and he had no real friends except for me. Everyone either feared him or hated him, but I admired his strength and intelligence. Slavik could spend hours talking about everything in the world, telling me about distant countries and mysterious events.

'I once read in the newspaper that the body of an unknown animal was found near Kherson. Hunters shot it, thinking it was a wolf. But how can there be wolves in Kherson?' Slavik giggled,.'That animal looked like a wolf, of course, but it was the size of a tiger, only not striped but grey. Do you know tigers?' I shook my head because I had never heard of tigers. Then Slavik told me about huge striped cats and promised to show me pictures of them in a book on zoology.

'And what about that beast near Kherson?' I asked, eager for more information.

'The scientists took it to the laboratory. They wanted to cut it up, but here's the thing: when they came in the morning, the beast was not there, and the guard who was supposed to guard the body lay bitten to death, with his belly ripped open.'

After hearing such stories, my blood froze in my veins, and at night I dreamed of the fierce mouth of a tiger-wolf, scratching the bedposts.

Sometimes we would run out of the gate, crawl through a small gap, and rush at breakneck speed away from 'home' until the teachers noticed our disappearance. Then we clung to the tram and rode either to Tsyganka or to more decent neighbourhoods of the town of M. and stole something tasty (Slavik was a master at this!). I especially liked to steal 'petushki' on a stick from the old Polish woman who sold them in Tsyganka. The main thing was to get the timing right, when she was surrounded by customers, to sneak up unnoticed and grab a handful of the amber lollipops. Then we would rush headlong, away from the swearing and screams of the old woman. I liked to sit on the damp ground, lick 'petushki' and listen to Slavik's stories. There were times when Slavik sniffed glue, but he wouldn't let me. After taking a couple of breaths, my friend would usually become cheerful and funny; the gloom temporarily left him and he admired the beauty of nature and the brightness of colours. However, after a couple of hours, he became sluggish and silent again. Then we silently returned to the boarding school and scattered, each about our own business. Nevertheless, I really loved our 'forays', because there, behind the gates, Slavik opened up another world to me. A world full of dangers and adventures, significantly different from the grey routine of our everyday life.

The order of life at 'Grey Willow' was simple and understandable to everyone, from the smallest of the children to the caretaker Nikichna. Wake up at 6:30, exercises, bathing, then breakfast. Breakfast usually consisted of oatmeal or buckwheat porridge with milk and bread and butter. At 8:00 a.m., the lessons began, at 11:00 there was an afternoon snack, milk with a bun (they also gave us fruit in summer), then we studied again until lunch, at 2:00 p.m., when we had 'ordinary lunch', as Nikichna put it: noodles soup, potatoes and cutlets or something like that, and sweet compote to drink. After that, until 5:00 p.m., we wandered around, left to ourselves. Some studied, some read in the library, some, like Slavik and me, wandered around the outskirts of M. After a light dinner (in the evenings the cooks did not spoil us too much) we were usually taken to the assembly hall, where one of the teachers read aloud a book in the twilight, often something about travels, like *Treasure Island* by Robert Louis Stevenson or *Hearts of Three* by Jack London. Lights went out at 9:30 pm. That was how boring and featureless our days were. Therefore the rare 'escapes' outside the gates brought me so much pleasure and joy, because it was possible to steal sweet 'petushki' and ride a tram.

3.

In addition to a huge list of standard subjects in the general school curriculum, the ignorant residents of 'Old Lady Willow' were given lessons on theology and ballroom dancing. Both subjects were introduced thanks to Klara Fyodorovna, who had been a famous dancer in her youth, and was a big believer in the divine laws. This lean old woman went to church every Sunday and was one of the few who regularly confessed to Father Vladimir. They usually talked during a slow walk or over fragrant tea, discussing philosophical topics which were incomprehensible to the common people of M.. Klara Fyodorovna, who had long been disappointed with modern life (which she often talked about), believed that religion was the only cure for all human diseases. Drunkenness, violence, profanity: religion had the power to treat them all, one just needed to give it a chance by letting God into one's heart. This belief had lived with the woman from early childhood, but she never forced others to 'believe', and one could refuse to attend theology lessons after the third compulsory lesson.

In spite of the 'free' schedule of visits, however, almost everyone attended the lessons on theology, which were taught by Father Vladimir. Some did so out of fear that this leniency was imaginary, and in the event of skipping class just once, one might get an earful from the headmistress, but basically everyone liked these unusual lessons. Father Vladimir was a short man of 'God knows how many' years of age, with thin hair and a dark face. He spoke softly and often smiled out of the corner of his mouth. There was something good about this man, something divine. Perhaps that is why we attended his lectures once a week so eagerly.

Slavik was one of those brave souls who skipped theology lessons, preferring to take a nap in silence and alone, or read a newspaper. In general, he read many newspapers, fishing interesting facts out of them, and sharing them with me during our forays into the city.

'These saints are only messing around with people's heads!' Slavik spat on the asphalt, wrapping his coat tighter. 'Vitka, they take money from people like us for the needs of the church, but instead they buy clothes and food for themselves.' My friend grimaced.

I disagreed, because Father Vladimir did not take money from us, but on the contrary, often brought something tasty (either apples from his garden, or cheese pies made by his sister). One Christmas, he even put on a real puppet theatre, showing scenes of the birth of Christ. I liked Father Vladimir.

'Well, who knows, maybe Father Vladimir is different. Maybe. Of course, baking pies for everyone is a good thing,' argued Slavik, agreeing with me (which rarely happened).

Unlike the theology lessons, Slavik loved the dance lessons, which were held twice a week. He danced fervently in general, breaking into a fiery dance at the sound of any music that was more-or-less rhythmic. On Wednesday and Saturday, a ballroom dance teacher came to us: Julietta Germanovna, a tall, wiry woman who wore her grey hair styled in a neat high hairdo. Madame Ju, as we usually called this unusual woman, spoke impulsively and loudly, waving her arms, drawing bizarre lines in the air with her thin hands. Madame Ju was in all respects a sophisticated person who did not tolerate ignorance and childishness. She wore a puffy black synthetic skirt.

'*Non! Non, mon cher garçon*!' Madame Ju clapped her hands. 'There are five '*pas*' in your waltz instead of three! This is an unheard-of audacity!' the woman exclaimed, pressing her hand to her chest.

Slavik admired these lessons. He hung on every word Madame Ju said with great enthusiasm (by the way, it was he who came up with such a name for the extravagant dance teacher), with difficulty trying to repeat the steps and movements she showed us. The woman appreciated my friend's efforts, and although she surely must have considered him completely devoid of talent, she never expressed her thoughts out loud. She praised Slavik's clumsy movements, which resembled the dying convulsions of a wounded animal.

But let's go back to the theology lessons and Father Vladimir. Professing Christian morality herself, Klara Fyodorovna never forgot that the Grey Willow Boarding School was an institution for children of different religions. For instance, a Tatar orphan Akim and his younger sister Miwa (and around five more Tatars, who appeared in M. out of nowhere) were Muslims. Samekh Bondar (though we called him Seryozha) was from a Jewish family, like half of the other guys (there were always many Jews in M. and there even was a synagogue on the outskirts); and a little girl, Undra, was Mongolian or Buryat, no one really knew. They said that she was moon-faced and funny because of her father, and her mother was ordinary, just like all of ours. So Father Vladimir said that the father of this girl was probably a Buddhist. In short, there were many different people mixed in here; it was therefore mandatory, once a month, for Father Vladimir, a learned man, to talk about other religions, about the exodus of Jews from Egypt and about the many-armed God Shiva. He brought books with pictures in colour, and we all looked through them one by one, staring at the gods of other religions. While he considered the Christian religion the only true religion and the one that was the closest to any believer, nevertheless this did not prevent him from introducing other worlds to us. Unlike Father Vladimir, Klara Fyodorovna did not consider Christianity to be the only true religion; she preferred to have 'God in her soul' instead, as she put it, and it did not matter what he was and how many arms he had. Therefore, we always celebrated Pesakh before Easter, and had cake for Eid al-Adha (no one knew how to celebrate this holiday the right way). In matters of religion, the spirit of democracy reigned in the school, which allowed me to grow up as an open-minded person, devoid of biased religious bigotry.

Certainly, there were children among us who despised the equality of religions and nations. Such children loved to beat the Tatars or stick a rag to Samekh's head, and then they rolled with laughter, pointing at him with their fingers: 'Hey you, stinking Jewish scum, you have the kippah stuck to your skull!' We could not stop their atrocities, and we didn't want to get into trouble, so we silently watched them bullying those that were 'not like everyone else'. Everything changed when one of those who despised equality, and there were at least twenty of them, decided to take on Undra. She was a small girl of seven years old, no more than a meter tall. She was nimble and funny, and everyone liked her. But one evening, after dinner, several guys started picking on her, calling her 'a slanted Chinese'. Despite her small stature and insignificant age, Undra had inherited a strong-willed character from one of her parents and did not tolerate insults. She spat deliciously at one of the offenders.

I'm scared to put into words what happened next. Three of them assaulted the girl, grabbed her by the hair and dragged her to the toilet. Undra struggled, screamed and scratched their hands, but in vain. There, in the toilet, for some reason they stripped her down to her panties, threw her to the floor and began to beat her. Undra let out a strangled howl, but the more sounds she made, the harder they beat her. Then we, those who had witnessed what had happened (just a couple of second-graders), ran for Slavik. A minute later Slavik was in the toilet. He rushed at one of the offenders, hitting him in the side. A scuffle began. But everything went quiet in a matter of seconds. The pale and suddenly frightened boy collapsed to the floor, his hand pressed to the place where Slavik had hit him. It was bleeding. I shot a glance at Slavik. He was stuffing something sharp into his trouser pocket.

'Help ...' The wounded boy groaned, rolling his eyes.

'Let's get out!' Slavik shouted, picking up Undra. We ran into the room of the older girls, who took first aid courses. They examined Undra and concluded that they could not do without professional help, so they took her to Klara Fyodorovna's office, who called an ambulance.

Despite the severe beatings, Undra recovered and returned to the boarding school a couple of weeks later. She never admitted who did this to her, but the stabbing of one of the students made Klara Fyodorovna consider her options. We committed to keep silence, refusing to talk. So everyone forgot about this issue over time, as if nothing had happened. Only one thing had changed: other religions were no longer despised. The boys were simply afraid to attack Muslims and Jews, fearing Slavik with a blade. And Slavik, although indifferent to the lessons of theology and religious issues in general, could not stand the abuse of girls.

'When I was as small as you are,' said Slavik, 'I once saw how my neighbour and his friends beat severely a neighbour girl of about thirteen. They beat her so much that she started drooling and stuttering.'

'Why did they do that to her?'I asked, frightened.

'Just because she did not want to kiss her neighbour, so he punished her. But don't worry, my stepfather and the girl's father taught these guys a lesson later.' Slavik grinned mischievously. By the unhealthy gleam in his eyes and the satisfied smacking of his lips, I guessed what exactly had happened to those guys, but I didn't want to hear it, so when Slavik spoke, I quickly covered my ears with my hands.

4.

There were few teachers at Grey Willow, so some of them taught several disciplines. For example, the history teacher could be the one teaching geography lessons, and the exercises teacher could be also teaching boys shop classes. In short, speaking in a modern way, the 'Old Lady Willow' suffered from a lack of personnel.

Our teachers, in their overwhelming majority, were so tired of the grey life in the town of M. that they simply did not have the strength for us. They were, of course, both rude and stern, but mostly indifferent. They didn't care much for us in their minds, let alone hearts.

However, there were also those who hated us. Rather, this was one person, but in her anger and cruelty, she could overtake more than a dozen of her colleagues. Oksana Gennadievna, the Russian language teacher. Over the years, I have often pondered how one very insignificant person could inculcate such a dislike for one discipline or another. I have carried my hatred for the Russian language through my whole life, getting a kind of thrill every time I think of its participial phrases and prefixes.

Oksana Gennadievna was below average height, with a loose, pear-like body and a chipped front tooth. Her short hair was always greasy and her lips were pale and dry. In a word, even Nikichna, who because of her good disposition found beauty in every person, didn't dare to call the Rusichka beautiful. Oksana Gennadievna hated us without hiding it. I do mean hated. Dislike or resentment are expressed in a different way – a person simply ignores you, patiently endures your presence; but hatred is a vivid feeling, requiring constant recharge with negativity.

Owing to the lack of both teachers and premises suitable for conducting classes, Russian language lessons were held in the Museum of the Great Patriotic War, which occupied one of the rooms of the school. After the end of the tragic events of 1941-45 that led to the death of a good half of the Soviet Union's citizens, the local authorities of the town of M. had decided to perpetuate at all costs the memory of those who had died for the freedom and honour of their homeland. However, not a single decent place was found in the town for opening an exemplary museum. Nobody remembers what was located in the premises of the current museum in the late 40s (most likely, one of the classrooms), but it was here that they finally decided to arrange the exhibition. It was a spacious room with large windows to the floor, but it was also dark, since the curly vines of grapes had long entangled the windows. There was a bulky dark wooden table in the middle of the room, part of the wall was covered with a camouflage net, and a couple of munitions shells were placed in the corner. Huge posters and photographs adorned those walls which were untouched by the netting. They pictured children in concentration camps, peeking out through the barbed wire which had been strung up by the Nazis, and soldiers, covered in blood and smiling from the trenches. There was little heroism in the selection of stuff; for the most part it was an illustration of the tragedies of the war. I remember when I first came to a Russian language class at the age of seven, I was shocked by what I saw. What scared me the most was a photo of a boy about my age, who was captured among those children. He was clutching the barbed wire with a thin hand and looking attentively into the camera. Nearby, an enlarged letter hung from the wire on a thick, frayed piece of cardboard:

Дорагая мама ... Мы т ... жд ... Ваня и мня увез ... холодно ... гдя т ... прощ ...

It was difficult to say whether the letter was written in this boy's hand, or what was in that letter in general. He had written it to his mother, and he must have been cold. Beside him there was also Vanya, as I called him, maybe a brother or a friend. I thought it was a farewell letter. That the boy and his brother Vanya were being taken away somewhere, that he felt very cold at that moment, and he was saying goodbyc to his mother, who, perhaps, was no longer alive ... Frightened by this boy at first, and especially by his gaze, over time I got so used to him that I no longer noticed the deep sadness and fear frozen in his bright eyes. Nor did I notice the bones protruding from under his torn shirt. I simply became akin to him, having studied every detail of his appearance and clothing. And I learned the text of the letter by heart. We met twice a week, and I even thought of a name for the boy: Sasha. I liked the name Sasha, it suited him, so twice a week for forty-five minutes, Sasha and I exchanged glances, and I knew that he empathized sincerely with my fears of Oksana Gennadievna, which she had instilled in my heart. Sasha knew what it was like to be tortured.

Oksana Gennadievna loved to notice obvious and not obvious defects in her students, both in their appearance and character. She called Tanya Kishchuk, a girl a couple of years older, a 'stutterer', because she could not always quickly pronounce the right word; and Fima Vodovoz, my classmate in the second grade (he was adopted at the beginning of the third grade), was named by her 'Tanyusha', since the teacher believed that the boy had a completely feminine character.

'You are soft like a little girl, Fima. You remind me of my neighbour Tanya, a sissy. Tanya played with dolls and carried in flea cats from the garbage. And everyone called her only this sweet way, 'Tanyusha'...' reasoned Oksana Gennadievna. We were silent. We were all silent. Both the living and the dead, looking at us from the cardboard photographs.

One of these windy spring days of my second grade Oksana Gennadievna called me 'handicapped' because I could not memorize one of the grammar rules.

'Handicapped children grow up to be freaks, Vitya. Their arms and legs are deformed, their forehead narrows. It is clear why your parents handed you over to us, no one needs a handicapped child. Perhaps, your mother has already given birth to a new baby ...' said Rusichka, and then kicked me out of the class. Without thinking twice, I quickly collected my notebooks and a textbook and left. I had a nasty feeling in my heart and I wanted to cry, so I wandered out into the street.

'Why so sed, Brave?' Nikichna croaked when I drew level with her dilapidated house. I just shrugged my shoulders silently.

'Probably had a lesson with Rusichka, heh?' The old woman chuckled. I nodded.

'She's a wicked woman, so very wicked.' Nikichna pursed her dry lips. 'Well, you, come on, let's go to my place, have some compote and cookies to chew. Come!' She lightly pulled me by the sleeve of my shirt, beckoning me inside her cramped housing.

The caretaker's house had one room and an annex, where there was a washbasin, a stool, and a wooden trough. The small room served as both kitchen and bedroom. There were a table and a couple of chairs in the corner, a wardrobe, and an ottoman on the side. Near the ottoman there was an old stove, which Nikichna used for heating and cooking food. The old woman also possessed a large chest where she kept the 'treasures' that she had accumulated over the years: cuts of fabric, new handkerchiefs, a little money for a funeral and old letters and photographs.

'Sit down.' Nikichna pointed with a crooked finger to the ottoman, where Licorice was sleeping having rolled itself up into a ball. Licorice was old, like its mistress, and lived out its years in peace, warmed by a kind caretaker. The question of who had called the cat Licorice was one of many other mysteries that had infiltrated the walls of the 'Old Lady Willow'. There were rumours that once, when the cat was still a kitten, one of the teachers' boyfriends had brought her a bag of outlandish licorice sweets from abroad, and little Licorice stole the bag and left sweets all over the yard. The rumour had it that it was on that day that she lost her eye and became lame, since the owner of those treats made her pay in full for what she did. Whether it was true or not, Licorice was Licorice, an old, one-eyed, lame and vividly ugly hazy-colored cat. When awake, she was the scariest cat I have ever seen.

'Here you go, kid.' Nikichna put a glass of compote and a vase with cookies in front of me. 'If someone had put such a pile of cookies in front of me when I was of this little age, I would have ... heh! I would have sold my Motherland! To hell!' The old woman laughed, watching me chewing reluctantly.

'They're delicious, thank you.' I smiled. I liked Nikichna.

'Heh, here it goes! No furrowed brow then, it doesn't look good on you!' She stroked my hand. 'Do not think bad of the Rusichka, she was offended by God.'

'God?'

'Yes, God, ya know, he blesses all people, but, you see, he must have forgotten about Gennadievna. These things happen with God, hands full, ya know! He forgot, and now she is angry that she is ugly as sin and she is not kind either. She wants to get married, for someone to love her, but where do you find such a brave man!' Nikichna threw up her hands.

'Good-lookings is not the main thing ...' continued the old woman. 'Take my Licorice for a change. You should look hard to find a more terrible cat, but her heart is warm, she is affectionate. She clings to me at night, and I can really feel how she shares her love. It's unpossible not to love my girl, even though she's a minger in her face, and also lame. It's not about the face, we all grow to look not nice. The main thing is here.'

Nikichna patted herself on the chest. I silently drank the compote and listened attentively to the arguments of the old caretaker about beauty and universal human values. She spoke slowly, at times falling silent for a minute or two, and then completely dozed off in her chair, tired of talking. I washed the compote glass, stroked Licorice and silently walked out into the street, slowly closing the door.

5.

Before the start of the third grade my parents gave me a stack of new notebooks with glossy covers (from abroad!). Themselves, they could not attend the September 1st celebration, as they were too busy. For all that, they loved me. Although my parents promised to take me away for all holidays and weekends, since the day I settled into the Grey Willow Boarding School they had only kept their promise no more than three or four times. Twice for the holidays in May, once for my birthday, and once on some other day. Each time they brought me sweets and new clothing. Mum mostly cried, hugging me to her chest, and Dad stroked my head. During the first year, I was still asking when they would take me home, but as time passed these and other similar questions passed my lips less often. All hopes vanished when the new pencil case arrived. I realized that they would never take me home. And it was then when I felt relief. Relief, because I accepted my fate, got over it and nothing tormented my soul any longer, nothing bothered me at night. Everything became extremely simple, as if it had always been so. As if there were never parents, but only Klara Fyodorovna, terrible Licorice, silent Sasha and my best friend Slavik. And also Solomiya Stefanovna, a teacher of the Ukrainian language and literature ...

Solomiya Stefanovna was a meek, quiet girl with a light blond braid and thick eyelashes that framed her large brown eyes. Now I understand that they were brown, but then they seemed the color of buckwheat honey to me, and her thick hair smelled of lavender. The older children called the extraordinary teacher Fauna for her natural beauty and love for all living things. Fauna, for this is how we will call Solomiya Stefanovna from now on, had the amazing gift to inspire peace in the heart and give joy. Klara Fyodorovna loved her very much and often took long walks with her. And all the children loved her, but not as much as I did. Fauna, sweet, kind Fauna became my first true love. Therefore, every week I gave her little presents: my own drawings, bouquets of dried leaves or something like that. Sometimes I brought her a handful of sweets sent by my parents, but Fauna refused to take them, though after lots of persuasion she offered to eat them together over a cup of tea. Then we went to her office, she boiled water and we drank hot tea with chocolates in our mouths. At such moments, Fauna told me about the books she read and about the great Ukrainians whom she admired. She had a velvety, gentle timbre of voice and an incredibly charming smile.

Slavik, like the others, considered Fauna sweet and did not laugh too hard or often at my feelings.

'Vitek, you have good taste,' he would mildly tease. 'People like Fauna are usually married and are not getting engaged in all sorts of nonsense.'

'What nonsense?' I asked, but Slavik always answered that I was still too small for such conversations.

'It is strange that no one has married our teacher yet,' continued Slavik. And it was really strange. However, I was glad that she did not belong to anyone and could spend time with me over a cup of tea. In the end of autumn, Fauna was the one who initiated a trip with some of her students to a concert that a Kyiv pianist performed in the House of Culture. God only knows how he found himself in our boondocks. In the very morning, we, twenty tomboys from eight to fourteen years of age, were given strict instructions on how to behave at the concert. No laughing, grunting or whimpering, poking fingers, yawning, talking or twisting the head. In a word, we should sit still and watch the pianist with our eyes and ears wide open, taking in the spiritual nourishment. When the evening approached, the nannies dressed us up, tied the boys' ties and tightened the tights on the girls. Half an hour before the concert, we left the boarding school in a single-file line, accompanied by Klara Fyodorovna and Fauna, and hurried to the House of Culture.

The elegant building with large columns greeted us with a huge signboard, which said in color: 'For the first time in the town of M., the great and spectacular pianist Something.' In the lobby, we handed over our outerwear to the cloakroom and entered the overcrowded hall. After counting everyone by our heads, Klara Fyodorovna and Fauna sat us down, while they themselves sat on the sides, cutting off our way out. A couple of minutes later the lights went out, the voices died down, and the pianist himself appeared on the stage, his shoes creaking solidly. This was a tall, stooped man in short trousers and a funny jacket. He bowed proudly and sat down at the piano.

Minutes felt like hours to me. I painfully tried to take in the spiritual nourishment, but it was like a piece of it got stuck in my throat. The pianist produced dismal wheezy sounds, leaning over the instrument, and the audience watched him with a mixture of delight and incomprehension. The inhabitants of the town of M. were narrow-minded people who saw nothing cultural ever, apart from amateur performances and French cinema. And here they had a Kyiv pianist and classical music at their disposal: one needs to be prepared for things like that. But Klara Fyodorovna and Fauna got real pleasure from the concert. They were well-read, educated, unlike many other teachers, and could perceive the beauty of what they heard. To my ears, though, the pianist continued to tap out the dreary melodies, while I fidgeted restlessly on my chair, fighting the urge to doze off. The music was lulling me to sleep, and the soft chair enveloped the body nicely. And when it seemed that I was about to fall into the arms of Morpheus, a suspicious creak, like a low thunderclap, came from the stage. The pianist's hands froze in the air, he lowered his head to the piano, and in a second the audience watched the base of the stool cracking and the great Kyiv pianist crashing down to the floor, with his feet up.

Fauna screamed, Klara Fyodorovna clutched her heart, and we, the pupils of the Grey Willow Boarding School, rolled with laughter like all the other spectators. The hall was filled with joyful chuckling and giggling; someone was wiping away tears, someone else was wheezing chokingly, trying to hold back a fit of laughter. The drowsiness vanished, and I willingly joined the others, pointing my finger at the pianist and hooting.

On the way home, Fauna was silent; she did not even want to look towards the 'faceless mass', which we were in her eyes. Klara Fyodorovna, on the other hand, reacted to the situation philosophically. She disciplined us for misbehavior and immediately forgot about what had happened. For her, we were foolish children who had little joy in life even without her preaching. But dear Fauna could not forget the situation so easily. Our 'savage' behavior, as she put it herself, hurt her badly. This made me feel bitter. Neither in those years, nor in many years after that, did I like to make people upset with my behavior. And then, at eight years of age, my heart was being torn into small pieces whenever I looked at Fauna. But I was afraid to speak to her. Slavik had taught me that when women pouted, the right thing to do was to leave them as they were, and try to ask for forgiveness after a while, but for now it was better to let her be alone with her resentment.

Falling asleep, I mentally replayed the events of the past day in my head, recalling with delight how the stool cracked under the pianist. Say what you like, but my first concert turned out to be, perhaps, one of the best in my life!

I avoided Fauna for several days, until Slavik said that now it was okay. 'But you can't possibly be thinking of going empty-handed to her.' He shook his head disapprovingly.

I suggested drawing a picture or collecting a bouquet from withered foliage.

'That is bullshit, Vitya,' Slavik disagreed. 'A woman has to be given a real gift after what've happened.'

'What kind of a gift?'

'Well, a perfume or a lipstick,' my friend suggested. But I had neither perfume nor lipstick, let alone enough money to buy them. Nevertheless, Slavik did not get upset by that fact; on the contrary, it excited him. He offered me to go to the local haberdashery in the town, where there would be a queue for some incomprehensible female things that everyone really needed, but were almost impossible to get.

The next day after lunch, we ran into the town and slipped into the haberdashery, perching ourselves at the hip of one of the customers, as if we were her children. The crowd was terrible, the women were shouting, pushing and filling the small store more and more. Having moved closer to the open counter, Slavik imperceptibly winked at me, nodding in the direction of coloured varnishes and small tubes of creams. But my attention was attracted by pocket mirrors lying nearby. The mirrors, studded with plastic stones and tied with thin satin ribbons, were beautiful. Slavik nodded approvingly and was soon holding one of them in his hands. Slavka was a quick and skillful thief; even I did not always notice how he did it, let alone the sellers. We ran out of the haberdashery and rushed back to the boarding school.

In the evening, plucking up courage, I went to Fauna's study, where she was checking notebooks.

'I'm listening to you, kid,' Fauna said in Ukrainian, lifting her head up from her work.

'I ... I just wanted to apologise ...' I blurted out.

'It's okay, it's nothing.' Fauna winked at me. 'I don't hold grudges ... It really was a little bit funny.' She closed the notebook, inviting me to sit down and have tea. It was then that I decided to take action. In his guidance, Slavik suggested that I open my feelings to Fauna, and present an expensive gift as a sign of eternal love. So I did. Stuttering and blushing, I confessed my love, expressing admiration with her beauty and kindness. From time to time, I would start screaming, but then I mumbled again, I waved my arms and laughed. In short, I behaved like a person truly in love. Having finished with the confession, I pulled a beautiful mirror, decorated with red muddy stones, out of my pocket, and with the words 'This is for you', I put it in front of Fauna.

She was silent. Then she picked it up, carefully examined the gift and smiled. 'I haven't seen anything more beautiful in my life ...' whispered the brown-eyed teacher. 'Let's have some tea, I want to tell you something.' Fauna took me by the hand and led me to the far corner of the office, where a boiler and a jug of water were standing on the table. We were silent for the entire time she was making tea. When the drink was finally brewed, and two slices of black bread were generously smeared with butter and put in front of me on a plate, Fauna spoke.

'A long time ago, I fell in love with a man,' she began. 'I lived in a different city back then, far away from here. He was a good man, he loved me too. Then, he proposed to me, and gave me a small silver engagement ring.' Fauna pulled out a chain from under her jacket, on which a small silver ring was hanging.

'My beloved one served in the military ... he was a marine officer. And so it happened that before the wedding they called him for manoeuvers. He promised to come back in three days, but he never did.' Fauna fell silent, tightly squeezing her ring.

'Why? Did he change his mind about marrying you?' I asked in horror.

'No, child, he loved me too much ... He died. A painful accident. There was a storm and he was carried away into the sea ... he drowned. So it happens, child.' Fauna passed her hand over my cheek. 'Many years have passed since then, but I could never love anyone else, for my heart has been devoted to that brave officer forever.'

'And you will never love again?' I asked her.

'Never, dear, never,' She smiled sadly, and I noticed how her fabulously beautiful eyes were filled with tears.

'Don't cry. Even though you may not fall in love, I will always love you and I will always wait!' I declared seriously. 'And I will always protect you and give you gifts.' I lifted my chin proudly, and Fauna, moved by my words, drew me to her and hugged me tightly.

'My amazing child.' She smiled, kissing my forehead.

That night, falling asleep, I thought a lot about the beautiful teacher, the love of my whole life, and about the man she loved, the brave officer who was swallowed up by the deep sea a few days before their wedding. I thought that, perhaps, it is simply impossible to love as much as Fauna loved. It is impossible to stay kind and warm when one has such a deep wound in one's heart. I thought that she probably often cried at night, rubbing a thin ring with her fingers. It was a shame that along with the death of the officer, also died Fauna's ability to love. She must open her soul, and if not to me, then to some other good man, she must accept his love. But remembering her look and confident tone, I understood that this extraordinary woman was firmly resolved to mourn for the dead groom until the end of her days. 'One day we'll meet in heaven,' Fauna said. And from that day on, I prayed every day for them to certainly meet in heaven. Not soon, but someday, after many years.

6.

In the evenings, when fog descended onto the town of M. (it was not in vain that it won the fame of being the foggiest town in the country!), I looked out of the window at the viscous mist, in which the crowns of trees could hardly be seen, and thought about my life. The present seemed to me one continuous hopelessness, slumbering behind an old high fence. And there, behind it, was a life that was just a little bit interesting, with sweet 'petushki' and a haberdashery. Slavik liked to repeat that 'we all came to this world with a purpose', and I kept wondering, what was my purpose ... I wanted to become a traveller, I wanted to make a lot of money and I wanted to leave the grey, foggy town of M. where people were born only to die one day. Life bypassed our town, and we only learned from newspapers and rare magazines about what was happening in the world, how everything was changing and transforming. 'Vitka, the good life is where we happen not to be,' Slavik laughed, listening to my reflections. But I didn't know how it was out there. And even more so, neither did I know where this mysterious 'there' was, and that's why it attracted me more and more every day.

In the meantime, another year passed. All my peers, who were already few in number, were adopted or taken home for permanent residence, until only I and the Tatar Akim remained. Since it was an utter luxury to teach only two boys, we were transferred from the fourth to the sixth grade. It was incredibly difficult to study, as Akim and I had an abyss in our heads a size of a whole year, but this did not bother our teachers at all. Therefore, we studied as best we could. I am not saying that we tried very hard, but we tried to handle it well enough to get our well-deserved 'satisfactory' grades.

If some of the teachers were satisfied with our efforts in general, the Rusichka was adamant. It seemed to me that twice a week she waited with special trembling anticipation for me and Akim, in order to once again shower us with insults. She called Akim 'a dirty infidel' for his dark skin and charcoal hair. When it came to me, she would call me 'handicapped' or a 'little freak' and poke her finger mockingly: 'Look, his little hands are already twisted!' Although they pitied me, everyone timidly erupted with laughter. I dreamed that Oksana Gennadievna would die. I sincerely wished her death, and not a quick and painless one; I imagined her tormented, writhing in pain. I smiled at these thoughts, hoping that she would never find love, never give birth to children, that she would always, always be alone ... and she would die an old, decrepit woman, forgotten and abandoned by everyone. These thoughts warmed my soul, which was tormented by insults: my imaginings helped me to overcome my fear of the teacher.

'Vitek, remember my words, someday one of the inhabitants will break her legs somewhere in a dark alley,' said Slavik, spitting on the ground. 'Such women do not stay on earth for a long time,' he continued, smiling. Rusichka especially didn't like Slavik, if I may say so. She generally disliked, and to tell the truth, even hated, everyone, but Slavik occupied a special place in her life. She beat him several times for the fact that he was not silent and always responded to insults. Once, she called someone a 'freak', to which Slavik laughed: 'Look at yourself, you snaggletooth!' Then Rusichka grabbed him by the collar and gave him a dozen slaps in the face.

'Remember my words, she'll get what's coming to her,' Slavik smirked, and I would feel better.

On November 7, 1994, on the day of the anniversary of the Great October Socialist Revolution, Oksana Gennadievna brought a baked duck to the lesson. In general, Soviet holidays were under an unspoken ban, Klara Fyodorovna did not encourage them, but she could not officially prohibit them either. We celebrated Pesach and Eid al-Adha and, so to say, we strove to keep democracy in everything. But if the director and many adherents of her policy had happily erased Soviet history from their memory, Oksana Gennadievna remained unconvinced. She honored the memory of Lenin, recalled the Komsomol with nostalgia and in general cited the Union as an example always and in everything.

'It was the Soviet soldiers who freed these unfortunate people!' she whimpered, pointing her finger at Sasha's photo. 'We, and only we, were those who won World War II!' She proudly lifted her massive chin, as if personifying the power of the Great and Terrible Union with all her appearance. Old Ivan Ivanovich, who was our history teacher, disagreed drastically with the Rusichka's false statement that 'we, and only we, were those' who had won the war. But the opinions of the old, experienced teacher were of little concern to her brainwashed mind. She believed and was happy in her belief.

That is why on November 7, 1994, Oksana Gennadievna, excited by the arrival of the holiday that was of such an importance to her, brought a baked duck with apples to the lesson to treat her students and talk about the revolution. Even then, it seemed extremely strange to me to dine in a classroom where images of people who were exhausted by hunger and concentration camps hung all over the walls. Be that as it may, I had never eaten duck before, especially baked with apples, and quickly forgot about Sasha and his sad hungry look. Having handed out a piece to everyone, Rusichka made herself comfortable at the end of the table, beginning a leisurely story about the revolution, mass demonstrations and the rule of a cruel tsar. Ivan Ivanovich had already told us all this, only in a slightly different interpretation.

'That year, the country got up from its knees and threw off the shackles that held it tightly!' Oksana Gennadievna spoke enthusiastically. 'We became equal, strong and real!' Her face was distorted by the grimace of an 'urban crazy' person. This exalted woman was so amusing that I choked on my duck, stifling laughter. The smile immediately left Rusichka's face.

'Do you find this funny, you, little freak?' she said through her teeth. I shook my head, still chewing on my piece of the bird.

'Ah, I understand,' she cracked out poisonously. 'You chowed down on the duck like an animal, as if you had never been given food, so you no longer care about values?!'

'I just choked ... Sorry.'

'You choked because you stuffed yourself!' She got up from the table, took her piece of duck, which had been untouched, and came up to me.

'Eat,' she said, placing her portion in front of me.

'I don't want to, thank you,' I replied. I really didn't want it. The duck was dry, with a strange sour taste. I didn't like it. I could barely swallow my own bite, feeling a lump in my throat.

'No, Vitya, you will eat.' She sat down next to me, moving the plate to the edge of the table. 'And while you're eating, I want you to think about those people who were starving and dying during the revolution. Eat.' She crossed her arms and I started eating. Swallowing dry, tough pieces of duck one by one, I felt Sasha's sad eyes on me from behind the barbed wire. I burst into tears.

'Why are we crying? Doesn't the duck taste good?' asked Oksana Gennadievna sarcastically. But I was silent, carefully trying to chew the 'treat'. When I finished the duck, the woman looked with disgust at my dirty face and hands and ordered me to go and get cleaned up. In the toilet, I vomited poorly chewed pieces of duck, which, by the way, I never had again. The very sight of this dish evoked persistent associations with war and revolution, and the sad face of my ghostly friend Sasha emerging before my eyes.

After washing my face and wiping away my tears, I returned to the classroom, where Rusichka continued her story. Frightened and hunted, like wild animals, my classmates sat silently in front of empty plates, their eyes lowered to the floor, nodding when necessary, and smiling when required. I looked at Sasha again and thought that he probably had the same thing going on. He was also afraid of angering the guards, and endured bullying. Only it was better for us. Oksana Gennadievna could not kill us. More precisely, she simply had no right.

On that day, several more children suffered from Rusichka, including Slavik. After lunch, despite the drizzling rain, many went outside to get some air. Hearing my story about the 'duck punishment', Slavik got furious, cursing and kicking the ground. Then he offered to run for a short time outside the gate. I agreed, and a little later we were riding the tram and eating the 'Golden Key' sweets that we'd filched. When it began to get dark, we took a turn towards the boarding school, but suddenly we saw the corpse of a dog at the very gates of the 'Old Lady Willow'. The dog was large, red-haired, with drooping ears and a long muzzle. His body was still warm.

'Why did it die?' I asked. Slavik bent over the mongrel and examined it carefully.

'Who the hell knows! There seem to be no wounds. Maybe it was old or sick.' He scratched the back of his head, kicking the dog.

'Why are you doing that?' I gently pushed him away.

'I'm checking. Maybe it's not dead. If it's alive, we'd go to Nikichna,' argued Slavik. But the dog was dead. Tears welled up in my eyes, and I choked out a sob, feeling exhausted by the past day.

'Hey, what's wrong?!' Slavik was surprised. 'Don't you cry! We will bury it now by all rights.' With these words, he raised the dead dog and carried it on his back.

'Where are you going?' I startled.

'What do you mean? To the school. We will bury it behind the yard, otherwise all sorts of louts will try to unbury it,' Slava replied, slipping through the hole in the gate.

Having borrowed a shovel and a hoe from Nikichna, we began to dig a grave behind the swing, closer to the slope. When we finished digging the hole, Slavik carefully put the mongrel inside, I said a prayer, we crossed ourselves and began to bury it. However, our actions attracted the attention of Rozalia Borisovna, the nanny. Seeing that we were burying the corpse of a dog on the territory of the school, she burst out swearing. For some reason, she decided that it was Slavik who was to blame for the mongrel's death, so she grabbed him by the hand, dragged him into the basement and locked him in one of the auxiliary rooms.

'Sit and think about what you have done! You monster!' Fat Rozalia Borisovna was screaming her lungs out. Slavik shouted and kicked at the door so loudly that I could hear him standing in the street near the unfinished grave.

The wind got stronger. It lifted the stale yellowed foliage in sharp gusts, spreading the leaves throughout the yard. I felt cold drops of rain penetrating my collar, and diligently began to shovel earth into the grave. I was on my knees, raking the loose, sticky soil with my bare hands. The rain was intensifying, and in the twilight of the autumn evening I could see a shapeless figure hurrying in the distance. The rain drummed on the ground, and then several small pieces of ice hit my cold hands. The hail began. The figure, hurrying to shelter from the rain, froze, then let out a heart-rending scream and rushed to Nikichna's tiny house with all her might, as it was located closer to the central entrance of the boarding school.

I recognized her. I recognized her voice and movements. Rusichka was beating on the door frantically, until finally the old woman opened it.

Having filled the grave to the brim, I hastily cleaned my soiled trousers and ran to the caretaker's house. I stood on tiptoe at the side window, pulled myself up with my whole body on the cornice and looked inside. What I saw frightened and amused me at the same time. The clumsy pear-like Rusichka was sitting in the corner of the room, legs tucked to her chest, and howling. She shook her head frantically, biting her lower lip. Nikichna tried to calm her down as she could.

'Oksanochka, darling, it's just a hail. Look at how frit you are! Do not be afraid.' The old woman tried to stroke Rusichka on the head, but she brushed off the kind gesture. I did not wait for the performance to end; instead, I ran headlong to the basement. Oh, I felt so good! I wanted to laugh until my stomach hurt!

‘Slavka! Slavka! Where are you?’ I cried feverishly, checking every door.

‘Here I am!’ I heard finally.

‘Slavka, you won’t believe it! Rusichka is sitting like a dog at Nikichna’s house now and howling! Howling like a beaten dog!’ I laughed, describing everything I had seen in detail and with great enthusiasm.

‘There you go!’ Slavik trilled with laughter. ‘Serves her right!’ He drummed on the door to the beat of the hail, and I smiled and thought about the right thing that we did when we decided to bury the dog.

7.

The town of M. was covered with snow. The New Year was approaching, resulting in heated preparations inside the walls of the 'Old Lady Willow'. The cooks experimented with new recipes for cake (there was a lot of cake over the New Year's holidays!), Klara Fyodorovna and Father Vladimir were preparing the holiday prayer, and Madame Ju was teaching a new dance. We rehearsed a lot, practicing singing and dramatic arts in order to meet the new year, 1995, with dignity.

New Year in the Grey Willow Boarding School was a merry and unpredictable holiday. Every year some kind of 'surprise' happened. For example, on the first year of my stay here, a real puppet theater came to visit us on New Year's Eve. And the previous year, the festive dinner had consisted entirely of sweets: pies, cookies and candy. In short, Klara Fyodorovna loved to treat us once a year. She also gave everyone gifts that the nannies hid under our pillows. There was a gift for every single one of us. Those were little things, of course. Colored pencils or socks; but it was nice to find them under the pillow. When it came to birthdays, we did not receive gifts due to the fact that, as Nikichna put it, 'you are umpteen, and there is not enough mooney', however on New Year's, Klara Fyodorovna spent a lot to create a little magic.

On December 31st, we usually woke up late, had something special for breakfast, like cakes with berry fillings or small pies with jam, and then hung around until lunchtime. Many pupils were taken home that day, and those who stayed were taken for a walk after lunch. The most interesting thing started at six in the evening. Around this time, we had our first dinner, then everyone went to the assembly hall, where we watched the New Year's performance, and there was a second dinner after that. At about ten in the evening we were invited to the cinema hall (we had one!), which was locked all year round: only on New Year's Eve did it open its doors to young spectators. We watched old French or Italian comedies and even westerns, and Soviet fairy tales. In a word, the things that the film lecturer could borrow from the local cinema for a while after providing some alcoholic drink as a bribe. Before going to bed, we were given a glass of warm milk and a piece of cake. And already in our rooms, we were opening up albeit insignificant but cute gifts. I remember that it was a coloring book in my first year, and another year it was a bright blue bath towel. It seems to me now that we received our gifts from those sales' representatives whom Klara Fyodorovna was able to trick into a free or minimum paid delivery of a certain amount of goods that particular year. The deputy director of a textile factory located in a neighbouring town, or the manager of a stationery store: our headmistress knew how to find the right approach to each of them. As they say, everyone had their own price.

My parents never took me home for the New Year. On that day they were always busy working. But they usually came to visit a week before the holiday. They gave me gifts, we walked around the school for half an hour, and they left to return in the spring, for my birthday. Most of the gifts were good, clothes or toys from abroad that aroused envy among my friends.

'Overseas clothes!' Slavik whistled, examining my jacket and frayed jeans. 'Cool!' He was not jealous, no. I think he just felt bad because his mum hadn't even brought a box of cookies all the time he was there. One day, therefore, I offered to visit her.

'Let's go and see. Maybe she got sick or she has no money at all.'

'My mother has never had money!' Slavik sniffed. 'But we can go. Maybe you're right, it could happen that the old woman did get sick.'

After lunch, we ran away through a crack in the fence as usual, and an hour later, we were at Tsyganka. The beggarly two-story building where Slavik was born and where his mother lived now looked so miserable that I immediately felt dreary. Auntie Alla, Slavik's mother, lived on the ground floor in a one-room apartment, which looked just the same way as the building itself. The woman did not open the door at once; we had to knock for a long time (the bell did not work). Then she opened it, sleepy and swollen. She smiled when she saw Slavik.

'Son.' Auntie Alla reached out to him, but Slavik recoiled.

'Well, so, how are you?' he asked matter-of-factly, crossing over the threshold. 'This is Vitka, my mate. Is there something to eat?' The woman shook her head.

'Maybe there is tea and biscuits?' Slavik insisted.

'Biscuits! How can there be biscuits in this house? I hardly scrape together enough money to buy bread,' Auntie Alla mumbled pitifully.

'From what I see, there is money for the medicine.' Slavik pushed an empty vodka bottle with his foot. The woman made a face. She was young enough and probably pretty in the old days, but now her face was drawn and the skin on her hands was dry and cracked. Auntie Alla looked wretched in a shabby robe and torn rubber slippers, her hair falling down her bony shoulders like thin icicles.

'There is some lemonade left and black bread with sugar in the kitchen,' the woman suggested. Having spread margarine on the bread, she sprinkled sugar on top and poured two incomplete glasses of lemonade that had long gone flat. Auntie Alla sat with us for a couple of minutes in the kitchen, while we chewed sandwiches, then she returned to the main room and fell asleep in a couple of minutes. We continued to sit in the small, cramped kitchen. Slavik twisted an aluminum fork in his hands, and I looked out the window at the children running around the yard.

'They say that there is a kind of lemonade abroad, which is black and very sweet. And there are so many bubbles in it that if you drink it quickly the foam goes right out of your nose!' Slavik suddenly began, examining the unfinished lemonade. 'I was told that they sell it in bright red cans and it has its name written in white, but I don't remember what it's called. I would like to try it ...' my friend finished dreamily. Then he shoved the plates into the sink, which was packed with dishes, and we left, having made a decision not to wake Auntie Alla. I don't know if Slavik visited his mother after that, but for some reason it seems to me that it was then when they saw each other for the last time.

After we had that conversation, the thought of that black sweet drink got stuck in my head, and one day I decided to call my parents about it. There was a pay phone on the first floor, not far from the main entrance, which anyone could use for calling free of charge. To my delight, my parents were at home, but they were in a hurry, so I got down to business immediately.

'Dad, you and Mum are going to give me something for the New Year, right?' I asked.

'Of course,' my father replied.

'You know, I don't really need anything. Just bring me some sweet water from your trip, it's black and very, very bubbly. In a red can with white lettering. I'm not asking for it for myself. I have a friend, he has no parents, and he really, really wants this kind of water. I definitely don't need gifts.' I was talking, and my dad listened to me in silence. He promised that if he saw such mysterious water, he would definitely bring it to me.

Mid-December arrived, and the Grey Willow was gleaming with colorful garlands. A decorated Christmas tree met everyone at the entrance;

it had been cut down by Styopka, the handyman, who dragged it on his own hump, despite the fact that it was huge and probably weighed a whole ton! The windows were decorated with snowflakes cut out of cardboard, and the railings were buried in snow, a fluffy white cotton wool. Each class of pupils diligently created wall displays, honed the New Year's dance with Madame Ju and wondered what kind of surprise was waiting for us this year. And the surprise didn't take long! Two weeks before the New Year, the teachers took us, the pupils of the 'Old Lady Willow', far out of town in small batches. A few hours' drive away there was a factory of Christmas decorations named after S.F. Suslikov. I was lucky to be one of the first pupils who got to spend half a day in this fabulous place. The director of the factory himself led the excursion. He took us to the factory floors, telling us how toys were made, and then he allowed us to decorate the large glass balls by ourselves. We put on long grey robes, rolled up our sleeves and sat at a huge wooden table, which was at least a dozen meters long. The table was littered with paints, tubes of glue, sparkles and rhinestones, and there was a deep drawer filled to the top with one-color glass balls in the middle. At parting, we not only took our articles; each of us also received a small box from the director, inside which was a skillfully decorated toy: a snowman or a Santa Claus (it depended). 'Something to remember,' smiled the director.

Talks about the Christmas toy factory did not die down until the New Year. Everyone was happy, even Slavik, who considered such entertainment to be the domain of children. By the way, he was cleared of the false charges of killing the dog after Fauna interfered, who was certain of Slavik's innocence. 'This kid is not like that, not like that' – the young teacher shook her head, and everyone believed her.

On December 29th, my parents came to visit me. They took me away for several hours, to a cafe where we drank tea and ate cake. I reluctantly talked about my disappointing school results, and my parents talked about distant relatives whom they had recently visited. Saying goodbye, my mother put in front of me a large bag, which my father had carried before.

'Here are some gifts for you and something for your friend.' My mother smiled, kissing me on the cheek. They wished me a Happy New Year and promised that they would come and visit very soon.

In the room, I examined the contents of the bag with great interest. There was a pair of sneakers and a toy railroad, a box of overseas chocolates and a bag of gumdrops. But the centerpiece of all that was a red cardboard box, which contained six tin cans of the same red color, with a white ornate inscription reading 'Coca-Cola' ... I can't describe how happy Slavik was! He drank the first can in one gulp, and foam went out through his nose. We laughed, enjoying the sweet drink, ate chocolates, and I thought that it was probably for the best that I was here and my parents were there. After all, otherwise there would have been no such sweets and delicious soda ...

8.

In May, right after my birthday, Slavik's mother died. He refused to go to the funeral. Instead, he ran away from the boarding school for the whole day, wandered around the city, sniffed glue and even drank beer with the local guys. Upon his return, neither Klara Fyodorovna nor anyone else scolded him.

The reason for Auntie Alla's death remained a mystery. 'They, such as she is, are responsyble for their death thamselves,' Nikichna said, but I did not understand the meaning of these words very well. Slavik did not cry, but now he rarely spoke and was gloomy. My parents, upon learning of what had happened, gave him a denim jacket, which cheered my friend up for a brief moment. He proudly walked in it through the corridors of the orphanage, showing off shiny zippers and fake pockets. But after a while, fed up with the new thing, Slavik became quiet again. One fine Sunday morning, he woke me up at dawn.

'Will you go with me to my mother's grave?' asked Slavik, and I agreed. We dressed quietly and sneaked out of the building unnoticed, slipped past Nikichna's house and disappeared into the good old crack in the blink of an eye.

The cemetery was an hour's ride away on the bus. We had no money for the trip, but Slavik managed to persuade the driver to pick up two more passengers; after all we were heading to the grave of his mother. When we left, the sun had already risen. The rays were mischievous, tenderly caressing the skin, and the wind ruffled an abundance of flowery bouquets. The air was filled with an amazing scent of lilacs that overgrew with hedges along the cemetery. Slavik broke off a couple of branches, and we went to look for the grave of Auntie Alla. She was buried far from the main gate, on the outskirts, along the sand embankment.

'They brought soil here and covered it with sand. Making space for new graves,' Slavik explained. He laid flowers next to the portrait of his mother, in which she looked young and beautiful.

'My mother was a beauty when she was younger,' Slava said, as if having read my thoughts. We squatted down and sat like that for a long time, examining the portrait of the deceased and enjoying the warm spring breeze that carried the sandy dust over the graves.

‘I think she is now in heaven,’ I said for some reason. Slavik shrugged indifferently.

‘Vitka, I do not believe in God and other nonsense. God, you know, if he were there, he would not have taken my mother away, he would not have let her drink. If God were there, there would’ve been no Rusichka, and Fauna would be with a man. No, there is no God. And if there is one, then he is cruel, this God of yours. I don’t need him.’ He got up, brushed the dust off his trousers and silently walked towards a small apple orchard. I hurried after him.

‘Where is your mother then?’ I would not stop.

‘Where? The devil knows where she is, this woman.’ Slavik laughed. ‘I think she has become a tree.’ He placed his palm on the thin trunk of a young apple tree. ‘My grandmother used to tell me that all the unfortunate people become trees when they die. Young, beautiful trees. They cling to the ground with their roots and bloom in a delicate color in spring. My mother saw little happiness in her life. My father left, my stepfather beat her, vodka became her best friend ... So I think that my mother has become a young apple tree, fragrant and tender. Look at the flowers on her, how fragrant they are! I think that her beauty ... the beauty that was given to her by nature, was revived here.’ Slavik gently ran his hand along a whimsical branch covered with blossoming buds of a soft pink hue. ‘Having become such a tree, it is simply impossible to be unhappy, because beauty is never unhappy. That’s for sure. And the place is good, it is quiet here. Mother’s soul is now at peace.’ He smiled. I listened fascinated to my friend’s story about the souls of people who were reincarnated into trees, and I thought about my grandfather, who, according to my mother’s stories, had been very unhappy. It turned out that he too had become a tree, maybe a maple or an oak, and now stands somewhere, shaking in the wind. I really liked the theory of Slavik’s grandmother about soul-trees.

‘So are all the trees someone’s souls?’ I continued the conversation as we walked back.

‘I guess they are,’ agreed Slavik. He himself had never thought about it.

‘And when we break branches or pluck leaves, do we hurt someone’s soul?’

‘I guess we do,’ repeated my friend.

‘Let’s not do this anymore, then,’ I suggested, and Slava agreed. We shook hands with each other for good measure, and said an oath, which we ourselves invented then.

I swear that I will not break tree branches.
Only if I am alone in the forest in the cold and I need to light a fire!
I swear that I will not hit animals, even the evil and the mad ones.
I swear that I will pray for the happiness of Fauna and Klara Fyodorovna, and when they die, I will pray for their rest.
I swear to hate Rusichka until my last breath, and even after I die!

We liked the oath very much, and, encouraged, we hurried to the boarding school before they missed us. Since breakfast was late on Sundays (at ten in the morning), we got there just in time. Having swallowed pancakes, generously laced with honey (apparently, the cook was in a good mood), we drank tea and went into the room where Slavik plunged into reading newspapers, and I played with some plastic toy cars presented for my birthday. My parents were unable to celebrate my twelfth birthday with me; instead they had given me a large cake and a set of toy cars. The cake was creamy, delicious, with the number twelve laid out with canned peaches.

'Sometimes I envy you, Vitka,' said Slavik. 'Your parents don't touch you – they only give you sweets and nice presents. That's the dream!' I nodded in agreement. In less than five years, I had been weaned off parental care, and off them themselves.

Having had enough fun with toy cars, I went to the library to look through the book on zoology, one of my favorites. However, when I returned a couple of hours later, Slavik was not in the room. Slavik did not say what really happened and how he had angered Rusichka in my absence, but we met after lunch (my friend was not there). Slavik's lip was broken, and there was a bruise glistening on his cheek. He flatly refused to explain it. One of the elders said that Slavik had dropped a broad hint at the Rusichka's frigid nature when she was scolding some second-grader in the corridor. I did not know what 'frigid' meant back then, and why she hit my friend because of it. Over time, of course, I found out and then I had a lot of fun, because whatever one may say, Slavik was absolutely right! But right then I was scared to look at the broken face of Slava, and it was even more scary because, frankly, none of the teachers or nannies cared.

At night, Slavik came to my bed. Covering our heads with a blanket, we chatted for a long time about all sorts of things, until he whispered: 'Vitya, I can't do this anymore.' He began to cry. Soon I was sobbing with him, stroking his palm.

'Don't cry,' I soothed my friend, fighting down my sobs. 'It won't help.'

'Let's kill her.' As if illuminated by an unexpected idea, Slavik froze and stopped crying.

'What are you saying!' I stammered out scared, widening my eyes in horror. But Slavik was already fired up.

'Nobody will know ... We can poison her. The grandmother told me how and what can be used to make it painless and avoid unnecessary fuss,' Slava reflected. But I was adamant here. Even though I hated Rusichka more than anything in the world, I flatly refused to commit murder. And I wouldn't allow Slavik to do that.

'We took an oath ...' I insisted.

'There was nothing about promising not to kill evil teachers,' Slavik retorted.

'If you don't stop, I'll tell everything to Klara Fyodorovna!' I exclaimed.

'And you call yourself a friend.' He crawled out from under the covers and went to his bed, throwing a haughty, contemptuous look over his shoulder. For a long time, I could not sleep, tormented by remorse that I had betrayed a friend, and fearing what I might agree to in the name of this very friendship. When morning was approaching, I managed to doze off, but not for long. Slavik woke me up, bowing low to my face.

'Since you do not want to kill Rusichka, then there is another option ...' he began. I pulled myself up on my elbows.

'Let's run away,' Slavik suggested somehow simply and routinely, as if we were planning to hit the road to the nearest grocery store for sweets.

'Where?'

'Just away from here ... Where Grad is.'

'And what is Grad?' I asked him.

'This is where all abandoned children live. There are no rules or penalties. And there are no adults.' Slavik smiled.

And this conversation became the beginning of a big adventure, in which, by chance, not only we, but also other pupils of the Grey Willow Boarding School were involved.

9.

We were planning an escape. We discussed all the nuances carefully and for a long time, thinking over the alternative ways of retreat in case we were caught; we rode the tram for hours, eating stolen candy and imagining how great it would be to wander the world in search of Grad. At night, I fantasized about uncharted lands we had yet to discover; about how we would live somewhere on the outskirts of the forest in a small hut, collecting brushwood and getting a goat. In short, my imagination painted amazing pictures of our future life. The escape was scheduled for mid-May: we needed to collect the necessary supply of food by that time. We began slowly stealing cereals, cookies and sweets from the kitchen. Slavik took a small pot, and I got aluminum dishes.

Meanwhile, spring delighted the town of M., smart and rosy like the cheeks of the saleswoman Galia from a local bakery. Spring flirted with passers-by, tousled her hair with her warm hands and generously spread her beauty around, young and naive. Even the 'Old Lady Willow' seemed a little cheered up after the arrival of the young lassie. The grey, inhospitable building brightened, freshened up in the rays of the soft sun, slowly rubbed away old scars, stitching them with bright spring threads. Small blue flowers bloomed on the grave of the mongrel Slavik and I had buried, and a carpet of pansies spread out a little further. They trembled amusingly in the wind, shining with variegated colors in the rays of the spring sun. They smiled with tiny faces like little fairies, winking at each other. How beautiful the spring was that year! I was twelve, enjoying the warmth, stealing food and devising an escape plan at night. Life seemed amazing ...

One day, having slipped away through the crack as usual, Slavik and I sneaked out to the cinema. *Crime and Punishment* with Georgiy Taratorkin as Rodion Raskolnikov was playing. I was unfamiliar with the plot and watched the movie with my mouth open. The film was fascinating and frightening at the same time. Even then, I had a persistent dislike for all kinds of violence, which only intensified over the years. And it was then, for the first time in my life, I felt disgusted. Disgusted by what I saw. My little, quivering child's soul, devoid of essential vices (except stealing sweets and hating Rusichka), resisted what I saw. I did not want to believe that such an evil existed, which could simply take a life without good reason. War was the 'reason'. Defending oneself and defending others was the 'reason', but what I saw was more of an expression of baseness. The beastliness of a human being, of a young intelligent man, frightened me. I thought that since the young Raskolnikov could take someone's life so easily, what was there to prevent Rusichka from doing the same thing. It may happen just like this: you will find yourself in the same room with her late at night, she will break loose, scream, swing, and that's it. Then, under the cover of night, she will bury your body next to the red mongrel, and in May forget-me-nots will bloom there, and Nikichna will water them. My heart was beating furiously! I understood that none of us was immune to this.

After leaving the cinema, I shared my concerns with Slavik. He listened intently, then shook his head busily.

'It makes sense what you're saying here, Vitka. We will never be safe. But I believe in punishment.'

'Murderers do not always get found,' I muttered timidly. 'My parents said so once.'

'People don't find them, but punishment does,' answered Slavik.

'What do you mean?' We slowly walked along a long alley, and I listened to my friend's reasoning about punishment.

'Punishment will definitely come for you if you have done something wrong ...'

'Like stealing food?' I whispered in horror.

'No. It's not terrible to steal, especially when stealing little and mostly food,' Slavik hastened to assure me. 'Punishment comes for murderers, rapists, all sorts of monsters. Well, those who beat children or abuse animals. There was a woman living in my house, who looked kind, and her husband was good, he loved her. But she killed him ...'

'How come?!'

'Just like that. For no reason, he just bothered her or something.'

'And she was not sent to jail?'

'No, there was no evidence. So she lived happily then. She buried her husband, and fooled around with other men. A couple of months later, she was stabbed to death by one of those men, in some showdown of drunk people. Then punishment overtook her. That man was jailed. I think that he had done something bad in his life too, so Fate pushed him to another crime, for which he paid with his freedom.' Slavik spoke, and I listened attentively, thinking that Fate is probably very cunning, since She can lull the vigilance of criminals and strike a fatal blow at the right time.

'And what, does She never forget about anyone?' I asked.

'No one! She has a special book where She has written down the names of all evil people. And for many years ahead, She has it planned, who and how she will punish. I know that, my grandmother told me,' Slavik said firmly.

We continued walking through the narrow streets of the town of M., fresh with spring, and talked a lot. About crimes and the punishment that awaits everyone who angers Fate. We discussed escape again and were excited about the hope of change.

When change came, it arrived with a young, pimply delivery boy. My parents were going on a long business trip, so no visits for at least a year. In the letter that was attached to the 'farewell' gift, they said that they loved me very much and that they would write and, if possible, call me, send gifts and pamper me, their only beloved son, in every possible way. I didn't believe a single word. Except perhaps what they said about gifts. I had long lost faith in their love, and I myself did not love them, because it is difficult to love those whom you see just a few times a year, and only for a couple of hours. The letter convinced me completely that running away was the right decision. I was only confused by the gift: a yellow budgie, which, according to the note, was called Lemon. He twisted his head amusingly, examining me, tweeted and jumped on a perch. Lemon was incredibly cute. My parents also wrote that Klara Fyodorovna had allowed me to keep it near the bed, but if other boys pestered the bird, she would always be glad to put it in her office, where I could come to have a conversation with a new friend. I liked Lemon, and the first thing I did was hurry to find Slavik, holding a small cage in my hands.

'We cannot take it with us.' Slavik sighed, sticking his thumb between the twigs. Lemon poked at him with its beak amusingly, biting lightly.

'A bird like this one cannot survive through the journey. You can't let it out from the cage, it will fly away and die. And carrying it in a cage is a torment for both us and for it. And what will you feed it with? Such parrots eat some special food, I saw boxes in the store. You can't dig worms for him in the forest, can you?' Slavik's words made me upset. I took Lemon to the bedroom, where I admired him a lot, gently shaking the cage. At each shaking, the parrot jumped on the perch and quickly shook its head. At night, I covered it with a sheet, as was indicated in the instructions, and in the morning I poured food into the feeder, which had come with Lemon. Very soon I fell in love with my new friend with all my heart, and the idea of separation from him became more unbearable every day.

'My grandmother loved birds very much,' Slavik said one evening. We were sitting in the bedroom, he leafing through the newspaper, and I stroking Lemon's finger through the bars. 'She said that birds are the souls of prisoners. Having died, those who have lived locked up all their lives are turned into birds ...'

'And who locked them up?' I asked.

'Not literally.' Slavik smiled. 'You can be locked up and live in freedom at the same time. It is not necessary to have shackles on your hands to be unable to reach the door. And outside the door there is an exit, freedom. Therefore, the souls of such people became birds to be able to soar in the sky, cutting through the clouds ...'

'Do you think that Lemon is someone's soul?' I looked at the silky breast of my feathered friend with interest.

'No, I don't think so. Lemon does not try to break free. From what I see, he doesn't really want to fly.' Slavik bent down to the cage, carefully looking into Lemon's beady eyes. 'He is definitely a real bird, you don't have to worry.' After his words I felt better, because the last thing I wanted to think was that the soul of someone who had suffered in a previous life was now suffering inside the tight cage.

10.

The escape was scheduled for May 20th. At night, after waiting for everyone to fall asleep, we were going to quietly sneak into the courtyard, where, a couple of days before we had hidden everything we needed behind Nikichna's house: food, dishes, clothes and some other items that we thought were necessary. Then, out into the town through the usual crack, and from there – on foot through the forest, without stopping. We planned to walk all night so that we could walk far enough before we were missed in the morning. Since May 21st was a Sunday and we usually got up later that day, we had several hours' headstart. Having had a good rest the day before, we readied our flashlights, which Slavik had got us in exchange for my cars, and were determined to walk until exhaustion hit us. At about two in the morning, Slavik pushed me lightly in the side. We tiptoed out into the corridor and soon found ourselves on the ground floor near the back door. No one locked the door usually so that Nikichna could get inside if necessary. Having pressed the handle, we were one step away from our long-awaited freedom, when suddenly someone called out to us. Startled, we turned abruptly, expecting to meet the angry gaze of a nanny or, even worse, Rusichka, but when the first wave of fright passed, to our surprise we saw Akim, the Tatar orphan.

'You fool, you scared us!' Slavik gasped. 'Why are you awake?'

'I want to join you,' Akim blurted out. Amazed, we looked at each other.

'What are you thinking! Go away, or I'll hit you!' Slavik swung menacingly, trying to scare Akim. But he was not one to get scared easily. Hot Eastern blood flowed in his veins, boiling up to meet any danger.

'If you hit me, I'll scream,' Akim said firmly, crossing his arms over his chest.

'Don't joke with me, Muslim muzzle,' Slavik hissed angrily, clenching his fists.

'I'm not joking, fatherlessness fool.' Now they were facing off, competing to see who was bolder.

'Akim, don't ...' A gentle voice sounded from aside. 'Leave them alone, let's go to sleep.' Miwa, Akim's younger sister, stepped towards us uncertainly.

‘What is she doing here?’ Slavik chuntered.

‘I won’t leave without my sister!’ Akim declared firmly, putting his arm around Miwa’s shoulders. The knee-high girl huddled close to her brother, hiding her doll face under his arm. In the moonlight, her long hair in a thick braid seemed darker than the night.

‘Akim, don’t be a fool,’ Slavik hissed trying to control himself. He was casting brief glances to Miwa, who at that moment looked like a fairy-tale girl, beautiful in her purity.

‘They hurt us here,’ the girl said quietly. ‘We will obey you.’ She looked at Slavik as if she was pleading. I don’t know how this little girl managed to charm my old friend, but that night he was drowned in a bottomless girlish gaze. Slavik scratched the back of his head, swore quietly and then nodded reluctantly.

‘Damn you! So be it.’ He waved his hand and pressed the handle.

Under the cover of the night, we made our way to the house of the caretaker, where we took our things, carefully packed into two army backpacks, which had been exchanged for a block of gum. Akim and Miwa were walking light.

‘You are not prepared.’ Slavik snorted contemptuously. ‘Do you think we’ll share what we have?’

‘We don’t need it, we’ll buy everything we need.’ Akim smiled, taking out a pack of small bills from his pocket. Slavik whistled.

‘Well, now we’re talking!’ He patted him on the shoulder in a friendly way. ‘We have to go without stopping for many hours. Don’t lag behind and look after your sister. I will not drag along because of her,’ my friend said forcefully and rushed towards the forest, illuminating the road with a flashlight. An hour later, however, Slavik carefully carried Miwa in his arms, while she snored quietly with her face buried in his chest. Akim and I walked a little further behind.

I peered cautiously into a Stygian darkness cut by the giant trees. The winding path zigzagged, forcing us to make an extra detour around the thicket, and then climb the mountain. I felt uneasy, and at the same time, I felt joy. Indeed, at that moment we were free, we were brave travellers who were not afraid of going forward. I watched how carefully Slavik wrapped sleeping Miwa in a denim jacket, given to him once by my parents, and was glad that there were now four of us. Now we were a real expedition, pioneers. As we walked further and further, I thought about my parents, whom it would hardly be possible to inform about my disappearance. Maybe in a couple of months, when they decided to call,

Klara Fyodorovna would tell them about what had happened. I wondered if they would interrupt their business trip, or actually feel relieved. I did not know and thought that I'd never find out. I also thought of Lemon, a kind feathered friend for whom I had found the most amazing of all possible hosts. The day before escaping, I had visited Fauna. She sat at her large teacher's desk, which was covered with books and notebooks. Putting the cage with Lemon on top of the books, I asked her to accept my gift. The girl refused at first, but then she agreed, taking a promise from me that I would sometimes visit him. This was the first time I had lied to my dear Fauna. And now, following Slavik, I thought about Lemon, who was dozing on the table of the kind teacher, and how for many more years he would be watching her checking stacks of notebooks day after day. I knew they would become good friends.

Part II

Escape, or Long-Awaited Salvation

Prologue

An old one-eyed cat sat on the windowsill, dozing in the gloom of a warm May night. The window was open, and a light spring breeze pleasantly caressed the grey coat of Licorice, the ugliest cat I have ever met. She was too old to hunt rats and too lame to chase pigeons. Therefore, all day long the old lady did nothing but lie on the windowsill, philosophically watching the slow flow of life in the yard of the Grey Willow Boarding School. Licorice knew all the school's secrets and mysteries. She knew who was going where under the cover of the night and how often the kids were running off to have a cigarette in the morning. She knew who was having an affair with whom, who had stolen a bag of potatoes from the kitchen, and why the history teacher had cried last Wednesday.

Licorice had seen a lot in her long feline life. Once upon a time, when she could still run friskily, the orphanage yard had seemed a huge world to her, and the people scurrying back and forth were giant wizards capable of performing miracles (for example, opening doors or getting mouth-watering chicken bones and sour cottage cheese out of nowhere). Over time, however, the cat realized that not all people were magicians. Having learned human nature, she treated almost all two-leggeds with contempt. The only exception was her human, a funny caretaker, and a lop-eared boy who sometimes visited their house. She could not stand the rest, rewarding them with a good portion of feline swearing and deep scratches. Becoming friends with Licorice was difficult, and few people tried. Sometimes, passing by the windows of Nikichna's house, the kids made faces at the cat, teasing it. At such moments, Licorice ruffled and strove to get through the window and teach hooligans a lesson. Her appearance became so formidable that the inhabitants of the boarding school immediately ran to get out of harm's way. Nevertheless, in ordinary life the old lame cat was a peaceful, imposing creature, who preferred a warm bed and greasy sour cream to any fights.

Licorice was dozing peacefully on the windowsill when a distant noise caught her ears. The old lady opened her olive-colored eyes wide, ears perked up. In the gloom of the night, she noticed four silhouettes creeping towards the fence, which she knew had a crack. Intrigued by what she saw, Licorice stood up, pressing her nose against the cold window, and watched carefully until the mysterious quartet disappeared around the corner of the house. Very soon forgetting about them, the cat jumped to the floor, slowly walked to the couch, on which Nikichna snored, jumped to her feet, washed herself for a long time, then stretched and fell asleep peacefully, curled up in a ball. Licorice knew how to keep secrets.

1.

At dawn, Slavik slowed down, offering to rest a bit and have something to eat. We readily agreed, as we were rather tired by that time. Slavik carefully put Miwa on the ground (the girl did not even wake up), then he took a pack of oatmeal cookies and water out of his backpack. After breakfast we rested no more than for half an hour, then set off again, not willing to be overtaken. After a while, Miwa woke up, forcing us to make another stop to eat. Even now, I don't know how far we had come, but the places, roads and small villages that we passed were unfamiliar. By lunchtime we were completely exhausted.

'We can't go further today, and the police are probably already looking for us in cars. They will quickly catch up with us,' Slavik reasoned. Ordering us to wait for him at the agreed place, near a fallen dry oak tree, he left in search of temporary housing. He did not return soon: the day was already wearing on when at last he reappeared.

'Faster, because all the nearby villages are already searching!' he commanded, and we ran after him, bending double. In about half an hour, our company found itself in front of a huge embankment with a lopsided door in the middle.

'This is an old cellar – they are no longer using it,' explained Slavik. 'We will sit it out here.'

'For how long?' asked Akim.

'We will sit for as long as necessary. A month if we need to!' snapped my friend.

'A month?!' Miwa cried in terror, pressing her tiny palms against her little porcelain face (her skin was light, unlike the skin of Akim).

'Well, I overestimated it a bit, maybe not a month.' Slavik smiled, winking at the girl. 'Less talking, let's go!'

And so we entered the pitch darkness of an abandoned cellar, which was supposed to be our refuge for the near future. It was difficult to say how big or small it was, as one pocket flashlight was our only light source. We were saving the others for later. Small, faded rays running along the walls helped us to piece together the image of our new home. The cellar was made of stone, roughly finished, and in some places the walls were already falling down. Tracks of mould ran along the cold floor, climbing up to the ceiling, which was shedding dust onto our heads. The stale, damp air made it difficult to breathe, and our skin was soon covered with sweat.

In the corner, there were several wooden boxes with rusted nails sticking out. 'This will do.' Slavik sighed, scratching the back of his head. 'It's disgusting enough for a dog to come here – I'm not even saying about cops!' He laughed, pushing one of the boxes with his foot. Having arranged the rest as chairs and beds, we laid out our modest belongings and began to cook dinner. Since we could not make a fire due to the peculiarities of our house, and were afraid to attract attention with smoke, for dinner we had dry chunks of black bread, cold canned meat and a few raisins. Unlike us boys, who listened keenly to every rustle outside the door, Miwa ate with delight and seemed to enjoy the unexpected adventure.

'Let's tell stories,' the girl suggested, chewing her raisins.

'Yes, horror stories!' Akim supported the idea.

'No ...' Miwa whispered, pursing her lips. 'Let's tell good stories.'

'About princes and princesses, right?' Her brother grimaced with displeasure. 'You girls always stuff your heads with fairy tales.'

'If she wants good ones, let them be good ones.' Slavik resolved the fight. 'It's deadly here, and with this stench, what kind of a horror story do you need?' The cellar really was not a pleasant place: besides the dampness, it smelled as if something had gone bad there, like a piece of meat had been lying around for weeks.

'Then you start!' Miwa clapped her hands happily, turning to Slavik. After thinking for a couple of seconds, he began:

'Once upon a time there lived a very beautiful and kind girl. Her name was Anya. Anya was not like everyone else. Just not like others. Even her name was special. After all, in fact, the girl's name was Antonida ...'

'What kind of name is this?' Akim spat on the damp floor.

'A special kind!' objected Miwa. 'Go on.'

'So that's it. She had a special name, Antonida. But, as I said, she was not a girl like everyone else. Therefore, barely reaching the age of three and finally realizing how ridiculous her name was ...'

'There you go.' Akim nodded.

'Shut up!' Miwa interrupted him.

'... realizing how ridiculous her name was, Anya stood in the middle of the room proudly, looked into the eyes of the surprised parents of hers and said: "From now on, call me Anya".' Slavik stood up to his full height, trying to clearly demonstrate how determined the three-year-old Anya was.

'Since then, she became Anya,' continued Slavik. 'In general, Anya always did only what she wanted. From the very day when she deliberately forbade everyone to call her Antonida or Tosya, as her mother often did, all the relatives, accustomed to the girl's oddities, did not contradict her, because they knew that Anya would still do as she saw fit.'

'What an amazing girl!' admired Miwa.

'As I said, Anya was very smart. Some even said that she was brilliant!'

'What means brilliant?' asked Akim before I did.

'Well ... it's like very, very smart,' Slavik replied thoughtfully.

'Oh.' We nodded.

'So, whatever Anya undertook, she immediately succeeded. Studying, sports ... She never had any problems with anything.'

'I wish I could do this too ... So that everything would always work out right away with lessons, and jump-rope,' Miwa said admiringly, wrapping her arms around herself. It was chilly.

'You foolish head, you don't even know how to tie your laces! A jump rope!' Akim was acting snarky.

'Shut up!' shouted Slavik.

'Yes, let him finish,' I added, having not uttered a sound before.

'So ... What was I talking about? Oh yes. So, for example, having barely finished sixth grade, Anya decided to transfer to another school, one with an in-depth study of languages. She just wanted to do it and that was it. And no one contradicted her. But, without even having studied there for two years, she moved to a third school. Nobody objected. The coaches predicted a bright future for her in swimming, and she simply said: 'I am tired of this. I want to skate.' And she skated. Beautifully, amazingly, as if she was born on ice, but before her relatives had time to blink an eye, Anya had already danced on the ballroom floor, easily winning prizes at the most prestigious championships ...'

'Brilliant!' Akim gasped. Miwa nodded her little head approvingly.

'And then Anya gave up everything. All awards and dances. She came to her parents and said: 'I've had enough. I am tired of this! I'd better learn foreign languages.' And she succeeded enough in this matter, receiving a number of diplomas, but then again waved her hand dismissively and ... got married. She just wanted to. And nobody disagreed. A year later, the marriage broke up, and Anya arranged a new wedding. But a week before the solemn event, she changed her mind, and left the institute where she was studying in the third year.'

'This Anya is weird.' I winced, not sharing the delight of my companions.

'Special,' Miwa corrected.

'Anya entered medical school, dreaming of becoming a surgeon ...'

'And what is a surgeon?' the girl asked.

'The kind of a doctor who cuts your belly and takes out your guts,' explained Akim.

'Why?!' Miwa's eyes widened in horror.

'Well, to wash them or throw away the extra ones. Or to find out why a person died. The bellies of corpses are cut open too, you know–'

Akim did not have time to finish as Miwa had tightly shut both her eyes and closed her ears with her hands. 'You're lying!' she squeaked.

'I'm not lying!'

'Surgeons don't cut corpses.' Slavik cut him off. 'That's what the morgue staffers do, those who work for mortuaries. Surgeons cure. Stop talking nonsense, or you'll get a slap.' Slavik shook his fist threateningly in front of Akim's nose.

'What happened next?' smiled Miwa, feeling our older friend's protection. He smiled back.

'After having studied for a couple of years, one morning Anya presented her parents with a fact: "I'll probably go to work." She dropped out of school, got a job as a waitress, then as a nanny, then as a guide ... And then, she gave up on everything again and left for Georgia!'

'Wow!' Akim whistled.

'Where is Georgia?' Miwa asked timidly.

'Far away,' snapped Slavik. 'A year later, Anya came back and signed up for dancing again. But on the eve of an important competition, she came and said: 'I've had enough. I am tired of living! I'm going to die tomorrow.' Everyone threw up their hands again, her friends laughed, and in the morning Anya died. Nobody believed it. Everyone decided that it was another quirk. And, standing in the cemetery, everyone believed that in another second Anya would open her eyes, roll them up and say: 'I've had enough. I am tired of it! I'm getting married in a month.' Only when her body disappeared under a layer of loose earth, did everyone finally understood what had happened ... That is how special Anya was. She always did only what she wanted, even died when she wanted to ...'

Silence reigned in the cellar for some time, until Akim broke it, swearing (and it was definitely swearing) in a language that we did not understand.

'What kind of a bad story is this? Once upon a time, an extraordinary girl lived, and then she just died, just like that! This is sillier than Miwa's favorite tales about pink princesses.'

'I liked it – it was a beautiful story.' Miwa sighed, enchanted, not taking her eyes off Slavik.

'The story is good, and if you were at least a little smarter, you would have understood what the point is.' Slavik made a displeased grimace.

'And what is that?'

'I won't tell you!' To add more contempt to his retort, Slavik raised the flashlight to his face, illuminating his tongue hanging out. Akim started swearing again.

'The bottom line is that Anya was free ...' I said slowly.

'What do you mean?' asked Akim.

'No one ordered her, no one told her when she had to eat, when to sleep, where to go and with whom to talk. Free, you know. She even died, not when it was acceptable, in her old age, but young. Because she wanted to herself,' I reasoned, tucking my knees to my chest.

'There! Unlike you, Akim, Vitek has a good head on his shoulders!' Slavik burst out laughing and patted me on the shoulder. 'My friend!' I smiled.

Tired after a day's journey, we decided to go to bed. Miwa and Akim settled down on one of the boxes, Slavik lay down on the floor, spreading the spruce branches that he had brought in advance, while I put myself on the heap of rotten boards piled up in the corner of the cellar. Slavik fell asleep instantly, snoring. After a while, I heard the even deep breathing of brother and sister. I myself could not sleep for a long time, thinking about the adventures of the past day and fearfully listening to the silence of the sleepy forest. It seemed to me that I heard someone's footsteps or a whisper. I was afraid that a police squad would enter and take us back to 'Old Lady Willow'. I loved the boarding school in my own way – it was never actually a boarding school to me. It was home. But I couldn't stay there any longer. I wanted to be free, like the girl Anya from Slavik's story. I wanted to go where I wanted to. To eat cold canned meat and chocolate cookies. I wanted to stay awake at night and urinate in the bushes. To spit, swear and do things that had always been forbidden. And even die if I suddenly wanted to. This is what I really wanted.

2.

We spent the next few days in our shelter, occasionally sticking our noses out to take a breath of fresh air or go in the woods. We dug a pit in the floor to use as a cesspool. Not very deep, so one could crouch over it without fearing of breaking one's legs in the event of rotten wood breaking. Nevertheless, on the second day, it was decided to do number two in the bushes, since the already horrible stink of the cellar was becoming simply intolerable. We endured to the last, and then, listening carefully, slowly opened the creaky door and, making sure that there was no one in the neighbourhood, ran half-bent into the bushes. We had breakfast with dried bread and drank a little water, being afraid to spend too much of it. We had cold canned food for lunch, and cookies for dinner. In the evenings (although it was hard to say whether those really were evenings, because we were surrounded by darkness all day long), Slavik entertained us with stories, for which Miwa was choosing a theme. If today she wanted to hear something kind with a happy ending, Slavik told stories in which the main characters found happiness despite adversity and obstacles. But the very next day, tired of the stench and mustiness, the girl could change mood and ask for something sad. Then Slavik started a melancholy ballad about unhappy love, death or betrayal. Miwa usually sobbed bitterly, and the next morning asked for a funny story, about grown-up fools or stupid kids. And then all three of us chortled (not out loud because we did not want to attract uninvited guests!), heartily laughing at the characters of the story.

On the fourth or fifth day, Miwa fell ill. Penetrating moisture and wet clothes broke her fragile body, and one morning we woke up to her violent cough.

'She has a fever,' said Slavik nervously, checking her forehead. 'It's bad.' He sighed heavily, squatting down next to her.

'Now what?' asked Akim.

'We should call a doctor,' I suggested.

'Are you crazy?!' Slavik twisted his finger at his temple. 'A doctor!'

'But she will die if ... well, without a doctor,' I babbled.

'True ...' Slavik said slowly, 'true. But we can't call a doctor – they will take us back then. If we find a doctor, then, well, we must kill him somewhere.'

'How?!' I gasped.

'What did you think?' Akim scoffed. 'Otherwise he will give us away.'

'Don't kill anyone ...' Miwa croaked, bursting into tears. 'Please.' She buried her face in Slavik's jacket, which she was using instead of a pillow.

'Hey, come on! Wait there. We are not going to kill anyone.' Slavik laughed. 'We need to put you in the sun, to warm you up.' After these words, he carefully took the girl in his arms and slowly walked towards the steps.

'Where are you doing?' Akim got scared, blocking the way to Slavik. 'You will be spotted!'

'Do you want your sister to die here?' my friend asked angrily. Having thought for a minute, Akim shook his head.

'There you are. Do not panic, they will not spot us. I'll be careful.' With these words Slavik, with Miwa in his arms, disappeared in the rays of the bright spring sun and did not return until the evening. By that time, Akim and I had got so worried that we were ready to start searching for them. When we saw the silhouette of Slavik in the doorway, we were very happy. But it was even better that Miwa was clearly recovering after a day in the fresh air. The fever had passed, and even her face (as far as one could believe the light from the flashlight) looked healthy.

'When will we leave here?' she asked, clearing her throat loudly.

'Hush!' Akim hissed. 'We will leave when things get quiet.'

'But it's so good up there ...' said Miwa sadly, pointing at the door with a tiny finger.

'Stop whining!' Akim pinched her painfully. 'Better go to sleep. Don't waste your energy.'

In the morning, to our great regret, Miwa, although she did not suffer from fever, coughed even more badly. Her throat emitted such eerie, hysterical sounds that no one who didn't know it already would have guessed that this was a little eleven-year-old girl. She sounded more like a huge man. Trying not to make so much noise, Miwa covered her mouth with her hands, hid her face in her palms, but everything was in vain. The cough echoed throughout the shelter, loudly hitting the walls, and, like a crystal glass, shattered into hundreds of sharp fragments. Each of us mentally prayed to God, Allah or anyone else, that no one would hear it up there, that they would not find us. But the cough would only get worse, and soon Miwa stopped even talking, as any attempt to utter a word was covered with the rapid wave of a deep rolling cough.

Akim was angry – he constantly pulled and hurt his sister, making her suffer severely. Even I felt stressed because of the situation, and sometimes I thought (although I felt bad afterwards!) that if Miwa died, we would all be safe. It seems to me that she felt it, so she avoided my company in every possible way and sometimes even feared to touch me. Only Slavik was lenient with the girl. Sometimes, during a particularly strong attack of coughing, he would take Miwa in his arms and rock her like a child, whispering something. Then the girl quickly fell asleep, and we sighed with relief (she did not cough only when she was sleeping).

A couple of weeks later, something happened that made us overcome our fear and leave our temporary home. Late in the evening, when everyone but me was already asleep, I heard footsteps outside the door. The soil, which was wet after the last rainstorm, was squelching, and someone was talking loudly. I hastily woke up the others, we packed our things and the four of us huddled in the corner of the cellar, hiding behind a pile of rotten boxes. After a while, the cellar door opened, and we heard someone coming down the steps.

'What a stench!' said a man in a raspy voice.

'Did some creature actually die here, or what?' a second man continued. He spoke slowly, drawing out every word.

'There can be anything in these cellars. It's good if it's just dead pigs and rotten vegetables, but there can be worse things.' The first man giggled.

'Stop that, we'll sleep here. The main thing is that it's quiet,' said the second man.

It seemed to us that they sat on the floor and began to rustle with packages, taking something out. Despite the fact it was pitch black, it seemed to me that I could see the horror frozen on the faces of my comrades. Squeezing into the very corner of the cellar, we did not know what to do next. But the situation worsened when I felt with my back, against which Miwa was pressed, how her little body shuddered, struggling with a surging coughing fit. She pressed her lips into my shoulder, but a slight thump could still be heard.

'Did you hear that?' asked the owner of the viscous speech.

'What?'

'Like someone clapping ...'

'Old cellars, even the walls whisper here.' While the strangers were talking about the source of the unknown sound, I felt not only Miwa's shudders, but my own heartbeat, which was so frequent that it rumbled crushingly somewhere near the Adam's apple, stifling my breath. Covering my mouth with my hands, I tried to calm it down, but nothing worked. At some point, Miwa made two or three sharp movements, squeezing my elbow.

'We're dead,' Slavik whispered, when suddenly the tremor stopped. The girl froze.

'There is definitely something in here,' the first stranger continued.

'Let's give you this something.' I heard Slavik's whisper again. As it turned out (I did not see it in the dark), he groped for a small stone with his hand and threw it in the direction of the intruders.

'What the hell!' cried the first one.

'I told you!' the second one replied. 'The hell with it! Let's get out of here.' And to our great joy, the two strangers left our shelter, frightened by some unknown thing living in a damp cellar.

When their footsteps died down, we finally crawled out of our hiding place. Slavik turned on the flashlight, discovering that the fugitives had left a piece of fresh bread and a bottle of tomato juice.

'Not a bad catch!' Slavik smiled.

'You are so cool!' I rushed to hug my friend, but our joy was interrupted by Akim.

'Shhh,' he whispered, 'it's ...'

'What now?' Slavik lit him with a flashlight and froze in mid-sentence. Akim's face looked like a death mask, horror frozen in his eyes.

'Miwa ...' He pointed to the corner where we had been hiding a couple of minutes earlier. Miwa was lying there. At first I thought that she was sleeping, but her posture was so unnatural, her hair disheveled hair and her arms arched, that Slavik and I tensed.

'She began to cough, and I got so scared that they would hear us. I covered her face with my hands, not strongly. She twitched and then froze ... She ... Did she die?!' Akim shrieked, trembling with his whole body. Without wasting a moment, Slavik rushed headlong to the girl's body, put his hand to her chest, then her ear; then he shook her, turned her over on the side, but she still lay motionless. Numb with horror, Akim bit his lips, and I cried.

'Do not cry! Come here quickly. You will help!' ordered Slavik, and in the blink of an eye I was near him.'Hold the flashlight and point at her face with the light.' Slavik handed me the flashlight and bent to the girl's lips, 'I saw this in an American movie.' After that he did something that looked like a kiss on the lips, as the older guys did. Then he hit Miwa several times in the face and chest with his palm, again and again.

‘What are you doing?!’ shouted Akim.

‘Get away!’ Slavik kissed the girl’s lips again. And so it went on until the cellar was filled with Miwa’s cough. The girl jerked abruptly and opened her eyes.

‘It worked, damn it!’ Slavik shouted joyfully.

Miwa coughed long and painfully. When the fits of coughing finally subsided, she began to cry bitterly.

‘I hate you! I hate you!’ she whined until another attack started tormenting her.

‘I did not want to. Believe me,’ claimed Akim, trying to touch his sister, who fearfully huddled up to Slavik.

‘You there, come here,’ said Slavik calmly. Putting Miwa aside Miwa, he approached the frightened Akim.

‘Vitka, light his face.’

I directed a beam of light at Akim, and Slavik hit him right in the jaw with his fist. Akim flew a couple of meters away, hitting his back on the rotten boards. When he propped himself up on his elbows, his chin was covered in blood, and a hole gaped in place of his front tooth.

‘If you touch her again, you will choke on your own blood,’ Slavik hissed furiously. His voice at that moment sounded really threatening. Miwa clapped her hands happily and threw herself on her protector’s neck.

‘If it was not for you! Oh, if it was not for you,’ she laughed, kissing Slavik on the cheek.

That night Slavik ordered Miwa to sleep apart from Akim. We confiscated the box he’d been sleeping on and put him on the damp floor.

‘In the morning we will have breakfast, collect our stuff and move on. We’ve been sitting here for too long,’ said Slavik. Everyone agreed with him. At night, I slept restlessly, constantly waking up from the rustling and then the furious howling of the wind. I tried to think about pleasant things, about Fauna and my feathered friend Lemon. But the wind brought me back to the reality of our fetid ‘home’, reminding me of how we had nearly lost Miwa. I felt extremely bitter from the thought that I had allowed myself to picture her death. That night, I vowed that I would never again let terrible fantasies into my heart, the ones that you don’t really want to come true. As it turned out, they can come true just as easily without our wishing them so.

3.

At that age, I did not know yet what a hangover was, but the way I felt the morning of the next day was similar to one: a heavy head, body pain and such a painful dryness in the mouth that I licked a damp wall because I couldn't find our water in the darkness.

'There is a freight train passing nearby. We will sneak to the tracks and jump up. Away from here,' Slavik reasoned during breakfast. We finished the food quickly and cautiously poked our noses out in the street, fearing an ambush. Instead of the expected gang of bandits or a police squad, however, we were greeted by the welcoming May sun, which seemed to promise hot fragrant summer tomorrow. The grass around our hideout was green, and the trees rustled in time with the wind. Seeing all this beauty, Miwa laughed joyfully. She looked dreadful, as we all did. Her face was a greyish, unnatural colour, her cheeks eerily hollow and there were dark circles around her eyes. The skin on her hands was dry and cracked, and Slavik even had some red spots on his neck.

'It's shingles,' he said, noticing my gaze.

'What's that?' I asked.

'It's a kind of a parasite, like lice, but it doesn't crawl. No worries, it'll die under the sun.' Slavik laughed seeing the fear on my face.

Either way, Akim looked the worst out of the three of us. The traces of dried blood could still be seen on his jaw, he spoke with a whistling sound because of the missing front tooth, and he was scratching all the time for some reason. I decided that on top of everything, he was being attacked by parasites.

'Maybe it's lice?' I asked Slavik, but he shook his head.

'We need to wash ourselves,' he said, pointing to the path leading to the railway. We went looking for a lake, which was supposed to be somewhere nearby, according to Slavik. We were glad that with every step we were moving away from the cellar, which had been our refuge all this time. Over the years, I have often recalled those days spent in pitch darkness, dampness and stink; how we ate cold canned meat and went to the loo over a hole in the floor; Slavik's stories and Miwa's laughter. This period left mixed feelings in my soul, a combination of disgust and joy, as if citric acid and powdered sugar were mixed in one glass, creating something unique, an acquired taste. Such are my memories, sweet-and-sour, with an admixture of bitterness, like a bad lemon.

We soon reached the promised lake. 'Undress yourselves,' ordered Slavik, and everyone undressed to their underpants, except for Miwa. She preferred to stay in a T-shirt. Slavik pulled a piece of laundry soap out from his backpack and handed it to me, as the first candidate for a thorough wash.

My legs were cramping in the water, which had not yet had time to warm up under the rays of the spring sun, but was still pleasant. The lake's freshness and sudden gusts of wind were most welcome after the musty cellar. My dry skin was moistened and cleansed of its ingrained dirt. Having washed myself thoroughly, I handed over the soap to Miwa, and sat down in the sun on the shore.

'Warm up properly,' Slavik admonished, watching vigilantly the girl's bathing procedures. Embarrassed by our gazes, Miwa went into the reeds, where she stripped naked to wash her clothes.

'Where are your parents?' I asked Akim while he was waiting for his turn.

'Who knows!' he replied indifferently. 'Our dad gave up on us a long time ago. He came from the Crimean people, and our mother was a bad woman and handed us on to our grandma. My grandmother loved Miwa and me, she baked cakes, but then one morning she didn't wake up and we ended up in a boarding school. Our mother might have left to go somewhere, or maybe she also died. I don't know, but if she is alive, I wish an impending and terrible death to her.'

The story of Akim upset me. Especially the fact that he wished his mother death. 'But she's your mother ...' I retorted.

'Only on paper. You know, everyone is given such a piece of paper at birth, where they write down the one who gave birth to you. So, she's a mother only on that piece of paper. You know, Vitka, I don't care about her, but Miwa feels sad without her mother, she even cries about her sometimes. Girls need mothers – they are somehow too gentle, they want to be held, they love to be kissed. I don't like that.'

'Me neither,' I agreed. 'Do you remember how your mother was?'

'No, I don't remember, but ...' Akim wanted to continue, but Miwa interrupted us. She ran out of the lake, wringing out her coal-coloured hair with her hands. The girl laughed, dancing in the rays of the mischievous sun. She was twirling around with her arms outstretched until she fell on the warm sand, and now she was burying her small palms and feet into it. Despite the indifferent feelings that I had for Miwa, at that moment I could not help admiring her! Her doll's face, recently haggard with disease, had transformed, and her white straight teeth looked like a string of pearls, which my mother used to wear on weekends. Miwa laughed and rolled on the sand in a childish playful way, amusing me and Slavik.

'What a funny girl she is!' My friend smiled.

Having washed ourselves up and dried off, we lit a fire and for the first time in a while we had warm canned meat with the fresh bread the uninvited guests had left in the cellar the day before. After drinking water from the lake, we moved along, trying to find a railway before the evening arrived.As we walked, I thought of the cold lake water, feeling its freshness on my dried skin. My face felt tingly and wrinkled because of the laundry soap, but I was happy that we no longer stank like the cellar: the smell of mould and human faeces.

At last we got to the railway, which ran ahead for hundreds of kilometers, already covered by darkness, foreshadowing an unforgettable adventure. The railway was invulnerable and lonely like 'Old Lady Willow', but unlike the grey building of the boarding school, it emanated calm. On that evening, looking at the rails and sleepers, I finally and irrevocably fell in love with the railway. Its brilliance resembled the flashing of precious stones, and its smell! An amazing smell of metal and creosote, which may feel harsh for some, but seemed surprisingly pleasant to me. After that, we moved around a lot on freight trains, and I fell in love with not only the smell of the railway and its rough beauty, but also the sounds it made when the wheels of the car were rolling over the joints of the tracks ... Those clickety-clack sounds, the monotonous song of the railway – perhaps annoying for many, but for me it was like a lullaby. It happened so often that I would fall asleep to it, breathing in rapid flows of summer wind, in which the smell of new-mown hay, gasoline, cow manure, goodness, field flowers and hundreds, yet thousands, of flavours, intoxicating and lulling, were mixed.

'Here it comes,' said Slavik, peering into the dark horizon. 'We'll jump up as soon as it starts slowing down.'

'Why would it slow down?' Akim asked with a whistle.

'There is a mountain ahead, it's hard to climb. My stepfather told me that trains often slow down before climbs, crossings and other obstacles.'

'Are we going to jump on the move?' Miwa squeezed Slavik's hand, frightened.

'Don't panic, little girl, it will pass by very slowly. I'll give you a lift.' My friend gave a gentle smile to the girl, and she looked away in embarrassment.

'And where do we jump on? The doors are probably locked ...' Akim chuckled.

'No, two or three of them are always open. The railway workers break the locks and then fix them again – they need the money. What other odd jobs can you do on a railway?' Slavik burst out in laughter. But despite his assurances, this adventure raised doubts in the rest of us.

'Okay, we will get there, and what about her?' Akim pointed at his sister. 'She is too small to keep up with the freight train!'

Hearing doubt in her brother's voice, Miwa pursed her lips and looked ready to burst into tears. 'Are you going to leave me?' she whispered, barely holding back her sobs.

'What are you talking about?!' Slavik barked and pushed Akim in the chest. 'We are not going to leave anyone. I will carry her myself, if need be.' After those assurances our little friend cheered up a little.

While waiting for the train, we sat down by the railway and decided to have a snack. Before Slavik could pull out a package of oatmeal cookies, however, we heard a characteristic roar in the distance, and soon we saw the two large yellow eyes of a freight train. The train was chugging down the tracks, and we, the four fugitives, awaited its arrival intensely. I don't know really, how Slavik managed to see a half-open car from afar, but he gave us the order to run just in time. Having taken Miwa in his arms, he overtook the car in several huge steps and, with a sudden jump, he grabbed the metal ledge with his hands, pulled himself up and disappeared into the blackness of the empty car. Without delay, Akim and I rushed after him. We nearly slipped, clinging to bulges and ridges, but were saved by some stranger's strong hand. Whoever it was pulled us easily into the car, and I hit my shoulder badly against its wooden wall. I quickly jumped to my feet, looking around cautiously, but it was so dark inside that I was not able to see my rescuer, and neither I was able to find my friends.

'Do not panic, boy.' An unfamiliar voice sounded somewhere close.

'All good, Vitka, this is one of us.' Having heard Slavik's calm voice, I immediately felt better.

'Who is it?' asked Akim, trying to see the stranger the same way I did.

'Your chief has just told you that I am one of you.' The stranger laughed. 'Sit down, kids, let's have some food.'

The stranger's name was Lacho – he was a gypsy and a frequent visitor of freight trains. Thanks to a kerosene lamp that he lit up, we could see his brownish face, affected with smallpox. Lacho had a repulsive appearance, his voice was low and growling, and his eyes were piercing. But he was kind to us – he even gave us condensed milk with black bread.

'Stuff yourselves, there may be nothing of this left by tomorrow.' He laughed, watching us shoving treats in our faces with delight.

'You are so pale, like children of the dungeon.' Lacho grimaced. 'Where do you come from?' We did not feel like answering this question, so Slavik invented a story about a sick grandmother, no money for buying a ticket, poor parents and so on. Surely, Lacho did not believe Slavik's fables, but he said nothing. He himself had wandered since childhood, so it was not likely that he judged other vagrants.

'We'll get off in the morning, at dawn,' concluded Slavik, wiping his lips with the sleeve of his jacket. 'And where are you going?'

'I'm going with the wind. We'll see what tomorrow brings,' Lacho replied mysteriously.

Having thrown away the empty condensed milk can, he pulled out a pack of marmalade from his pocket and, hearing our enthusiastic exclamations, poured its contents on the floor in front of us. While we were chewing orange and lemon slices, Miwa examined Lacho's neck carefully.

'What is that on your neck?' she asked in her childlike way, pointing at a red line, a healed scar.

'This?' The man grinned. 'This is a reminder of Tamara.'

'Which Tamara?' Miwa continued the conversation.

'Don't bother him!' Akim snapped.

'It's okay, do not worry,' smiled Lacho. 'Dear, do you want me to tell you a story about the beautiful Tamara?'

Miwa nodded happily. 'Tamara was sixteen, and I loved her with all my heart,' began Lacho, leaning on the wall of the car. 'She was beautiful, and a talented dancer. Gorgeous too, with dark hair that fell on her shoulders in large curls, slightly slanting sky-blue eyes and a radiant smile. The first time I saw this girl spinning in a dance, I was lost. The very next day, I proposed to her, but Tamara was in no hurry to get married ... Or she was simply hiking up the price.' The man uttered a laugh. 'She had fire inside of her, it was passionate, incinerating. In a few days Tamara surrendered to me ...'

'Surrendered?' repeated Miwa.

'Hmm ... well, yes, it's like she agreed to be mine. However, Tamara was too young and naïve. There was a lot she did not notice and did not understand. She was loved by many, many wanted to be with her, but even I did not want her as much as my brother did.'

'You fell in love with the same girl?' Akim gasped.

'Yes, we fell in love with the same girl.' Lacho sighed sadly. 'But she chose me. After a few days spent in love and adoration, Tamara went with her friends to a neighbouring town to earn some money by dancing. But she never came back ...'

'What happened?' Miwa was wary.

'We searched for her for a long time, crawled every corner, looked into every crack, but Tamara had disappeared, as if she'd evaporated in the air. And a day later, a local boy who was digging the ground for fun, came across a piece of fluffy black hair ... He called the elders, and we dug out Tamara ...'

'What do you mean, you dug her out?' Slavik asked in shock.

'With shovels.' Lacho spat on the floor. 'She was strangled and buried among the rosehip bushes not far from our camp. The irony is that Tamara loved rosehip – she used to gather it, dry it out and then prepare a broth against the cold.

'Did you find out who did that to her?' Miwa rounded her eyes in horror, her legs curled up beneath her.

'Very soon, my dear, very soon. One night I woke up in excruciating pain. Someone had tried to cut my throat.' Our new friend rubbed the terrible scar on his neck. 'This someone turned out to be my very own brother.'

We froze, frightened by what we were hearing.

'But how come? Why?' I mumbled.

'You wouldn't understand, kid. He loved Tamara more than he loved freedom, he went mad from the desire to have her. He strangled her, buried her in the rosehip bushes, and he wanted to deprive me of life to prevent me from clouding his eyes. After all ... it was me who took his love away. Since then this scar serves as a reminder of my love for the beautiful Tamara. And of herself, full of life and beauty. When my heart is yearning, I rub the scar, and here I see Tamara dancing in front of me, playfully letting her hair down, and laughing so loudly ...'

'And what happened to your brother?' Slavik said.

'He was hung on a pine tree that very same night,' said Lacho indifferently. 'A cur's death for a cur.' He chuckled again.

I fell asleep quickly, thinking about the beautiful Tamara, who was destined for a short, but bright life. I was glad that she'd had time to fall in love and to be loved, and I hoped sincerely that death from being strangled was not so painful. Falling asleep to the tunes of the railway, I saw a dancing dark-skinned girl before my eyes, who raised the hem of her colorful dress flirtatiously and laughed infectiously. I wanted with all my heart to believe that this mysterious girl had died quickly and painlessly.

4.

At dawn, Slavik woke us, ordering us to have a quick snack with crackers and get ready to jump. We obeyed, sleepy and rumpled after a night spent on the hard floor (even though we were no strangers to it).

'Where are we going to get off?' asked Akim.

'If memory serves me, in ten minutes there is a small village. An old woman I know, Grandmother Marusya, lives over there, so we can refill our supplies of food and water and sleep in normal beds,' said my companion. Miwa clapped her hands happily. She did want to have a sleep in a soft bed.

'Jump out only when the train starts moving as slowly as possible, otherwise you will smash your heads,' Lacho's hoarse voice sounded from the corner of the car.

'No need to tell!' Slavik waved him off. We got ready, and when Slavik said 'go!' everyone jumped, except for me, because Lacho was tightly clutching my hand.

'Let me go!' I cried.

'Don't be afraid,' Lacho said affectionately, 'you listen to the old gypsy's parting words.' He smiled. 'When the crucial moment comes, take a step back. It's important,' he said and lightly pushed my fragile body. Not having enough time to tuck, I hurt my spine against the ground and travelled a few meters on my back.

'What took you so long?!' shouted Slavik from afar, seeing my floundering body. My friends approached me while I was still shaking the earth off my clothes.

'I thanked Lacho for the food,' I lied.

'The right person to say thanks to. Gypsies are crooked people – you've got to keep an eye on them because if you turn away for a moment they'll put a knife in your back and steal your stuff.' Slavik carefully stroked the collar of his denim jacket.

'Well, all right then, let's go find Grandmother Marusya. If this is the right village, of course,' I replied stiffly. Slavik chuckled thoughtfully. And we moved in the direction where, according to Slavik, there was a village in which lived the mysterious grandmother.

‘This old woman has a cow and a few dozen chickens. Maybe some other living creatures have appeared there since I last visited.’ Slavik spoke as we walked.

‘Does she have a dog?’ asked Miwa. ‘Or a cat?’ The longer I knew that girl, the more reassured I was about how tender and gentle she was.

‘Of those she has enough!’ Slavik said. Miwa laughed happily.

‘I’ll be playing with them soon, and petting them,’ she reasoned.

‘Wait with those dreams of yours – Grandmother Marusya may be dead already, or this may be the wrong village,’ Akim suggested.

‘Why are you always jumping down her throat?’ Slavik angered. ‘Even if she has died, won’t we find a dog to pet in the village?’ Akim looked down – he did not want to argue with Slavik. In less than half an hour, we saw the outlines of small houses in the distance. Slavik emitted something like a victorious battle cry, throwing a contemptuous glance at Akim.

‘There is no guarantee that the grandmother is alive,’ Akim muttered in my ear. I agreed, as yes, there was no guarantee. Although, frankly, I didn’t care whether the grandmother was alive or not. After all, there are dogs to pet a dime a dozen in any village, and we could just steal the food. We did not need any grandmother for that.

Upon reaching the house of this mysterious person, possibly a relative of our Slavik, we stayed waiting behind the gates while he went to investigate. The yard looked homely, and the hut looked fine too. Somewhere from the depths of the yard one could hear the barking of a dog and the clucking of chickens.

‘She does have a dog,’ Miwa screamed happily. ‘I want to pet it as soon as I can!’

‘This dog is angry, just listen to it growling,’ Akim retorted. ‘It will grab you and bite off your head!’ A snide grimace distorted his face when he saw Miwa’s frightened look.

‘Don’t worry, I think that the dog is good,’ I said, protecting Miwa, rather to my surprise. This was unusual, because I was spending more and more time with her brother, we talked a lot and over time we had become almost thick as thieves; on the other hand I was indifferent to his sister as I’ve already mentioned. But even I was tired enough of his constant insults and bullying of the girl. Miwa smiled gently and after a short period of silence she agreed that ‘the dog definitely was good’.

‘Well, guys, come on in.’ Slavik’s long nose appeared from behind the gates. ‘Grandmother Marusya is waiting.’ Feeling happy that Slavik was not mistaken, we ran into the yard where we saw the grandmother, a decrepit woman, sitting on a bench beside the house. She was of small height, slightly hunched over, wearing a bright scarf on a white head and bulky men's boots.

'These are my friends,' Slavik introduced us. The old woman remained silent for a long time, examining us with interest.

'Still small,' she finally said, smacking her lips. 'There's no use.'

'I can work for two, and the boys are really tough, don't judge by the looks. The girl can feed chickens and collect eggs. Do not think of us as children.'

'Children are children.' The grandmother grinned, 'That's okay, you silver-tongue, settle down. Tomorrow there is going to be lots of work.' She got up from the bench, helping herself with a wooden cane.

'Do you want to see the dog?' she asked, having noticed Miwa's interested glances, thrown in the direction of the dog kennel. 'Come on, I'll introduce you to each other. His name is Jack, he is a cross between a German shepherd and a mongrel. He is terribly angry but loves children.' With that, the old woman leant on Miwa's fragile shoulder with the hand which was free of a crutch.

'Slavik, whose grandmother is this?' asked Akim.

'She is a distant relative.' Slavik waved. 'We should spend some time in a normal place and replenish our supplies. We will be doing some little work for the old woman in return. We will spend a week or two here and we will be on our way. Just let Miwa's coughing stop,' my friend concluded, looking anxiously after the girl.

5.

Grandmother Marusya's house was small and well-groomed. Two rooms, a spacious veranda and a small porch. We, the three boys, settled down on the veranda. Akim and I stayed on a cot, and Slavik got an old mattress on the floor. The grandmother put Miwa on a couch in the house. In addition to the angry dog, Jack, the old woman kept a dozen chickens, and for as long as we lived with Grandmother Marusya, we ate scrambled eggs for breakfast made with fresh eggs. She took milk from a neighbour (her cow had died a year ago) in exchange for pickles, which filled the cellar of her small house, and she baked bread herself.

The woman looked as old as life itself. She moved slowly, leaning on a cane, constantly muttering something to herself and smacking her lips. Her skin was like baked apple peel, and her fingers were so twisted that they looked more like the twigs of a tree. She was usually silent, rarely started a conversation, and then mainly with Miwa, to whom she had become closely attached from the very first day. While the grandmother could shout at me and the others if she noticed that either of us had done a poor job, at the same time she just stroked the head of our young companion and combed her thick hair.

My and Akim's duties were to clean up the yard, dig the ground, get rid of weeds, cut off dry branches and fertilize the soil with a smelly liquid, which the grandmother strictly ordered to be carried only in gloves. Slavik was repairing a rickety shed between the house and the chicken coop, where the old woman kept her most valuable things. In my opinion, this was all just trash and debris. Slavik's task was to fix the end wall by filling up cracks and holes.

The old woman kept Miwa by her side, sometimes asking her to collect eggs in the henhouse or to go over to the neighbour's to get milk. The girl goofed around all day playing with the dog, or entertaining us with amazing songs in a language that Slavik and I did not understand. Miwa's voice was sonorous, still quite childish, but not devoid of the strength inherent in experienced singers. Slavik said that in the future she would become a great singer, to which Miwa blushed, hiding her eyes modestly. I liked our new life: although it was not quite the same as I had imagined it to be, I felt good. Despite the gloominess, Grandmother

Marusya was not doing any harm to us. We had our bellies full of food and slept in a clean bed, which the old woman regularly refreshed by doing laundry on the back porch. She paid for the work done with canned food and cookies and gave us money every few days so that we could run to the store to buy ice cream and soda. Even years later, I remember that delicious chocolate-covered ice cream and that sugary fruity drink sizzling in my mouth. I liked living the way we lived then.

Despite the good food and a warm blanket, Miwa still coughed sometimes, but Slavik assured her that this was normal, a 'residual phenomenon'. I did not know what a 'residual phenomenon' was, but the confident tone of my friend spoke of his own absolute awareness. This was calming and gave hope that any day now the girl would feel completely well and we would be able to continue our journey.

Once, on our way home from the store, all smeared with ice-cream, we took a turn towards the forest to play catch, Miwa's favorite game. Having run to our hearts' content, we fell on the soft grass, exposing our faces to the warm rays of the June sun, which was playfully making its way through the lush crowns of trees.

'We will have to leave soon,' Slavik began. Miwa stopped laughing and propped herself up on her elbows. She looked attentively at Slavik.

'Why?' the girl asked. 'Can't we stay with Grandmother?'

'No, we have our own way. Furthermore, here we can also be found sooner or later, and they will make us go back to the boarding school. You don't want that, do you?'

Miwa shook her head. 'Grandma is good,' she whispered sadly.

'I know, but we have a long road to Grad ahead,' Slavik continued mysteriously.

'Grad?' the brother and sister asked at the same time. Slavik smiled.

'What is this Grad?' Miwa sat down on the grass with her knees drawn in. 'Tell us!'

'Grad is the place where all abandoned children live. They beat no one there and there is a lot of food. You can also play and sing all day. This is how Grad is ...'

'What a magical city ...' Miwa drawled dreamily.

'Vitka and I even took the oath of the Children of Grad. We can teach you,' Slavik smiled slyly.

'Teach us! Teach us!' Akim and Miwa began to shout. It was then that Slavik first delivered the oath to us all, the one invented by us at the grave of his mother, adding 'Children of Grad!' at the end.

I swear that I will not break tree branches.
Only if I am alone in the forest in the cold and I need to light a fire!
I swear that I will not hit animals, even the evil and the mad ones.
I swear that I will pray for the happiness of Fauna and Klara Fyodorovna, and when they die, I will pray for their rest.
I swear to hate Rusichka until my last breath, and even after I die!
Children of Grad! Children of Grad! Children of Grad!

Our friends liked the oath very much, Miwa jumped up and began to dance cheerfully, bursting into joyful laughter. Akim proposed to write down the oath on paper and seal it with blood. Everyone liked the idea, so we hurried to the house of Grandmother Marusya, where Akim, as the most literate among us, wrote down the spoken words. We all signed it, and then pierced our fingers with a needle and dripped a little blood.

'The oath is now sworn and sealed and cannot be changed. We must strictly follow it!' concluded Akim, having rolled the sheet of paper into a tube and tied it with a handkerchief.

'What's next?' Miwa asked.

'Next you have to stop coughing, and we will move on further,' answered Slavik.

On that day, we all fell asleep thinking about the upcoming adventures and about the mysterious Grad, which we had to build if we couldn't find it. I imagined several well-kept houses, like Grandmother Marusya's house, with a large vegetable garden and cows. We would have a dog and chickens to always feast on fresh eggs, and we would hang a swing on a thick branch.

In my fantasies, there was a lake or a river nearby, which I could run to and swim in (if only someone taught me how to do it!), and in winter we would light fire in the stove, bake fragrant sweet bread and eat it with strawberry jam. I even felt the taste of it, a sweet, fresh berry flavor combined with an airy bun, crunchy on my teeth. Our Grad was wonderful, and I was eager to hit the road!

6.

A couple of weeks later, thanks to the efforts of Grandmother Marusya, we no longer had any trace of our basement pallor. Our cheeks had acquired a natural children's glow, and the skin on our hands had become smooth again, as it should be at our age.

'My poor children,' the old woman would say at times, putting fresh baked goods on the table. But, on the contrary, we did not consider ourselves poor – we rejoiced in the long-awaited freedom, warm summer and upcoming adventures.

One evening I accidentally overheard a conversation between Grandmother Marusya and Slavik. They were sitting at the chicken coop, and my friend was smoking a cigarette.

'Leave the girl to me,' said the old woman. 'She will be my joy.'

'No,' Slavik snapped.

'She is small, she will not bear your adventure. Where are you taking her?! Do you understand it yourself?' Always calm, she switched to a strangled cry.

'Miwa will stay with us, period. And if you put pressure on me, we'll leave tomorrow.'

'No no! I won't!' the old woman hastened to assure. 'Stay a little longer, give me time to spend with the little one. She is so pretty!'

'Yes,' agreed Slavik.

'You did not fall in love, did you, Svyatoslav?' The owner of the small house smiled. It was then that I first learned how thc full name of Slavik sounded.

'Why would you even think that?!' he cried out. 'Did you lose your mind or what?' Then I heard hurried steps and quickly took cover behind a spreading raspberry bush, until I was convinced that Slavik had disappeared inside the house.

After what I'd heard, I had many questions about the relatives of Grandmother Marusya. Did she have a family, children? And if so, where were they now? It was hard to imagine this gloomy, dry old woman smiling happily surrounded by her grandchildren, but curiosity kept bugging me. Therefore, one day, when Grandmother Marusya was sitting basking in the sun, I decided to have a talk with her.

'Grandma, may I ask you something?'

'Well, go ahead,' she answered indifferently, not inclined to have a conversation with me.

'Do you have any grandchildren of your own?'

The old woman looked at me questioningly, crossing her arms on the stick. 'And what do you care?'

'No reason ...'

'My dear, even kittens don't come into the world for no reason.' Grandmother Marusya laughed. 'Well, if you're so curious about this, then you probably know that to have grandchildren, one should have children first.'

'And a husband?' I wouldn't stop.

'Do you see any old man dozing on the bench here?'

'No ...'

'Exactly.' The old woman smacked her lips. 'But I did have a husband, a Nightingale of a man. He was a healthy fellow, a hard-working man. He couldn't sing for the life of him, but my goodness did he have the gift of the gab!' She smiled affectionately. 'He had a thick mustache and wore ankle-length pants. He was a good man, a faithful husband ...'

'He died?' I asked, wanting to hear the rest.

'Yes, Vitka, he died. He died a long time ago, when my hair had not yet turned white, and my back was straight. One day he came back from the factory (there used to be a bread factory twenty kilometers from here), and he complained about having a pain in the chest. He lay down on the bed, while I was putting dinner on the table. I came to call him, and he was already lifeless. This is how my Nightingale passed on, quietly, folding his hands on his hurting chest ...' Grandmother Marusya fell silent, dropping her chin on her hands. I was silent as well, waiting for her to continue. The way the old woman spoke of her late husband was so kind and sincere, that I wanted to keep listening.

'Yes, it happens sometimes. The man had not turned forty yet. He lay down and died. My neighbour, you know, kept buzzing that some envious people did that to him, that they conjured him to death. As if we had lived too well, me and my walrus-whiskered one ... But as for me, this is all nonsense, Vitka. It just happens like that. People get sick, people die. Even the healthiest and the best ones. So they were destined, and you can't escape destiny,' reasoned the old woman. 'I only regret that we never had children. I was afraid that we would live from hand to mouth, and always waited for later, for us to come into some money. After I buried the Nightingale, I sat on the porch, and, you know, there was not even one tear of despair. Life collapsed in an instant, and it all happened so fast that all the sobs stuck in my throat. I thought at first about drowning myself or running my neck into a noose, but the Nightingale would not have approved of that. He was a devout man, he believed that killing oneself was a great sin. So I threw myself headlong into taking care of the household and the wounds healed little by little ... But I have been trampling this land for nine decades now, I am tired.' Grandmother Marusya smiled, straightening the hem of her long, just-washed bathrobe.

'Why didn't you get married for a second time?' I asked delicately. The old woman stared at me displeased.

'This is how they do it now – the bed has not yet cooled down, and women are already starting tricks with other guys!' She fell deep into thought. 'There was one gentleman, for many years he followed me, until he got tired of this and married a neighbour. She gave birth to three ... But I have no regrets. I loved the Nightingale, very much. Even now, when I'm talking about him, something is breaking right here.' The old woman put her hand to her chest. 'And you know, Vitka, this only happens once in a lifetime. And not for everyone. God willing, you will fall in love like that too, only to live in perfect harmony all your life, and sire a bunch of children.' The mistress of the small house smiled affectionately, stroking my head. 'Well, that's it, you discovered all the secrets of an old woman, now run to the chicken coop, collect some eggs, and I'll bake a sponge cake with raisins for you.'

While I collected eggs, diligently trying not to disturb the precious layers, I had an image of the handsome Nightingalc in my mind, a tall man with a moustache who loved Grandmother Marusya too, I was sure about that. Probably in those years he called her Masha or Mashenka, maybe he held her in his arms (after all, he was strong!) and kissed her on the lips. I was sad that he died so early and did not have time to do much in his life. I felt sorry for Grandmother Marusya, who, although she was expecting death now, actually died many years ago when she found her lifeless husband on the bed.

In the evening, we ate a delicious sponge cake with herbal tea. Everyone was in high spirits, even the old woman herself. She laughed and made fun of Akim's whistling speech. A couple of times she winked at me conspiratorially, and then my heart felt so happy. She and I had a little secret of our own, that no one knew about.

A couple of days after Grandmother Marusya told me about her husband, the weather changed and long showers began. Slavik felt extremely frustrated about this, as he had planned to hit the road any day now. This was now not possible, though. The humid cold air provoked another manifestation of Miwa's illness, from which she had seemed to have recovered. One morning, however, we were awakened by a prolonged coughing fit coming from Grandmother Marusya's room. Miwa could hardly endure the weather change – her face was pale and drawn, she began to have violent coughs during the mornings and evenings, and at night, she shivered. The old woman brewed some herbal infusions for her. They improved the girl's condition for a short time, but eventually the disease took over again. This could not change Miwa's cheerful disposition, however. She rushed around the house, inventing entertaining games in which she involved everyone, even Jack, who had temporarily settled with us in the veranda when rain flooded his kennel.

'Slavka, she can't go with you, the girl is weak. Her lungs are very bad,' the old woman whispered in the veranda, squeezing Slavik's elbow. He shook his head nervously.

'She will get better, just keep brewing more of those herbs for her!' Grandmother Marusya did not argue. Instead she moved towards the drawer, took a handful of dried herbs from different iron and glass jars, mixed and pounded them in a mortar and said some kind of spells. Then she poured boiling water over the leaves, steeped the concoction it, and little by little gave it to Miwa to drink.

'Grandma is so wonderful! She is treating me!' Miwa hung around the old woman's neck. She did this so often that the old woman's desire never to part with the little Tatar girl was growing stronger and stronger every day. Eventually, it all ended with a big scandal. Not afraid to be heard by the rest of the household, Grandmother Marusya did not ask but demanded to keep Miwa with her, threatening Slavik with the police.

'I'll report you!' she screamed.

'And what, then we will all be taken away! And your precious Miwa too,' Slavik hissed in response.

But Grandmother Marusya was not one of those people who could be intimidated by a fourteen-year-old boy.

'I will call the boarding school, they will take you away, and I will adopt Miwa. Believe me, this is how it is going to be,' snapped the grandmother, 'so think carefully, Slava.'

It was then that Akim and I began to persuade Slavik to give in to the old woman.

'Miwa has fallen in love with the grandmother, she is a gentle girl, she is drawn to such people. Leave her, she will be fine here. And then the grandmother will leave her the house and the chickens when she dies,' said Akim.

'Could you abandon your sister?' Slavik was indignant.

'We are not abandoning her. We are leaving her with a good person. And it will be easier for us to be without her, because she is getting sick all the time. We will visit her, be her guests,' insisted Akim. I agreed. Slavik listened to us attentively, snapping his fingers nervously.

'Let's see,' he finally said and went out into the courtyard, where the downpour never stopped. His tense face and hard look did not bode well. I knew that, but Akim was glad that Slavik had agreed to at least think about it. While I was waiting to see what kind of trick Slavik would pull just to twist the old woman around his finger, the unexpected happened. One night, as the rain subsided, Grandmother Marusya died.

Miwa woke us up at dawn (she always got up with the mistress of the small house to help in the kitchen), and whispered in a trembling voice that 'Grandma is not breathing.' Frightened, Akim and I did not even want to approach her bed. Slavik carefully examined everything and covered the old woman's face with a sheet.

'Don't cry. She was old, her time has come,' he reassured Miwa, who was sobbing bitterly, burying herself in his chest.

'That's enough, calm down. It's time to go. Akim, write a note to her neighbour saying that the grandmother is lying here, and it's time for us to ditch this place,' Slavik continued busily.

'Just like that? Maybe I'll go call the neighbour now?' suggested Akim.

'No! The whole village will get here, and the doctor will come. Then the police ... It is dangerous for us to stay here.' Despite the cynicism of our senior friend, he was right. We quietly left the yard taking the food supplies, which would last for no less than a month, and some of the old woman's warm clothes (it was not as if she was going to use them anyway).

It was damp outside. Silently opening the gate, we tried not to disturb the peacefully dozing Jack. Miwa was crying, and I was saying goodbyes in my head to the small house and the gloomy old woman. When we were already on the country road, I turned around, and it seemed to me that I saw the broad-shouldered Nightingale – his face beaming holding the hand of a fragile girl with a long blond braid. They waved after us, wishing us luck. I no longer worried about Grandmother Marusya – she had become Masha again, young and beautiful, and most importantly, there was a man next to her whom she had loved all her life.

Jack's howl pierced the sleepy street. And we continued our trip without looking back.

7.

Having entered the wilderness, we quickly moved away from the village, our passing covered by the shadows of giant trees. Miwa sobbed constantly until the first halt, which we took only a couple of hours later. Slavik tried to calm her down and convince her that Grandmother Marusya was at peace.

'She's in heaven with her husband now,' I said, patting Miwa on the back.

'Did the old woman have a husband?' Akim was amazed.

'At some point, long time ago,' I answered shortly. I did not want to give up Grandmother Marusya's secret. I liked being the only one who was filled in on the story.

We put our stuff next to us and made a fire to heat some canned fish. After our snack, Slavik suggested we take a half-hour nap in order to regain strength and then not make a stop until lunch. Having rested, we hurried towards the unknown again.

After getting on the road, we met a man on a cart. He kindly agreed to give us a lift for a can of stew. After a couple of hours of the old nag's slow pace, we gained strength, and when the time came to jump off near his village, we were full of energy again. To everyone's delight, Miwa no longer coughed. Her illness had cleared up, it seemed, in the warm summer air.

'It's all because of the dampness,' Slavik said, observing the girl. 'Her lungs love dryness, and she coughs from the rain.'

By the evening, we had wandered far enough into the forest to hide from unnecessary glances. Slavik looked for a suitable place to spend the night, illuminating the road with his pocket flashlight. Now we walked slowly, dragging our feet, as we were feeling tired after the day. When it got completely dark, Miwa started whining.

'I'm cold,' she said, tugging at Slavik's sleeve. 'When are we going to stop?'

'Once I find a suitable place,' my friend answered.

'What does 'suitable' mean?'

'You will see. Stop whining, you are already a grown-up girl,' snapped Slavik, pulling the girl by the hand. Miwa got upset because of the comment, and now she walked after our guide, her head bowed and it seemed that she was crying again. Just very quietly, so as not to bother anyone else. Miwa's attitude to Slavik surprised me. She argued with Akim all the time, she would even shout at her brother, but she obeyed Slavik unquestionably. When it came to me, our relationship was full of indifference. Miwa did not even notice me sometimes, as if I were an imaginary friend. But the girl hung on everything Slavik said, catching his every word and gesture. He was the only one who could make her laugh; he was the only one who could calm her down and caress her. Now I understand that a children's love was being born, growing and getting stronger in front of me. Also now I understand that Slavik was ready to cripple anyone who would dare to say anything bad to this fragile girl.

'Stop!' Slavik's muffled cry distracted me from my surging thoughts. We stopped and watched my friend listening to the night air.

'There is someone there. Stay here, I'll find out,' he commanded, dissolving into the darkness of the night. After a couple of minutes, he returned with a broad smile.

'You would not believe who I met! Lacho is here with friends! Come on, they'll give us shelter for tonight.'

Having come to the edge of the forest, we saw a huge bonfire, shooting multi-colored sparks. The view was fascinating. A small pig was roasting on a spit, exuding an amazing spicy smell; a van was parked a little further away, and people, mostly short and dark, stood on the roof of the van, around the fire, and around the edge of the clearing.

'What a reunion!' exclaimed Lacho, standing up to meet us. He wore a green vest over a tattered grey T-shirt and dirty trousers.

'Make yourself comfortable, kids, the piglet is about to be ready.' He sat us down closer to the fire, from which a pleasant warmth emanated. I instantly felt blood rushing into my face and a leaden weight in my legs.

'How have you been this whole time?' asked the gypsy, giving us a glass bottle of lemonade. 'Would you like anything stronger?' He turned to Slavik, who nodded affirmatively. Lacho brought him an opened bottle of vodka. Slavik took a sip and drank lemonade after.

'Can I?' Akim eagerly looked at the bottle.

'Help yourself,' Lacho grinned snidely, passing him the drink. However, unlike Slavik, after the first timid sip Akim started coughing and spat on the ground. This scene amused all the gypsies, especially Lacho. He laughed hoarsely, clasping his stomach in his hands.

'We lived well,' Slavik finally answered, when the general fun had subsided a little.

‘I’ve met my relatives,’ Lacho replied. ‘They want to go to Romania. I’m thinking of hitting the road with them.’

‘Where is Romania?’ Miwa asked, wrapping herself in a striped blanket that a young gypsy woman had given her.

‘It’s far, kid,’ smiled Lacho.

‘I read in the newspaper that there is devastation and poverty in Romania now,’ said Slavik busily.

‘We also have devastation here.’ The gypsy shrugged. ‘You won’t scare us with it, but it would be good to have a look at another country.’

Slavik nodded silently. Then the old gypsy gave everyone a piece of the piglet, which was laid out in portions on pieces of brown cardboard. The meat was juicy and toasty, seasoned with aromatic herbs. We ate greedily, wiping our greasy lips with our sleeves and drinking soda after. While we gorged ourselves silently, something lively started moving around the fire. Several young girls were pulling their girlfriend by the arms, begging her to do something. She coquettishly refused, turning her head away.

‘What’s happening?’ I asked.

‘This is Valenta, one of our young girls. They are asking her to dance. She is our best dancer. The cunning thing knows that, so she makes others beg her,’ explained Lacho.

Valenta did not look young at all. A confident hard look, a sarcastic grin and lush breasts were not the hallmark of young beauties according to how I imagined them. Nevertheless, she was sixteen. Valenta could be called attractive, at least for her slender legs and a thick black braid that gleamed in the light of the flame. The dancer was clothed in a long orange dress trimmed with lace on the sleeves.

‘Dance, beautiful, do not languish,’ Lacho said slowly. ‘Please my eyes.’ He licked his dry lips in anticipation, examining Valenta. The girl threw back her head and laughed, lifting the hem of her dress.

‘Music!’ she shouted, and the edge of the forest filled with the lively sound of a violin. The gypsies clapped their hands, stomping and shouting something in a language that I did not understand. Valenta began to dance, bending to the beat of the music.

‘She is so good!’ Lacho said, applauding the girl’s talent.

‘Have you lost it, or what?’ Slavik giggled.

‘Few gypsies would refuse such a girl,’ smiled Lacho. ‘But she is out of my league. With a fiery beauty, you can be burned.’ He licked his lips again, reminding me of a hungry cat, waiting for an unsuspecting tit.

Lacho made a bed for us near the fire, laying two old mattresses on the ground, and several woolen blankets on top. Miwa, despite Akim's protests, lay down beside Slavik and pressed herself against his chest. I lay down on the edge, watching the gypsy camp slowly fall asleep. When everyone seemed to have settled down, and I heard Akim's puffing next to me, I noticed a dark figure slowly creeping towards the forest. It seemed to me that it was Lacho, but I couldn't say for sure. After a while, another figure followed him, holding the hem of a dress so bright that even in the darkness, illuminated only by the moon, it shone orange. Then I turned over onto my other side, giving my imagination the opportunity to continue the story in which Lacho and Valenta got married and left for Romania together (it would be good to know where this mysterious country was!), where they built a house and had many beautiful swarthy children. I do not know whether it turned out to be this way, because in the morning we said our goodbyes to the gypsies forever and never met Lacho again.

Before we left, Lacho whispered to Slavík that there were rumours about four missing children in local villages, so all the locals were on the alert. After relaying this information, Slavik suggested we wait a couple of days in the forest in order to think over a further action plan.

'If we don't want to get caught, there's no need to rush,' reasoned our senior friend. So we set up a temporary camp in the very thicket of the forest, where few people visit. Lacho had given us one mattress and a canvas awning. We stretched it between two thick branches, making an improvised roof to protect us from the sun and rain. Not far from our shelter, Akim found a meadow with strawberries, which we attacked eagerly, unable to stop until we had eaten to the full.

'I like our life so much!' Miwa exclaimed, stretching out to her full height on the mattress.

'We have a wonderful life.' Slavik smiled. 'But when we get to Grad, it will become just magical.' He lay down next to Miwa, touching her hand with his shoulder.

Akim did not like this. 'Decent girls don't behave like that,' he hissed so that Slavik would not hear, for he was afraid of him.

'Like how?' I asked, not understanding his indignation.

'They don't lie on a mattress with men.'

'Why not?'

'Because you can only lie on a mattress with your husband,' Akim snapped and went for a walk because he did not want to see his sister behaving with Slavik in such a frivolous way.

8.

We spent almost a week in the forest, eating berries and canned food taken from the house of Grandmother Marusya. Every day we went to the river half an hour's walk away, but we covered the distance merrily and quickly. Miwa often sang wonderful songs on our way, which were well known only to her people. Her voice was fine and clear, like spring drops. Sometimes we spent the whole day on the bank of the river, splashing in the water and basking in the rays of the gentle sun. June was drawing to a close, and Slavik was determined to find Grad, where a new, even happier life would begin, before the start of July. When we returned to our camp, hungry and exhausted from bathing, Slavik made a fire, and we decided what we wanted to have for dinner today. We put several cans in a row, someone closed their eyes and waited for others to swap the cans, and then pointed a finger at random. In such a funny way, we decided what we would eat: pork or fish, or maybe even pea soup. We loved our carefree life so much!

A week later, though, Slavik announced that it was time for us to leave. We packed our things obediently and set off with our guide at dawn. We needed to reach the railway again in the evening.

'The train will not slow down for many kilometers, so jumping on would be like heading off a cliff. We'll have to be civil, with tickets and a train conductor,' explained Slavik. 'Lacho said that the police were looking for four children, three boys and a girl. We need to disguise ourselves so that no one suspects anything'.

We really liked the idea of dressing up. Everyone chattered excitedly, deciding which image to try on. When we asked Slavik where we could get new clothes, he replied that he would solve everything. The main thing, as he said, was to get to some village there was always some good stuff in villages ...

After half a day's journey, we noticed the outlines of a settlement ahead. Slavik took us into the forest, ordering us to wait for him as always, and not stick our heads out if possible, since people might be wandering around the village. Unconditionally obeying our senior friend, we took refuge among the spreading bushes. Slavik was not long in coming back. He returned smiling radiantly, pleased with the rich pickings. He was carrying a large parcel and a food net was hanging behind his back.

'A good supply of condensed milk and bagels, gingerbread and stewed meat,' Slavik listed proudly, 'and some other small stuff. Tea for a little princess.' He bowed artistically to Miwa, who happily clapped her hands. She was very fond of tea.

'What about the disguise?' asked Akim.

'This is the most interesting part,' answered Slavik, dumping the contents of the package on the ground. A pile of dirty grey clothing formed at our feet.

'It's mostly girly clothes!' Akim was surprised, checking the 'catch'.

'What did you think, just changing your clothes for another guy's things?' Slavik laughed. Akim was right: the clothes were mostly female: dresses, skirts, scarves ...

'You two must dress up as girls,' ordered Slavik, unable to contain a smile at the sight of mine and Akim's astonished faces.

'I will not be doing that!' Akim shouted, kicking the clothes. 'This is humiliating!'

'Oh come on now ... Just for once,' I began hesitantly, realizing that Slavik wouldn't make us do it for no reason. He had good arguments for everything.

'Vitya, he does it on purpose! Why don't you change yourself then?' Akim was not calming down.

'Because you all should be accompanied by an adult boy, you big thicko! Do you know what they do to pretty girls on trains? No? And you don't need to know that! I said: change your clothes!' Slavik barked, pushing Akim in the chest.

'Don't hit him!' begged Miwa, grabbing Slavik's hand. Despite her constant quarrels with her brother, she loved him.

'I will not beat him if he stops whining and obeys me.' Slavik smiled, stroking Miwa's hand.

'Stop whining!' repeated Miwa in her gentle voice, giving maximum seriousness to her face. 'We want to get to Grad, right?'

'Right.' Akim nodded, still grimacing at the thought of a woman's skirt and a flowered scarf.

'Well done.' Miwa smiled, clinging to her brother's chest. 'I love you very much, Akim, very, very much! You are so great.' The girl showered her brother with affectionate words, which soon had the desired effect, and Akim agreed to try on a new image.

'Beautiful!' Slavik nodded approvingly, examining me and Akim, dressed as girls. I was wearing a washed print dress, while Akim chose a knitted sweater with buttons and a brown skirt.

'You, Vitka, need to put a kerchief on your head, otherwise you look too much of a boy with those protruding ears of yours.' Slavik rummaged through the pile of clothes, pulling out a linen scarf embroidered with a red thread.

'You look like a very pretty girl now.' He smiled, patting me on the shoulder. 'Hey, don't wilt, it's temporary. And what I need to do is to age myself a little.' Having said that, Slavik smeared a little ash under his eyes, giving his face the effect of fatigue, and put on glasses. He put on trousers like grown men wear, and a jacket that fitted him perfectly. Then he greased and combed his hair back from his face. After such manipulations, one might guess that he was seventeen, or even more, if one did not look closely.

'How beautiful you are!' Miwa could not resist, admiring Slavik, to which Slavka smiled with satisfaction. And although Miwa was the only one not affected by the changes, she also had to change into new clothes, and her hair, always gathered in a tight braid, was twisted into two pigtails, which made her face look rounder. In this updated form, we continued our way to the railway, where we had to buy four tickets with Akim's money (as we knew, he had enough of that!). The very next day, Slavik said, we would be very close to Grad.

Where exactly Grad was located, no one knew except Slavik. I watched in bewilderment his decisive actions and words, as if Grad was a well-known place on a map. This is how confident my friend was in mapping the route. He constantly talked about a new home, a new life, so fabulous that we would certainly forget about all the bad things that had happened to us. Once, I even dared to ask Slavik about where exactly Grad was. But he just dismissed me kindly, saying that it wouldn't take long for the day to come when I would see everything with my own eyes. Therefore, we were carefree in our ignorance, each imagining a new home in their own way. We even expanded our vow with a list of 'Wishes' into which each of us contributed three wishes. According to Miwa, one of the obligatory points should be having a dog; Akim wished to arrange a beer day on Sundays; and I wanted to set up a vegetable garden where I could grow tomatoes.

Some 'wishes' could not withstand Slavik's criticism, and some he willingly accepted. For the time being, he kept his own desires secret, intriguing the others with this. Slavik had long been the unofficial leader of our group, which meant complete obedience to him. It suited us all, except for Akim. Miwa loved our guide more and more every day and was ready to do anything to make him happy, and I liked all Slavik's decisions, they were very 'grown-up'. Only Akim, who had long held a grudge against our senior friend, was dissatisfied all the time with everything that Slavik proposed or did. Now it seems to me that, because of his hot-tempered character, Akim was simply unable to obey someone else. A knocked-out tooth and utter inability to take his sister lightly only added fuel to the fire that caused Akim's frequent mood swings. He could shout at Miwa unexpectedly, or pretend that he did not hear when someone spoke to him. Akim was friendly only with me. We often wandered together in the forest, chatting about everything in the world. It seems to me now that Akim found comfort in our conversations, forgetting for a while his childhood grievances and disappointments. Even at the time, I was pretty sure of that.

So we appeared on the platform in our new look, waiting for the eight o'clock train, which would take us to Grad the next day. Or to the place next to which Grad was located. It seemed to me that we looked frankly like caricatures, but soon I noticed that no one waiting for the train was paying attention to us. Dressed in their own grey and inconspicuous clothes, people were eating seeds, smoking and having leisurely conversations, without even dignifying us with a look.

'Are these your sisters?' asked a middle-aged woman, the only one who was interested in our company. She sat not far from us on an oblong, roughly fashioned box.

'Yes, I'm taking them to our grandmother,' answered Slavik politely, giving his appearance even more 'adultness'.

'Pretty girls.' The woman smiled. 'Only this one is not like the others.' She poked her finger at me. I got very nervous, deciding that this nasty woman had figured us out and now she was about to call the police.

'The thing is that we are not all siblings. We are cousins, actually. My mother's sister married a Tatar, so some of us are white-skinned, and some are dark,' Slavik answered calmly, causing admiration to rise in our eyes. He had come up with a lie on the go, so simply and easily!

‘I see.’ The woman nodded. ‘Well, you should be careful with the kids, so as not to allow them to get kidnapped!’ she admonished. Slavik reassured her that he would not take his eyes off his sister and cousins.

When the train arrived at the platform, we felt much calmer, and now everyone was able to tell a lie without blinking an eye. Slavik’s confidence was infectious. He looked reserved and serious and played the role of an adult guy perfectly.

The reserved seat third-class sleeper car was dirty and shabby. It exuded a poisonous cocktail of a variety of odors, from the stench of dirty socks and rancid oil to a suffocatingly sweet women’s perfume. Despite this, the surroundings delighted me. Never before had I ridden in a real carriage with shelves and tables! Even the disgusting stench could not spoil my mood, this being how grand was my first impression of the reserved seat carriage. Slavik settled down in the bottom bunk with me, Miwa and Akim occupied the upper shelves. By nightfall, brother and sister dozed off, and we chatted quietly, discussing how wonderful our Grad would be.

‘Do you have any matches?’ an unfamiliar blonde girl interrupted our conversation, bending over Slavik.

‘There you go.’ He pulled the box out of his pocket and handed it to the girl.

‘Will you go for a smoke?’ she asked, giving an appraising look to my friend. She looked no more than fifteen. Strongly rounded cheekbones and green eyeshadows added some maturity to her face. The stranger had an ample bosom and long legs, the slenderness of which was mainly emphasized by faded leggings. I was surprised that the girl’s T-shirt barely covered her breasts and displayed her rounded belly for everyone to see.

‘So will you?’ she asked again, shuffling along impatiently.

‘Let’s go,’ Slavik grinned, biting his lip. Then he turned to me, strictly forbidding me to go anywhere. I nodded obediently.

‘And don’t let our Tatars get away,’ he threw over his shoulder, following the stranger. Probably more than twenty minutes passed, but Slavik still did not return. Concerned, I decided to go to the vestibule to see if everything was all right with him. Quietly rising from the shelf, so as not to disturb Miwa and Akim, nor the passengers sleeping next to me, I tiptoed to the vestibule and looked out the door window. What I saw discouraged me. In the corner there was the girl, legs apart. Slavik hung over her, pressing his hips against her belly (it seemed that this was the belly, it was hard to see). At the same time, both were silent, making strange chaotic movements. The blonde girl hugged the back of my friend with her arms, and he held her bare legs (she was no longer wearing leggings!). Embarrassed by what I saw (although I did not fully understand what was happening), I imperceptibly retreated to my shelf. Slavik returned soon. The smell of cigarettes and flower soap emanated from him, and his whole appearance was blissful and contented. I pretended not to know anything and soon forgot myself in a restless sleep.

9.

In the morning we were awakened by the general turmoil in the carriage and the loud conversations of our neighbours. The train had arrived at our destination, so we quickly packed up and were on the platform after a couple of minutes. The clock showed about seven in the morning, and we decided to wash ourselves and have breakfast somewhere along the way. Hastily, we moved away from the station in order to get to Grad quickly, our fabulous future home. Except for Miwa, everyone was in high spirits. Contrary to usual, she was gloomy and silent.

'What happened? Are you not feeling well?' asked Slavik, concerned about the girl's mood.

'I'm fine,' Miwa grumbled, kicking the sharp stones that she found along the way with her small foot.

'Well, *I* see that something is wrong ...' Slavik persisted. Akim and I were silent, deciding not to get involved in the conversation of the 'lovers'. The nature of their relationship was little understood to us, so we were powerless here.

'I told you, I'm fine!' Miwa blurted out in anger, which made everyone freeze. Miwa never raised her voice at Slavik. She was always gentle and courteous with him. Slavik froze, grabbing Miwa's hand.

'Let's go talk,' he said, pulling Miwa to the side.

'I do not want to talk!' Miwa tried to free her hand, but Slavik was holding it tight.

'Akim! Help!' The girl turned, begging, to her brother, but he only spat indifferently, saying that this was not any of his business.

'It hurts!' shouted Miwa. In fact, it did not hurt, and Slavik would never have harmed her in his life; her pain was more of a hysteria, caused by some unknown reason. However, after having a short talk with Slavik alone, she changed, became cheerful and smiling again. This little incident did not go out of my mind, and, having caught up with Slavik, I asked in a whisper what had happened.

'Girly nonsense.' He waved me away. But Slavik confided in me later that Miwa saw him go to smoke with a stranger on the train, and she did not sleep during all the time that he was not there, anxiously awaiting his return. Miwa even smelled the flower soap emanating from

Slavik's clothes. That's why that morning when we got off the train, she behaved so strangely. Our girlfriend's little heart was contracting because of overwhelming jealousy. A disease common to all lovers.

On the day of our arrival at the station, the weather changed. Clouds spread in the sky and soon a fine summer rain began to fall, which did not stop all day, forcing us to make an unplanned halt. We quickly pulled up the tarpaulin roof, which we took with us. Unfortunately, we'd had to leave the mattress due to its voluminous dimensions – on that rainy day it could have been very useful to us. So while Miwa and I sat under the roof, making a fire, Slavik and Akim hastily gathered branches intended to serve as a bedding instead of a mattress. The ground was wet and disgusting to sit on. And as Slavik said, it was really dangerous for Miwa's health. Having built an impromptu flooring, prickly but dry, we warmed up a can of pork, and made sandwiches with condensed milk for dessert. Afterwards Slavik boiled rainwater in a tin can, into which he then threw tea leaves. Instead of sugar, he poured a little condensed milk in the can. Passing tea in a circle, we gradually warmed up. Soon our cheeks turned pink, and the branches ceased to seem so prickly.

'Some vodka would be nice now.' Slavik smacked his lips.

'With beer!' Akim licked his.

'When we settle in Grad, you will have a beer. Definitely,' assured Slavik, stretching his legs towards the fire.

Contrary to our hopes, the rain did not stop, forcing us to spend the night under a canopy and keep the fire going if possible, so as not to freeze. We, the boys, took turns on duty around the fire, throwing branches on the embers, thanks to which some kind of warmth remained in the 'house' until dawn. The rain finally stopped in the morning. After breakfast with bagels and sweet tea, we set off.

10.

Klara Fyodorovna loved to repeat a piece of life wisdom, transmitted to her by her great-grandmother, a saying that only those parents were wise who accepted the wisdom of their own children. Over time, the woman rephrased the statement, replacing 'parents' with 'adults', which was more acceptable to the ears of the boarding school inhabitants. For us, the children of Grad, Slavik was an adult. He knew the answers to almost all life questions; he knew how to do the right thing and what justice was. As we traveled, Slavik taught us when to keep quiet (in his opinion, almost never), and when to punch someone in the nose. Not to ask for mercy if you get into trouble. If someone beats you, but you can't give back, endure it, don't cry.

'The offender can break his hands and beat up your face, but he should not hurt your pride. Hold on to the last, do not cry,' said Slavik, showing me and Akim some self-defense techniques, which, as I eventually realized, were more like the techniques of a surprise attack or, better to say, an unfair fight.

But, according to Slavik, the concept of 'honesty' and 'justice' did not exist on the street.

'You need to endure the beatings, and if you were not killed, then hunt down the bastard and take revenge! Take revenge, put him, if not into a grave, then at least into a hospital.' We swallowed every word of our senior friend. Slavik seemed strong and fearless to us. And he accepted our 'wisdom', if you could call it such. Of course, most often he had the last say, especially when it came to Akim, but he respected our opinions, which was new to me personally. Our teachers and educators at the 'Old Lady Willow' were more often decrying us; they had half an ear, and even that one was stuffed. The exceptions were Klara Fedorovna and Fauna, but even they were often condescending to the 'wisdom' of their wards. As for our parents, it seems to me that they never listened to us at all. When talking to me, Mum either cried or was surprisingly detached, while Dad mostly muttered under his breath and coughed when I dared to 'reason'. Nevertheless, they hugged and kissed me, which, as I now understand, replaced the need to talk. For any tactile contact can temporarily replace the need for emotional communication.

Mum once told me how happy she was when she found out that she was pregnant, how Dad carried her in his arms and kissed her not yet rounded tummy. When at night unrestrained melancholy rolled over us as we all realized anew that we had been abandoned, memories of this story warmed my young heart. Not all mothers are happy with their pregnancies; the thought of having a child does not cause tears of happiness in all of them. But mother had cried with joy, and my father carried her in his arms and even bought a bouquet of roses (an unprecedented luxury for them!).

It's great when you are welcomed yet unborn, it's so great. Everything that happened later, the boarding school and the life of a pseudo-orphan – it just happened, it was no malicious intent of my parents. But the love that you are given in the womb, and love after birth are different things, and sometimes it happens that love becomes different after you are born. Then it's better to just have a hug and stay apart.

Having had breakfast with bagels and sweet tea, we set off. Miwa coughed violently again. The damp, rainy night had done its job, and now our girlfriend was constantly shuddering with all her body, trying to restrain her coughing fits so as not to upset Slavik.

'It's a pity that Grandmother Marusya 'checked out'. We could have left Miwa with her. It would have been good for her there. Now looking at my sister hurts,' Akim whispered in my ear, casting anxious glances at the girl, who turned very pale.

'Wouldn't you have missed her?' I asked.

'I would. Probably,' Akim drawled thoughtfully. 'But I could visit Miwa with you on her birthdays or on other holidays. She would be happy in the village, in a warm bed and among the animals. And now we are forced to trudge because of her slow pace and listen to her continuous coughing.' He rolled his eyes irritably, looking towards his sister.

'I don't get why God created girls,' Akim said out loud. 'They are sickly and weak. What's the use of you?' He jokingly pushed Miwa in the side. She raised her eyebrows in a non-joking manner.

'Babies appear in our tummies. If it weren't for us, there would be no you either,' Miwa threw at him contemptuously, quickening her pace.

'And how do they appear there?' I asked, remembering how happy my mother was with her pregnancy. Silence reigned for a minute; even Slavik was silent.

'This is magic,' Akim continued. 'They say that when a man and a woman lie close to each other, and if they also hug each other, then in the morning a child appears in the woman's stomach.'

'Is it only at night or at any time of the day?' I specified.

'At night, of course. All the magic only happens at night.'

'Nonsense!' Slavik snorted. 'I'm sure that babies appear in the stomach from kisses, when you use a tongue.'

At this phrase, everyone present felt dizzy. 'When a man's saliva enters a woman's mouth,' Slavik continued remorsely, 'some chemical processes take place, and after a while a small worm appears in her stomach, which, if fed correctly, begins to grow into a child.'

'How should you feed him?' Miwa asked, amazed.

'How? Well, with different sweets, white bread,' Slavik listed competently.

'I thought that babies appeared in the stomach from peas ...' Miwa conjectured.

'Peas?' Slavik was surprised.

'Yes. One girl told me that her mother, in order to get pregnant, ate a bag of peas. It began to sprout in the stomach and grew into a child. I don't eat peas after that!'

'Nonsense!' announced Slavik. 'It's all about saliva, not peas and magic.'

'And what if you don't feed it with sweets?' asked Akim, seriously thinking about the words of our senior friend.

'Then the worm will remain just a worm, it will not grow. It will live all its life in the woman's stomach until it dies.'

'Wow!' Akim whistled, 'this is how ...' Deeply shocked by the new information, which had opened our eyes to much hitherto unknown, we did not even notice how we walked without stopping until the evening. The sky was turning grey, and the outline of a forest appeared on the horizon, towards which we headed. Having entered its depths, we walked quite a bit longer, until the night haze became an obstacle to further progress towards the goal unknown to anyone except Slavik.

'We'll spend the night right here, and tomorrow there will be a new life,' Slavik said mysteriously, lying down on the warm ground. None of us understood the meaning of what he said then, but in the morning the fog of incomprehension cleared away and a truly new life came into our view.

Part III

Children of Grad

Prologue

Not far from the village named after a famous Soviet general, who lived for several years in that very village, so the locals say, in former times there used to be a *khutor* by the lake behind the forest There were three neat, bleached houses, fenced off from the bustling world by a wicker fence, and a stable and a wide vegetable garden, which the owners shared. People say that this *khutor* existed from time immemorial, until a new Soviet power came, which was not happy about the bright life of the locals, because people were not supposed to live in perfect harmony (with orchards, dairy cows and aggressive roosters). Therefore, the *khutor* began to slowly wither away, until one day it was completely empty. The happy landlords moved someplace else, the cattle scattered, and when it came to the roosters, the local villagers decided to 'take their heads off' and make soup out of them. The farm became overgrown with weeds, the barn was leveled to the ground, and the fence completely decayed. Only the three houses, like ghosts of the past, continued to gaze at the country road silently, sullenly seeing off the random travelers.

In winter, these ghosts dressed in white fluffy coats, which gave them a fabulous look. On days like this, they were like the huts of hard-working dwarves or like the local Snow Queen's tiny kingdom. In the spring, having received a new portion of chips and cracks, the ghosts became a haven to swallows, which nested around their roofs, and nimble squirrels climbed through the windswept cracks and multiplied there gladly. With the arrival of summer, the bushes of raspberries and currants, once planted by the industrious hands of the owners of the farm, grew wildly, climbing up to the windows and doors of the ghosts. When the turn of the golden beauty came, the gloomy ghosts transformed, because autumn was their favorite season. In it, just as in their old walls, one could feel sadness and the certain hopelessness of the inevitable. Autumn carefully covered their roofs with a shaggy gold veil, blowing a cool breeze inside the cracks.

The ghost *khutor* lived out its days this way. It had long been accustomed to the unhurried flow of life and was only waiting for the strong walls of its houses to finally give up standing and, after another invasion of mischievous squirrels, collapse under the burden of time. One year, however, became special for it, because along with the warm breath of summer, four uninvited guests arrived: a brother and a sister of Eastern appearance, a short, lop-eared boy and a young man with a small birthmark under his right eye in the form of a spilled star.

1.

Slavik woke us at dawn. His eyes glittered with excitement, and his knees trembled as if he was ready to start dancing at any moment.

'Grad is already very close! There is a lake nearby, and it's right behind it!' Slavik blurted out, barely restraining himself from screaming. Without hesitating for a second, we jumped to our feet, hastily packed up our belongings and ran as fast as we could towards the lake.

'How do we swim it?' asked Akim, stepping ankle-deep into the water.

'We will have to bypass it,' answered Slavik, and we hurried after him, anticipating the unforgettable sensations that our new life would bring. Even Miwa, only yesterday frail and pale, could now get a head start on her own brother. A gentle blush covered her cheeks, and her breathing quickened, as was common for healthy children spending time on the playground. We rounded the lake and found ourselves on a country road that zigzagged into a thicket. After running a dozen more meters, we reached a dense undergrowth, dazzling with all the colors of summer. Slavik stopped, caught his breath and finally said triumphantly, spreading the branches with his hands: 'Our Grad!'

Beyond the thickets, we saw the place we had been trying to reach for so long, about which we had for so long dreamed and fantasized. We saw our new life: Grad. The city was small: there were only three huts, surrounded by raspberry bushes. Despite its overall poor appearance, Grad concealed a certain charm that only we, the children of Grad, could see. Actually, I had imagined it somewhat different, more attractive, but this Grad was appealing in its own way. We burst into laughter and rushed headlong to inspect our new home. Intoxicated with happiness, we made our way through the thickets without feeling the thorny branches clinging to our hands and scratching our skin. We were as happy as only children can be. Selflessly and to the bone!

The three houses were practically mirror images of each other. Each had two rooms, each had a porch and a cellar. The only difference was that just one of them remained practically intact, having stood the test of time. It was this house that we decided to make ours by universal agreement. The walls of its neighbours were not as strong and had partially collapsed.

Having calmed down a bit after the first burst of joy, we moved our things to the house, where we decided to have breakfast. Having settled down on the porch, Slavik opened a can of condensed milk with a knife, and Miwa began to tear the stale loaf of bread with her small hands.

'I want meat ...' Akim drawled dreamily.

'We'll get some chickens, and you will have your meat,' Slavik smiled, stuffing a generously oiled sandwich into his mouth.

'And a dog? Will we get a dog?!' Miwa got worried, dropping a piece of bread from her hands.

'Of course we will. This is a mandatory item in the life rules of Grad.' Slavik smiled cunningly, pleased with how the girl's face lit up. She happily clapped her hands, barely restraining herself from throwing herself on the neck of our older friend.

After breakfast, we began to inspect our new house. Despite years of desolation, it had survived well, except for the walls, riddled with cracks, through which we could see the weedy vegetable garden. One of the rooms even had a bed and a huge wooden dresser, which looters had apparently not been able to drag out into the courtyard, so heavy was it. This antique piece of furniture delighted our Miwa, a little connoisseur of beauty. It was royally beautiful with its carved feet and drawers and ornate handles, as befitted a soulless inhabitant of Grad. The bed, on the other hand, could hardly be called magnificent, but it was solid and wide, proper enough to accommodate four thin guests. Some of the windows still had decaying curtains, which turned to dust at a single touch.

We were lucky to find some canned meat in the cellar, and although it was expired, according to Slavik, it would be 'as good as new' after being boiled. To his delight, behind the cans of stewed meat Slavik also found a bottle with a cloudy liquid, stuffed with a corncob.

'That's what doesn't go bad for sure!' he exclaimed, licking his lips.

'What is it?' I asked.

'This, Vitka, is a cure for all diseases, a way to cheer up the mood and warm the soul. The best invention of mankind!' Slavka carefully wiped away the thick layer of dust that covered the bottle.

'Aunt Larissa said that the best invention of mankind was a washing machine,' Miwa said pensively.

'Like Aunt Larissa had ever seen a washing machine!' Akim quipped.

'Maybe she hadn't seen it, but she'd heard a lot about it.' The girl stood her ground.

'Yes, that is a good thing,' agreed Slavik, thinking. 'Then let me tell you so, a washing machine and moonshine are two of the greatest inventions in the world. That's for sure!'

2.

After a good night's sleep, the next day we started cleaning the new house. We found tools in one of the cellars and, having washed off their stubborn dirt in the lake, we put them into action. Miwa and Akim beautified the house, clearing out years of decayed foliage and wiping off the dust; Slavik patched holes and cracks the best he could, and I was assigned a mission to deal with the vegetable garden.

For some reason, I had always had a craving for my own garden. Once, before the boarding school happened, my parents took me with them to a village to visit distant relatives. It was a time when rural gardens and vegetable gardens were especially generous with a variety of goodies. Our relatives had a small orchard, a couple of apple trees and cherries, but their garden was impressive. It had all sort of things! All kinds of greens, carrots, cucumbers and several varieties of tomatoes warmed with the summer sun from yellow to dark red. Noticing the delight on my face, the owner of the garden took me by the hand and led me between the rows, allowing me to pluck and try whatever I liked. And I must say that I liked every vegetable, every stem. Swallowing juicy fruits, I thought that when I grow up and start a family, I will also have my own vegetable garden, only there will be even more varieties of tomatoes. It was the tomatoes that I liked the most. Their sweetish scent filled my heart with joy, and their expressive taste brought a truly gastronomic delight. Tomatoes have become my passion! I love them in any form: fresh without anything or in salads, salted and pickled, stewed ... Tomatoes not only do not lose their amazing taste in the variety of ways of cooking them, but acquire new, bright notes.

Thus, I picked up a hoe and began to clean the place where there was once a vegetable garden. Having spent almost the whole day uprooting weeds, in the late afternoon I was able to clear only a small fraction of the land, which in the future would be planted with tomatoes as per our 'Wishes' list. 'Coeur de boeuf' and 'pomo d'oro' to begin with, and then we would see. I also planned to sow dill and parsley, lettuce and carrots and beets. Cucumbers and radishes were on the secondary list. It was important not to forget about potatoes, so that we could have a nutritious dinner on the table on winter evenings. Thinking about the future brining, sealing jars and harvesting, I spent the whole day in the yard.

Tired and worn out, I put my hoe aside only when Miwa called for dinner. Brother and sister had done their best to make the house look presentable. Lake water and a bar of laundry soap had brought a fresh smell to the main room, which was intended to serve as both dining and living room. Akim had ripped the decayed curtains off the windows and swept all the foliage out beyond the threshold. The house was now livable.

'Tomorrow we'll have to go to the village to buy some things for the the house and the garden. What do you need?' asked Slavik, turning to me. I replied that I wanted to clean up the garden, and plant and sow whatever I could at this time of year. The only problem was that I did not know well what that would be.

'I will talk about this with the locals. Maybe someone can advise us,' Slavik reassured.

'I know for sure that you can plant onions now. Some varieties. Nikichna told me once,' Akim shared.

'Perfect! So, we need to buy bulbs from some old woman.' Slavik tore off a small piece of wallpaper from the wall and handed it to Akim so that he, as the most literate of us, could write down a shopping list

'Put it there. Onions.' Akim pulled out a stub of a pencil from his pocket. He always carried it with him in case he 'had to write something down'.

'First: onions,' Akim repeated, carefully scribbling.

'And other vegetables available for sowing,' Slavik continued.

'We need soap and new curtains,' Miwa suggested.

'I need nails and some tools. At least a hammer,' our senior friend said seriously. He'd had trouble all day with rusty nails, which he'd hammered with a piece of brick due to not having a hammer.

'We need to buy some food. And a new kettle,' Akim summed up. 'It will be enough to start with, we are already about to spend a lot of money on all this.' He gently patted himself on the breast pocket in which his savings were kept.

'If we don't have enough money for something, we will make an exchange, or steal it in a pinch,' Slavik answered calmly, stirring a stew of chicken stomachs with buckwheat in a battered kettle. Our dinner gave off a pungent smell and looked even worse.

'Stealing is a sin.' Miwa shook her head displeased. She possessed a subtle, gentle soul and condemned any sinful behavior. And stealing really was a sin, even when it came to food.

'It'd be better to die of hunger then, right?' Akim snapped, rolling his eyes. 'For how long will righteousness feed you, eh?' he grinned maliciously.

'One can earn money to buy food,' Miwa persisted.

'And you know exactly what it is like to earn money!' Slavik laughed. Fragile, sickly Miwa had never had to starve or work for food. Neither had myself or Akim. Such a dilemma was fully lived only by Slavik, who'd had to take on any, even the most dirty and vile, work from an early age in order to get a piece of bread with margarine in gratitude. If he was not able to work, he would fall asleep hungry. But it was not always like that. Later a stepfather appeared in his and his mother's life. Although he was cruel to his stepson, he provided food regularly, lavishing them even with such delicacies as gingerbread and boiled sausages.

'But I can ...' Miwa chirped, ashamed by Slavik.

'You don't need to.' Slavik smiled, patting on her shoulder. He nodded at me and Akim. 'There are me and the boys for earning money. You'd better spruce up the house, hang the curtains, feed the chickens. It's not a girly thing to make money.'

There was no table, so we sat on the floor. Despite the smell, as disgusting as its taste, we ate our dinner with delight, smearing the remains from the kettle on rancid crackers.

'We need to buy some more bread and breadcrumbs tomorrow.' Akim put a note in his list.

'And more candles. We must use our flashlight more efficiently,' Slavik said, extinguishing our only source of light. 'Let's go to bed.'

The four of us got comfortable on the bed, which smelled damp, chatted for a while and, one by one, began to fall into a swcct, languid sleep. I was the last one awake. Despite my fatigue, sleep did not come to me. There were too many thoughts in my head, starting with a detailed list of the necessary vegetables and ending with deeper reflections about Grad and our future life in general. I imagined myself already quite adult, with stubble on my face and broad shoulders. Imagined deftly picking an early crop of tomatoes. Perhaps there would be more of us here by then. Perhaps I would find a wife in a neighbouring village who would agree to live in Grad in seclusion with my friends. I imagined her being like Fauna, with eyes the color of buckwheat honey and a light blond braid that gave off a subtle lavender scent. I thought it would be good to plant lavender bushes at the doorstep. That plant looks beautiful. Thus I fell asleep, thinking about tomatoes, my future wife and lavender.

3.

In the morning, Slavik and Akim went to the nearest village to buy, exchange or steal everything we needed from the list. Miwa and I stayed to keep charge, and, at her request, I put off working in the garden for a while to help with cleaning the house.

'Then I will help you with planting onions,' she assured me. My task was to run to the lake constantly and bring water. Although Miwa tried to use it consciously, the water turned black very soon due to the heavy pollution of the house. It took ten minutes to get to the lake, and the same amount of time to come back. A whole half of the day was dedicated to this continuous running. Slavik and Akim returned after lunch.

'Dear mistress, here we come!' Slavik shouted triumphantly when he saw Miwa. The girl was standing on the dresser, washing the mould off the wall with a rag. He pulled a piece of lace from a large sack and spread it on the floor.

'New curtains! You just need to cut it.' Seeing the intricate beige lace, Miwa gasped with delight, swaying on the dresser.

'That's so beautiful!' She deftly jumped to the floor, scooped up the fabric and, wrapping her arms around it, began to circle the room joyfully.

'I'll sew it on with threads, it will be fabulous!' She laughed. 'Where did you get such beauty?'

'We took it from an old lady as a payment for some work,' Akim lied, since in fact he had stolen the fabric in the local haberdashery, while the saleswoman, a pimply girl, was chatting with Slavik.

'We brought you soap and something to eat. And here are your onions, Vitka.' Slavik handed me a basket filled to the brim with bulbs. 'Here's some more for you, everything is detailed here. What can be planted now and which way.' After the bulbs he gave me a small bag full of beet and carrot seeds. It also included detailed instructions, written in neat, flowery handwriting.

'We wandered into the yard of a widow – she has a beautiful garden! We bought everything from her and asked her to write instructions, because we are kind of bad at this.' Slavik smiled.

'She said that we can ask her if needed. She has a large supply of potatoes in the cellar, and we agreed that we would come back and buy a bag. Because yesterday's meat from the can is still growling in the stomach,' Akim grimaced, patting himself on the stomach.

'And how is it there in general? In the village?' Miwa asked, still clutching the lace fabric.

'The village is of some size. There are a couple of shops, the local farms are quite good. We've got our eye on some chickens in that very yard, we will need to buy or exchange them. But this is after we build the chicken coop. Maybe in a couple of weeks.

'I love fresh eggs!' Miwa licked her lips.

'Who doesn't?' Slavik laughed. 'It's ok, we will live like kings and queens!' He smiled with satisfaction, examining his and Akim's 'catch'.

After the guys came back, the need for my house cleaning services disappeared. Miwa plunged headlong into a new task: decorating windows. She measured the fabric, cut and sewed a sort of curtain (the guys had brought her a sewing kit with threads and needles in a small wooden box), then put it against the window and fixed it again. I isolated myself in the garden. Having completely cleared a small piece of land from weeds, I began to dig it up. Thanks to a shovel brought from the village, the process went much faster now. Before dinner, I had put part of the garden into the proper form for sowing, clearing and digging, the ground not just loose, but fluffy, like a porous soufflé. Throwing off my holey shoes, I walked with pleasure barefoot on the soft, delicate soil, drowning in it. I breathed in the scent of the damp ground heated by the summer sun, experiencing an all-consuming joy. My heart was bubbling in anticipation of a sown vegetable garden and a future rich harvest. I thought about how on winter evenings we would cook borscht (if only I could learn its recipe!) from carrots and beets from my garden. And onions can be fried until golden brown and put on brown bread. Standing almost ankle-deep in the ground, I felt the taste of fried onions, thoroughly salted, and fresh brown bread: a wheat or rye loaf.

Although there was no table in the house, there was a large stove, similar to the one in the house of Nikichna, our caretaker. Only ours was peeled and cracked due to many years of life alone. As it turned out, however, the stove was still working properly. We burned branches that Akim brought from the forest, boiled potatoes in a new kettle, and fried a dozen fresh eggs (just laid today!) in a frying pan, those which Slavik 'nicked' along with the basket when the hostess turned away.

We ate, I must say, with an unprecedented appetite! The potato burned the larynx but was so tasty (or was it just us feeling hungry for fresh food?) that we swallowed it, not paying attention to the pain. And the scrambled eggs, generously seasoned with parsley, were good. For the first time in a while, there was deathly silence between us, because we were completely focused on our dinner.

Having eaten to the full, we sat down by the stove and, like forest snakes that had just swallowed their victim, slowly digested what we had eaten.

'It's been a long time since I've overeaten so much!' Akim stretched out his legs. He had hiccups. 'Will you pass me a beer?' He turned to Slavik. Slavik did not hesitate and pulled out three glass bottles from behind the oven.

'To Grad!' Slavik smiled, toasting with Akim. I refused beer and drank rosehip tea with Miwa.

'It's bad for you,' said Miwa meekly, glancing at the bottle in Slavik's hands.

'Well, it's not like I'm too much of a drinker,' our senior friend replied.

'Promise me that you won't drink too much.' The girl frowned.

'Of course, I promise.' Slavik gently ran his hand through her hair.

Slavik really did limit himself to only one bottle, while Akim drank two, after which his speech became terribly funny. He staggered and giggled for no reason. And he smelled quite unpleasant. Therefore, that night Slavik did not allow Akim to sleep in bed with us. He was not very offended, just lay down on the bare floor and instantly fell asleep.

After sitting for another half hour, the three of us also decided to go to bed. Having washed her face before going to bed, Miwa pressed against Slavik's shoulder and he put his hand on her back. After wishing each other good night, my friends fell asleep. I, as usual, could not sleep for some time, looking at the new curtains on the windows. Crookedly sewn and also crookedly hung, in general they added comfort to the room. Of course, it was clear that the girl was holding a needle and thread for the first time ...

4.

After a quick snack early in the morning, I ran into the garden to start sowing seeds. Strictly following the instructions (soaking some seedlings in the evening, sowing at a certain distance from each other), I plunged headlong into gardening activities, only taking pauses to drink water or grab something to eat.

Akim, who suffered that day from headaches and general malaise, barely crawled out into the courtyard close to dinnertime, and he only did that because Slavik threatened to drag him out by the scruff of his neck. Sitting on the steps, he greedily drank the lake water brought by Miwa in a clay pot.

'What the hell?' asked Akim, addressing the question to somewhere in the void.

'This is because of beer, idiot,' explained Slavik who considered it an obvious fact.

'How do I get rid of it?'

'Drink some more beer, it will help. Go to the house. There is a bottle hidden in the wardrobe for cases like this one,' answered Slavik. The prospect of a drink cheered Akim – he quickly went into the house and returned with a bottle of warm beer.

'Want some?' Akim offered Slavik, but he shook his head, grimacing.

'It's warm. It's not tasty.'

Having drunk a bottle of beer almost in one gulp, Akim cheered up significantly. His strength returned to him, and literally an hour later he, together with our senior friend, was busily walking around the house, making a list of necessary furniture. But only necessary items, namely those without which it would be extremely uncomfortable to live. Thus, another bed (or just a mattress), a table and four chairs were added to the list. Miwa asked for shelves to nail up on the wall.

'You can put jars and dishes on them, it's convenient,' she persuaded until the boys gave in and the shelves were included in the list of 'only the most necessary'. The question remained where and how to get all these necessary things. Akim offered to buy chairs from one of the locals. Any would do, the main thing was for them to have four legs. We could make a table by ourselves – we just needed a solid board and four logs. And we didn't really need a second bed as much: a mattress or an old carpet would be a great alternative. Having studied the list again and discussed all the details, Slavik and Akim left for the village after lunch.

A few hours later, they returned with four chairs and a piece of plywood, a potential countertop for our future dining table. I noted reluctantly how strong my friends were, being were able to drag all this stuff on their backs! It was just a small matter of finding the legs for the table. Slavik himself took over this matter. Armed with an ax, he went into the forest and returned, dragging long, thick branches. It must be said that Slavik was busy until late at night, having refused dinner. He huffed and groaned, pounded with a hammer and swore. All this continued even after we fell asleep. I don't know whether Slavik was making the table until morning or not, but when we woke up, we gasped with delight, as there was a large table on high wooden legs by the stove. Of course, like Miwa's curtains, one could not call it a work of art, but it was stable, had four strong legs and, most importantly, it was comfortable to sit at it. Finally we could eat at a table!

But I was jumping the gun. While Slavik had just started tinkering with the table, Akim nailed to the wall of our living room the oath of the 'Children of Grad'. He put the crumpled piece of paper into a frame, for which he had exchanged a can of stew in the village. He smoothed, pressed and hung it on the wall between two windows. Beside the oath there was an honorary place dedicated to the list of 'Wishes', where each of us was permitted three wishes regarding our life in Grad. Not everyone had had time to decide on their wishes, so there were dashes next to some points (for now). Altogether, it looked like this:

AN OATH OF THE CHILDREN OF GRAD

I swear that I will not break tree branches.
Only if I am alone in the forest in the cold and I need to light a fire!
I swear that I will not hit animals, even the evil and the mad ones.
I swear that I will pray for the happiness of Fauna and Klara Fyodorovna, and when they die, I will pray for their rest.
I swear to hate Rusichka until my last breath, and even after I die!
Children of Grad! Children of Grad! Children of Grad!

WISHES OF THE CHILDREN OF GRAD

Miwa	1) get a dog;
	2) buy a gramophone;
	3) go to bed whenever you want
Akim	1) beer day on Sundays;
	2) permission to swear on Saturday and on holidays (non-religious);
	3) get chickens
Vitya	1) grow a vegetable garden (tomatoes!);
	2) buy the magazine *Murzilka*;
	3) –
Slavik	1) –
	2) –
	3) –

The only one of us who had no idea what he wanted was Slavik. Although at times it seemed to me that he was just holding fire, waiting for some important moment or event in order to voice his 'wishes'. And, as it turned out, my feelings did not fail me. But more on that later.

Satisfied with his work, Akim went out into the yard, where I was covered in dirt, learning the hard work of the agrarian.

'When will the beets come up?' he asked, taking a handful of ground in his hand. 'So fluffy!'

'We will be lucky if we can harvest them in September,' I replied, wiping the sweat from my forehead. Akim whistled.

'Wow! So long ...'

'We will only be able to harvest onions soon.' If they sprout, of course, I thought, examining the basket of bulbs.

'What do we need onions for?'

'You can fry onions in butter and spread on bread. They are delicious and can be stored for a long time ...'

'When there's nothing to eat in the winter, and so it will be, you'll say thank you to Vitka that he was digging doubled up, and planted onions,' Slavik interjected into our conversation, coming out into the yard to stretch his back.

'I didn't say that I was against onions,' Akim hastened to assure him. 'But this whole venture with the garden, it just takes a long time. It would be easier to steal food from the locals.'

'It is not good to pilfer stuff too often, or someone will notice and start to dive into it, look for the one who did it. Eventually they may reach our Grad. We don't need that. Therefore, we should steal only trifles and infrequently. And, in general, we should not appear in the village for some time, otherwise they will suspect something. They will start searching, sniffing around, those wretches. I know these rural people, they always stick their noses where they shouldn't. They give you no space. So, any stealing should be rare and small. Yes, and next time I will go to the village with Vitka, your face is so noticeable, Akimushka.' Slavik laughed at the last phrase, pleased with the indignation of our Tatar friend. Akim refrained from answering, though, because he had to agree with what Slavik said. To be too noticeable meant to jeopardize everything we had been working for. Therefore, he just grunted in displeasure and answered casually 'as you wish', after which he went into the house to help Miwa with the cleaning.

'You see, Vitka, that's what respect means,' said Slavik when we were left alone.

'Respect?' I asked.

'Yes, respect. He wanted to answer me but said nothing. And all because he is afraid. And if he is afraid, that means that he respects me. Fear breeds respect.'

'But in Theology lessons, we were told that fear is the path to hatred ...' I began hesitantly, remembering Father Vladimir's parting words.

'No,' snapped Slavik, 'I'm not talking about that fear. Fear can be different. You can be afraid of a dark gateway, because you may be beaten there; or of hunger, because you can die. This is one fear. I'm talking about fear of someone who is head and shoulders above you. Above you with his brains. Who is always right and always knows what needs to be done. You are afraid of him because of his Greatness. Greatness! Do you understand this, Vitka?' Slavik came up to me, looked straight into my eyes, and then began to measure my garden with wide steps.

'Those who are led are always afraid of those who lead.'

'Who?' I asked, not understanding the meaning of what he said.

'Well, there are those who lead and those who follow them. I am the leader, Vitka, but Akim is the one who follows the leader.' Slavik smiled with satisfaction.

'And me?'

'What about you?'

'Am I following you too?'

'You are my right hand, Vitka. That is different. You walk hand in hand with me. Without you, everything would be different, I would have been well on the other side by now!' Slavik smiled, firmly shaking my hand, 'I'll never forget this, never. You are my friend forever!'

To say that I felt pleased is to say nothing. Hearing such words from Slavik, our unofficial leader who knew the answers to all questions, was the highest measure of recognition.

'You are my friend too,' I replied with an embarrassed smile. We stood for a long time, silently examining either our shoes, or the lumps of ground in the garden. I felt good in my soul. Because it is always good when you have a real friend who appreciates you and for whom you, despite his Greatness, are equal to him. It costs a lot!

'And Miwa?' I asked unexpectedly.

'And what about Miwa?' Slavik smiled slyly.

'Is she like Akim or like me?'

'Miwa ... Miwa is different,' Slavik answered mysteriously. 'You know, she is a special girl. Still just a girl. But damn special.' He smiled again and said nothing more. I remained ankle-deep in the ground, trying to penetrate the unsaid.

5.

Miwa really wanted a dog. Since Slavik had promised to fulfill her wish, a couple of weeks from the day we started arranging our new home, he brought a small smoky-grey puppy from the village. Outwardly, it somewhat resembled a Caucasian shepherd dog, but was clearly a half-breed. Cute and very funny, it ran around the yard to the joy and delight of our little girlfriend. Miwa named it Bagel because she claimed the puppy smelled as good as fresh bagels. So we got a puppy called Bagel, who whined at night and asked to sleep with his mistress.

'Don't let it get accustomed to your hands. We will need a guard dog, and not a pocket pug,' Akim muttered. But Miwa did not listen to him and took the puppy with her under the blanket (another thief's trophy of my comrades), arguing that we did not need 'a guard dog, but a friend'. And friends should not be left to sleep on the floor, especially when they are so small and defenseless.

While Miwa spent her days playing games with Bagel, we boys started building a chicken coop. Having disassembled a mountain of old boards that were once a barn, it took us a week of continuous work to build a pretty decent coop, a little bigger than Slavik's height. We stuffed boards inside and put a large rusty basin for water on the floor. On one side, Slavik pulled up netting, stolen from one of the locals.

'That will serve as a fence for the chickens so they don't run away. They're stupid birds,' he explained. After evaluating the results of the work, everyone was satisfied. We were absolutely fine with a chicken coop like this one, even though it stood at a crooked angle and the wind blew straight through it due to the abundance of cracks.

'How beautiful it is!' Miwa admired it, running around the new building. 'It's just amazing!' She laughed joyfully and, picking up Bagel in her arms, whirled for a long, long time, relishing the charm of the life of the children of Grad.

In August, I harvested my first thin crop of onions. Miwa put the bulbs carefully in a wooden box and took it to the cellar so that in winter there would be 'something to spread on bread'. Some greens were also suitable, which, as Slavik suggested, could be dried and mixed with lard in boiling water during the times of cold.

'That will be a nutritious broth,' said our senior friend knowingly. Thus, by the end of the summer, we, like real adults, began to think about our supply of food for the hunger season. By that time, Slavik had brought a dozen chickens from the village, who were cheeping around the clock in the chicken coop.

'As they grow up, we will chop off some of their heads, and put the carcasses into jars. It will go well in winter!' reasoned Akim, licking his lips. This is how our life went on. When we were not busy with preparations for the winter, each one idly wandered about his own business. Miwa most often played with Bagel or walked with Slavik, picking flowers in the forest. I liked to spend time in the garden or read till I wore out old issues of the magazine *Murzilka*, which was not so easy to get. Sometimes I also liked to run around with Bagel, throwing him a small stick. He was an affectionate puppy and always licked the hands of those who frolicked with him.

Akim's main fun, despite the beer day established only on Sunday, was to drink beer, and sometimes moonshine somewhere in the forest (God only knows where and how he got it!). When there was no work, he slept until lunchtime, and then left in an unknown direction and returned late in the evening already tanked. A couple of times Slavik bludgeoned him, strictly forbidding him to get drunk to such a state and so often. There was no complete ban on alcohol in Grad, since Slavik himself did not mind having a couple of bottles of beer or a glass of homebrew (a half-blind grandmother in the village sold it for a penny). The physical punishment helped for a short period of time, then Akim came home late and drunk again. Sometimes, however, he could give up drinking for several days after the tearful persuasions of Miwa, whose heart ached for her brother. She usually sat at his feet, covering the boy's fingers with hot kisses, and whispering something in a language that Slavik and I did not understand. Her speeches were like a prayer, her voice even and velvety. After this, Akim usually did not drink for some time and was even extremely gentle with his sister, but then everything repeated and Miwa cried again, burying her forehead in his sharp knees. At such moments, I could carefully examine her doll-like face, framed by lush, coal-black hair. Despite her oriental blood, Miwa's skin was porcelain with a slight blush on her cheeks, as if painted with bright paint. Small plump lips, wide eyebrows and a neat, even nose made her really look like a doll. It was impossible not to admire her beauty. Sometimes I let my fantasy go wild and imagined her as an adult girl with long legs and lush breasts. In my mind, Miwa's waist was thin, and her hair was certainly loose. Miwa was a beauty, one couldn't argue with that. Slavik, just like me, noted this fact, but as time went on, more so, and the girl spent most of the time with him. Not surprisingly, one evening Slavik dumbfounded us by wishing to sleep with Miwa in a different room, on a different bed.

'From this day on, Miwa and I sleep together. Just us,' he said in a businesslike manner. Miwa, unlike Akim and I, took the news calmly, since she had long been aware of Slavik's plans.

'What do you mean?!' Akim shouted. He was sober that evening.

'I mean what I said,' Slavik answered calmly. 'I want to sleep with your sister in the same bed, separately from you, in a separate room.'

'Miwa!' Akim turned towards his sister. She sat on the floor stroking Bagel.

'What 'Miwa'?' the girl mimicked.

'You cannot do things this way. You are not his wife. Only a wife can go to bed with her husband separately from everyone. Otherwise it's shameful! Only street girls do that!' shouted Akim, indignant at his sister's behavior.

'Oh, stop it!' Miwa dismissed. 'What is that nonsense?'

'We decided so, period.' Slavik's voice acquired metallic notes. Akim understood that there was no point in contradicting, otherwise he could get a smack in the mouth. Slavik had long consolidated the position of the unofficial leader of our Grad. As a senior friend, he was our leader and patron. Akim, however, who had been nervously swinging in his chair, got up calmly and began to slowly pace the room.

'Well, since you decided so, I will not argue,' he hissed through clenched teeth. 'But I will not give my blessing until you, Slava, marry my sister,' he snapped, measuring Slavik with a haughty look. Slavik widened his eyes in amazement.

'And who will marry us? We are not mature enough for this yet.'

'Not mature enough to get married, but mature enough to lie in one bed?' Akim's face turned purple.

'Either you marry her or blame yourself!' he shouted, clenching his fists. For the first time, Akim had expressed direct disagreement with Slavik.

'Boys, stop it ...' Miwa was frightened when Slavik approached her brother, clenching his fists.

'I can marry them,' I said, which attracted everyone's attention. 'Well, I know different prayers and I attended an engagement ceremony once ... I know what to say,' I continued.

'In order to marry someone, you have to be a priest,' Akim snapped.

'In order to marry someone, you need to know the right words. And the right words come from God, they are powerful and sacred. If you say such words, they will consolidate marriage, and marriages ... You know, Akim, they are made in heaven.' My short speech amazed everyone present to the extent that the fists of my friends unclenched by themselves, and Miwa smiled.

'Well, since you know the right words, come on, marry us,' shrugged Slavik.

'To begin with, you have to propose to Miwa, then you have to woo her, and then comes the wedding ...' I started long explanations.

'And how do I do the proposing thing?' Despite the fact that Slavik knew the answers to all questions, he was weak in matters of 'going after' someone.

'Well, you need to give her a ring. This is the first thing. Then you should come with flowers and ask if she wants to marry you, and if she agrees, then you can woo her ... But usually you have to woo the parents too ...'

'So to hell with matchmaking!' Slavik cursed.

'No, it is not possible without matchmaking.' I thought about it. 'I can be instead of your parents, and Akim from the bride's side!' Everyone liked my idea, and we began joyful preparations for the upcoming matchmaking. That night Slavik and Miwa slept separately – we persuaded them to wait only one day, until the wedding. The next day there was a lot to do: get the ring, prepare a festive dinner and, most importantly, a wedding dress; so that night we could not sleep for a long time, excited by the upcoming event.

6.

Slavik got up before dawn and, quietly gathering himself so as not to wake anyone up, left in an unknown direction. When we got up (and it was about eight in the morning), the water he'd boiled to make tea had already cooled down. Miwa chatted tirelessly, discussing the cut of the future dress and how it was to be sewn from scraps of the fabric that was used for the curtains. Since Miwa did not know how to sew, she preferred a canopy-style cut. Throwing lace on her shoulders, she tied its long parts at the waist, from which the fabric fell in waves, imitating a fluffy skirt. We invented beads from wild berries and flowers, stringing them on a thread so that we had something to put on her neck. Miwa kept her hair a secret, because, as she herself said, 'there must be a mystery to thc bride.' While our girlfriend was busy with her own toilet, Akim and I went to the village to collect 'holiday' snacks. Of course, we stole the bulk of the products in order to save money, which was already scarce. Marshmallows, marmalade and a couple of chocolate bars were complemented by cinnamon rolls, vanilla cookies and a bottle of red wine. Akim said that the holiday was not a holiday without champagne, but since it was not in the store, he had to settle for red wine with a brown bear on the label.

'We need to wring a chicken's neck for soup, add your onions and some potatoes. It will be excellent for a hot meal!' declared Akim as we were returning back. So he did as soon as we returned. After breaking the chicken's neck, he skillfully plucked and gutted the carcass, then threw it into the kettle, warmed up the stove and set the soup to boil.

By the time the chicken broth boiled, Slavik returned. It was impossible to recognize him! Dressed in brown corduroy pants and a matching jacket, he held an armful of daisies in his hands.

'Where is my bride?!' he exclaimed playfully. Miwa's head, decorated with a wreath of wildflowers, appeared from the window of the house. She coquettishly covered her face with a piece of translucent cloth.

'Who's asking?' she replied.

'Here I came to ask for your hand, beautiful. Will you marry me?' Slavik approached the window, leaning his elbows on the rickety windowsill. As befits a decent girl, Miwa paused to consider the proposal.

'I will,' she finally whispered.

‘And what’s next?’ asked Slavik, turning to me. Akim and I stood at a distance, watching this unusual scene.

‘Give her the ring,’ I hissed, annoyed that Slavik was at a loss at such a crucial moment.

‘Oh yes!’ Slavik cursed, then rummaged through his pockets and pulled out a small bag, from which he took out a thin bracelet with shiny stones.

‘Sorry, I didn’t find a ring, but here’s this instead,’ explained Slavik, making excuses. He handed Miwa a gift, and she gave him her hand in return. Fastening the bracelet on her thin wrist, Slavik uncertainly kissed the bride’s hand.

‘Is that correct?’ he asked again. I nodded approvingly. After the bride gave formal consent, matchmaking began.

‘The hunter is ours, the sable weaver is yours!’ I laughed, dancing in front of Akim. I scattered in compliments to the groom, embellishing all his advantages and keeping silent about his shortcomings. Akim listened attentively, occasionally asking leading questions.

‘Is your hunter strong enough? Is he capable of protecting my sister?’

‘He is strong as a bear!’

‘Will he be kind to my sister? Will he not hurt her?’

‘He will not hurt a stray dog – he will caress anyone!’

‘Will he be able to feed her?’

‘No one will lack anything with him!’ I answered confidently, and Akim gave up.

‘So be it!’ He smiled. ‘Let them marry.’ He brought out a plate of buns and wine in glasses made from newspapers.

Such a light lunch was supposed to symbolize our unity already as a family. After drinking the sweet drink, I eagerly swallowed two rolls. Now the most crucial moment came: the marriage itself.

From the back of our house, among the thickets of raspberries, Akim and I made our way to a secluded place where it was possible to conduct the ‘sacrament.’ Sheltered from the burning sun by the branches of an old linden tree, this place was really special; it was comfortable there.

‘Stand facing each other, and I will speak the words,’ I ordered, placing myself one step ahead of the ‘young couple’. Akim stood on the sidelines, tightly controlling everything to make sure that all was correct.

‘Miwa and Slavik,’ I began, looking carefully at my friends, ‘do you understand how important and serious this is?’

After hesitating for a moment, both of them nodded. Miwa could not help smiling – this was such a joyful day for her. The wreath she had woven with her own hands that morning gave her face an innocent look, and her hair was twisted into a tight knot which made her look a little older. As if she was Slavik's age, and not an eleven-year-old girl. After a few more general questions, I began to pray.

'Always give thanks to God the Father for everything in the name of our Lord Jesus Christ. Submit to one another out of reverence for Christ ...' I muttered, shaking my head up and down. From time to time, I baptized the young in the same way as Father Vladimir did during the divine services. Having finished my prayer, I baptized my friends for the last time, wishing them a long and happy life.

'Now you can kiss each other to seal the union,' I smiled.

'What if they make a baby?' Akim was frightened.

'They're husband and wife now,' I insisted, 'this is how it's supposed to be. Only without tongue.' Akim had no choice but to agree. Leaning over to Miwa, Slavik kissed her on the lips and the girl's cheeks flushed. She pushed him away playfully.

'Well, that's enough.' Slavik smiled.

'It's time to set the festive table!' Akim exclaimed, hugging the newlyweds.

The evening was approaching. Slavik brought the table with four chairs out of the house to eat in the garden in honor of such an event. In the center of the table was a kettle of steaming soup made from chicken and onions. Next to it was a plate of buttered bread, and bowls of marshmallows and marmalade. An open bottle of wine and a bar of milk chocolate completed the still life.

'So yummy!' Miwa looked around the table with an admiring glance. 'I've never seen such beauty before!' She was delighted, clinging to Slavik. 'How good it is that we decided to get married!'

'That's for sure,' agreed Slavik, devouring soup and bread. The festive dinner turned out to be very joyful. Sweet wine which Akim generously poured into glasses, also contributed to the merriment. We laughed, Slavik entertaining us with stories of unprecedented adventures and fabulous creatures that lived far away. Miwa danced to Akim's outlandish singing (long, rather melodic in a language that Slavik and I did not understand). She whirled, waving her lace skirt from side to side, and was so energetic and infectious in her fun that Slavik and I joined in. The dances did not end until late at night, when Akim got tired of singing. We finished our wine, deciding not to clear the table, and went into the house. Since Slavik and Miwa were now husband and wife, they could sleep together, separately from everyone. Akim and I had to give them the bedroom. We lay on the floor in the living room, using an old dusty blanket instead of a mattress, which smelled of mould and sheepskin.

'It's okay, we'll make ourselves a bed or get a mattress,' Akim said, pulling a T-shirt over his nose so as not to feel the 'scent'. The muffled conversation of the 'newlyweds' was heard from behind the closed door, and from time-to-time Miwa burst into laughter, or the bed creaked. I was incredibly interested in what they were doing there.

'You think they are kissing?' I asked, lightly pushing Akim in the side. He just grunted in displeasure.

'I hope not.'

'But they are husband and wife, they are allowed to. Moreover, without a tongue ...'

'Miwa is still too little, she can't,' muttered Akim.

'Husbands and wives all kiss, that's why they get married.' I continued to argue until I heard the quiet snuffle of my neighbour. I tossed and turned for a long time, pondering whether all husbands and wives really kiss, and why people get married at all. To kiss? Thanks to Slavik, we already knew that children appear in the stomach from kisses with the tongue. It was clear to me why they do it then. But in respect of the usual kissing on the lips, there were many questions. Why do people do it? Maybe it's nice, or maybe it's just necessary, like brushing your teeth or washing your face in the morning? I had many questions, but I fell asleep without finding the answers ...

7.

Summer was drawing to a close, and the spirit of autumn was already in the air, stealthily approaching the threshold. Unable to withstand my and Akim's whining, Slavik dragged home out of nowhere a fairly tolerable mattress, which we put on heavy wooden boxes that we found in the cellar of one of the houses. So we got our own nice bed.

Miwa's health deteriorated because of the dampness of nights. At night she would cough, and her cheeks turned pale again, as had happened at the very beginning of our journey. Slavik was worried about his 'spouse' and even got some herbs in the village, a broth of which Miwa obediently drank every day before going to bed, following his instructions. The truth is that it did not help her get better, though it did not allow the cough to get worse.

Akim got drunk every day. Despite the official permission for Slavik and Miwa to sleep together, which was sealed with the correct words and the necessary ritual, he still could not bear the fact that his sister went to bed every night with Slavik, a guy. However smart he was, Akim still hated him at heart. Now I already understood that Akim openly despised our leader, but was powerless because of his authority. And although Akim was never too attached to his sister, perceiving her, as it seemed to me, as a burden rather than a full member of our brotherhood, he nevertheless considered her behavior insulting. Not because he was worried about her, but because by it she expressed disobedience to him, her older brother and a man. My precious Fauna once told me that in the world of Akim and Miwa, girls should be meek and obey the elders of the family in everything. But we lived in a completely different world, far from the one whose traditions Akim so zealously tried to observe. A couple of times, after drinking heavily, he tried to start a 'conversation' with Miwa, to instill shame in her. She only laughed it off, however – considering herself Slavik's 'legitimate' wife, she now only obeyed him. Akim was written off. Humiliated and depressed, he disappeared all day in the wilderness, where he had his own stash of moonshine and beer. Slavik did not care much about the behavior of our friend, but sometimes would not let him into the house to spend the night. Then Akim slept in the chicken coop, and in the morning, smelling of droppings, he might twist the head of one of the chickens out of anger. After several such incidents, Slavik hung a lock on the chicken coop, and now if Akim did not get into the house, he slept in the open air.

'Not everyone knows how to drink,' Slavik started a conversation one day, after once again not letting Akim inside. He had replied with filthy curses and kicks at the door, frightening Miwa. But soon he got tired and went to sleep on the porch.

'We had a neighbour, Valik Ostroukhov, he could belt down a bottle of vodka in one evening, wash it down with beer, and then add wine on top. And what do you think? He got up stone-cold sober and went to work. He was a watchman in some warehouses. He could drink a bucket, and he was barely even buzzed,' argued Slavik, chewing brown bread. 'Then there were those, of course, who were checkered by one glass. Akim is one of those. Bad blood.'

'He and I are of the same blood.' Miwa pursed her lips in offense.

'You are not. You are not like that.' Slavik smiled, pressing the girl to his chest. 'It happens in families. One turns out fine, and the other one takes on the worst. It's like a rejected puppy. Now, now, Bagel, we are not talking about you.' Slavik gently patted the worried Bagel by the ear. The teenage puppy stretched out under the table happily, its long tail between its legs.

'Do you think I know how to drink?' Miwa asked.

'I don't think you need to try it. That is an ugly thing, when girls drink vodka in glasses. It leads to bad consequences.' Slavik shook his head disapprovingly.

'And I?' I asked.

'What about you?'

'Do I know how to drink?'

'Well, this is a moot point, Vitka. As I see, you are not into that. And if you get drunk like Akim, who will take care of the garden? You've got good onions!' my elder friend laughed.

'Slavushka,' said Miwa, 'why haven't you written your wishes yet? Don't you want anything?'

'But I have everything.' Slavik spread his hands. 'A wonderful house, best friend, a beautiful wife and a faithful dog. What else does a man need to be happy?' He winked at Miwa, who blushed when she heard a compliment addressed to herself.

'Everyone wants something,' I drawled, drawing patterns on the surface of the lard with my fingernail. Slavik looked at me attentively.

'Well, since you insist ...' Slavik got up from his chair, rummaged in his pockets in search of a pencil, but, not finding it, pulled out a small coal from the oven. For a couple of minutes he silently stood in front of the list of 'Wishes'.

'I want new clothes every spring. Especially trousers and pajamas,' he finally announced, dragging out a funny scribble in coal dust.

'And I also want to be obeyed, because I am older than the others,' he continued and, having met the tacit consent of all those present, filled out No. 2.

'And ...' He paused to think. 'I want Miwa to always be my wife.' He glanced tenderly at Miwa, which made her cheeks flush.

'She's your wife anyway, and the right words sealed the marriage,' I said.

'Yes, but people sometimes leave their loved ones. They get divorced and don't love each other anymore ...'

'I will always love you! I swore an oath,' Miwa hastened to assure. 'I will always, always be your wife.' She ran up to her 'spouse' and, standing on her tiptoes to seem at least a little taller, she pressed herself against him as tight as she could.

'And will you always be my wife?' Slavik smiled.

'Always, always,' Miwa buried her face in the chest of her loved one, gently purring, like happy cats do. Watching this touching, but overly explicit demonstration of affection, I thought of Akim, who was now asleep on the porch, shuddering from gusts of cold wind. What would he say if he witnessed such a scene? It seemed to me that this would not give him joy ...

Having finished writing his last wish, satisfied, Slavik reread the entire list once again.

WISHES OF THE CHILDREN OF GRAD

Miwa	1) get a dog;
	2) buy a gramophone;
	3) go to bed whenever you want
Akim	1) beer day on Sundays;
	2) permission to swear on Saturday and on holidays (non-religious);
	3) get chickens
Vitya	1) grow a vegetable garden (tomatoes!);
	2) buy the magazine *Murzilka*;
	3) –

Slavik 1) new clothes every spring, especially trousers and pajamas;
2) obeying ~~*me*~~ Slavik because ~~*I*~~ he is older;
3) Miva ~~*will be*~~ is my wife forever

Unlike Akim, Slavik did not have the necessary knowledge of grammar to fill in the list the first time without mistakes, which is why it turned out with errors and crooked. Nevertheless, he was pleased with himself, because he couldn't even remember the last time he had written anything at all.

'By the way, you still have one more wish,' Slavik noted after reviewing the list.

'I'll save it for a rainy day.' I smiled. Slavik rolled his eyes theatrically.

'When it was about me, you pushed me, and here it goes, 'for a rainy day',' he mimicked kindly.

'Don't tease him, let him have one wish for a rainy day.' Miwa smiled. She sat down on the floor next to Bagel, who slept blissfully, twitching his paw in his sleep.

'When will we buy a gramophone?' asked the girl, fingering the dirty tufts of fur on the back of the dog. Slavik and I looked at each other in bewilderment. We had completely forgotten about Miwa's wish to have a gramophone in the house.

'Soon,' Slavik dropped casually.

'In a week?' asked Miwa.

'Why exactly in a week?'

'Because it's my birthday in a week.' Miwa smiled happily, straightening the thick braid that fell on her chest. 'I would like to receive a gramophone and a couple of records as a gift ... With beautiful French songs ... Like those that Madame Ju played for us in her lessons. They are all about love.' The girl closed her eyes with pleasure, remembering the wonderful lyrical songs that sounded from the fashionable electrophone of the dance teacher, Juliette Germanovna.

While Miwa was moving her sharp shoulders to the beat of an unknown melody that sounded only in her head, Slavik and I looked at each other in confusion, hardly imagining where we would find a gramophone and records with French songs within a week ...

8.

The third day after the events described, Slavik and I went by train to a small town two hundred kilometers away from Grad, where, according to our calculations, it was possible to get a gramophone. We firmly refused to take Akim, as he reeked of alcohol. He was not particularly upset, looking forward to long hours of sleep.

Since we had run out of money a long time ago (Akim still had it, and regularly replenished his stocks of strong drinks, but flatly refused to share any with us), in order to buy tickets, Slavik had to sell the denim jacket my parents had given him, to a local peasant who was hanging around at the station.

'It's a pity,' I said with chagrin, when we had two tickets in our hands. 'It was a good jacket.'

'Forget it. It'd be too tight next year. Even though I am an adult, I am still growing.' Slavik laughed, straightening his bony back. We got into the carriage of the beaten-up electric train and after a couple of hours alighted on the platform of an unknown settlement.

First, we went to the local market to ask where one could buy records and other musical accessories. The market was practically adjacent to the railway station, so it took no more than five minutes to walk there. Everywhere there were sellers with goods for all tastes, so to say. Rubber slippers in hot pink and light green were lying right on the ground. A little further off, a young woman was selling dried herbs, and nearby a man of about fifty was selling old books (the wealth of the old days). The range of products in the market mostly suited casual passengers. Choosing a middle-aged woman from all the hucksters, Slavik twirled a bar of flower soap heated in the sun in his hands.

'How much is the soap?'

'It's expensive,' the huckster mocked. 'It's unlikely that you have that kind of money lying around in your pockets, kid.'

'It is up to me whether it is lying around or not. Can you tell me, madam, where can I find records here? And is it possible to find them at all?' Slavik frowned, deciding that this would bring seriousness to his looks.

'Records?' the woman laughed loudly.

'In this whole place, only the prosecutor has such an apparatus for records ... What is its name?' A young woman joined the conversation.

'A gramophone,' said the bookseller.

'So, my dear, there are no records to be found here. Unless to listen to as a guest of the prosecutor's.' The woman wiped away the tears that appeared from her laughter.

'Well, thanks for that too.' Slavik bowed and pushed me to the exit from the market without letting me say a word.

'Where are we going? We must go back,' I protested, surprised.

'Why is that?' my friend asked.

'Well ... there is no store here that would sell gramophones ...'

'But the prosecutor has a gramophone.' Slavik winked, twirling a bar of floral soap in a colorful package in his hands. 'Miwa will get this from you for her birthday.' Seeing bewilderment on my face, he smiled. 'You have to give her something.'

After walking about ten minutes, we reached a small shop, which, in addition to bakery products, also sold alcohol and cigarettes. Slavik asked an old woman dozing on a bench nearby how to get to the house of the prosecutor, a man, judging by the reaction of the old woman, who was respected and important.

'You go straight to the crossroads, there turn right. Go to the church, and take a sideway there and stay left, you will see through a small fence a garden with tall plums, this is what you need. This will be the house of the prosecutor, our Ivan Ivanovich ... What do you need from him?' the old woman decided to ask, but Slavik and I were already in a hurry to the crossroads.

'We have a package for him,' my friend waved her off. The old woman called us a couple of times, but very soon not only her silhouette, but also her voice disappeared into the hot day.

As the old woman said, having covered the entire route, we found ourselves near a house with tall plums.

'Now what?' I asked.

'Now you stay quiet somewhere nearby, and I am going to explore,' answered Slavik and in one fell swoop jumped over the low fence. I took refuge in the shade of a spreading tree that grew across the street from the prosecutor's house. However, not even a few minutes had passed when Slavik's head appeared over the fence.

'Come here.' He waved his hand, and I hurried to climb (not without the help of my friend) over the fence. The prosecutor's garden smelled of ripe fruit and a pleasant coolness created by a variety of trees. Plums, apple trees, apricots and pears: there were fruit for all tastes. Ripe fruits covered the sagging branches, and along the path to the house bright buds of flowers glittered. The garden was well kept and rich. Surprised by its beauty, I whistled with envy.

'We will also have one like this someday.' Slavik patted me on the shoulder. I just shrugged. One can only get such a garden after many, many years of hard work. Perhaps when Miwa is a grown woman with large breasts ...

'There is no one at home. There is no dog in the yard either. So the gramophone is ours,' said Slavik, slowly sneaking up to the house.

'Do you want to steal it?' I was surprised.

My friend grimaced. 'No, Vitka, I'm going to buy it, for Christ's sake!'

'But you can't do that ...' I faltered.

'Do not lecture me about morality and about God and sins!' snapped Slavik, casting an angry glance at me. 'Do we steal food? Yes, we do. And you are not complaining.'

'But without food we die.' I objected.

'You cannot justify one theft and condemn the other. That's not very grown-up!'

I did not calm down. 'The gramophone is probably expensive ... The prosecutor earned money to buy it, and we will just take it and steal it!'

'Listen.' My friend stopped and, squatting down next to me, he spoke: 'Remember, Vitya, judges, prosecutors, lawyers and other lawyers are thieves and criminals. They should not live in houses with a beautiful garden, but rot in prisons. Not buy gramophones, but eat the ground! Do you think he earned money for a gramophone the right way?'

'I don't know,' I choked.

'No, he did not. He sued someone for a bribe, who is now rotting in the clink, but this one is listening to records!' Slavik hissed, clenching his fists.

'What does a bribe mean?' I asked. Slavik smiled and became kinder for a moment.

'You foolish head, you are small yet, you do not know much. A bribe, Vitek, is when you fulfill someone's request, usually a bad one, for money. And then other people suffer. Lawyers are all bribe-takers. I know that. But don't worry, we will only take a gramophone and records. Maybe something else. Something that we need, food or warm clothes. We will not take anything else, we are not thieves.' Slavik patted me on the back, assuring me that we were definitely not doing anything wrong. And I believed him. It took him no more than a minute to open the door lock, and then we sneaked inside.

The prosecutor's house smelled of dried lavender and felt pleasantly cool. I was surprised how clean the rooms were, and how all the things lay in their places with geometric precision, as if aligned with a ruler. We found the gramophone in the living room, where on the wall there was a huge portrait of an elderly mustachioed man with a hard look and a ruddy woman with thin lips. Most likely these were the owners of the house, the prosecutor and his wife.

'Here is our catch!' Slavik ran his hand over the grey box, which looked like a portable suitcase. 'In good condition, even though it's old!' he exclaimed enthusiastically, taking the musical unit in his hands. 'A wonderful gramophone! So, go choose the records, and I'll go to the kitchen for food.' Slavik pointed to a stack of records that lay on a fancy carved table next to the gramophone.

While my accomplice rattled jars and doors, I went through the records, among which there were both familiar names and outlandish ones written in an incomprehensible language. At the boarding school, we had English lessons once a week, and on weekends Klara Fyodorovna taught us German grammar, so I could distinguish the alphabet of these two languages. The names of some of the records had unusual letters, however, with curls and tails. One of these showed two doves, so I decided it was definitely about love, and put it aside. After spending about fifteen minutes on the task, I had compiled the correct, in my opinion, selection of records, ones which would suit Miwa's taste.

'Well, did you find them?' asked Slavik, appearing in the doorway. In his right hand he held a shopping bag, in which he had hidden the gramophone. On top of it he had placed some cereals and sugar. 'We'll also take a couple more sweaters and a blanket – these are necessary things,' said Slavik, putting the 'most necessary' into his bag. 'I've made you a sandwich with boiled sausage in the kitchen, go eat some.'

He didn't have to persuade me. I dashed off to the kitchen, where I eagerly swallowed a thickly cut piece of sausage with a fresh loaf. Having washed down lunch with water from a jug, I wiped my lips with the sleeve of my shirt and again caught myself thinking how neatly everything was arranged in this house. All the jars in the kitchen were put in order from high to low, all labelled neatly with their contents. The floor was squeaky clean, and the tablecloth on the table looked like it was fresh from the store, without a single fold and starched. Then I thought that, even though prosecutors are all bribe-takers, they are damn accurate in matters of everyday life.

Leaving the prosecutor's house, we looked around and listened to see if anyone was in the garden. Fortunately, the yard was still empty. We stuffed ripe red apples into our pockets and hurried to the station. On the way, Slavik said that we needed to hide there and try not to get noticed by the locals, especially our familiar hucksters. After some discussion, we decided to lie low and not appear at the station but take a train from a village half an hour away.

Slavik carried the bag all the way, and I was once again surprised at his physical strength (the gramophone was quite a heavy one!). We didn't have a return ticket, but my friend managed to somehow persuade the conductor to give us a ride. Just a couple of hundred kilometers. He fed the man some kind of tale about a sick mother and recently deceased father, about hungry children and a legless grandmother. In a word, he filled the conductor's head with so much nonsense that we, 'unfortunate half-orphans,' were allowed to go without tickets, and they also gave us tea. Truly, Slavik was the best scoundrel I knew!

On August 29th, Miwa's birthday came. We set a beautiful festive table, even better than the one at the 'wedding'. There was an abundance of fruit, boiled potatoes with corn, and a waffle cake with boiled condensed milk into which we inserted eleven candles stolen by Slavik from a church shop, which served to crown everything.

Miwa had been dressing up since morning. She wore a fancy hairstyle, decorating her hair with wildflowers and little dark berries. She smeared her pale cheeks with beetroot juice and lowered her eyes with a thin layer of soot. It looked beautiful and funny at the same time. The soot with beet juice made our friend's face brighter and more mature, but the application technique left much to be desired. The streaks and stains demonstrated the clumsy hand of the make-up artist. Nevertheless, Slavik admired her. Akim made only sarcastic comments, whispering in my ear that his sister was like a 'dressed up doll'. I personally had nothing against dolls and did not understand Akim's indignation. But in those days, he often grumbled for no reason, especially when the last vapors of alcohol disappeared and he needed to go to the stash to get a new dose, the location of which was a mystery to the rest of us (and we did not try to find out).

During the celebration, Slavik showered compliments on his 'wife', kissed her little hands, and pronounced each next toast in her honor. We drank beer. When it came time to present the gifts, Miwa could barely contain her excitement. I was the first to give my gift, a bar of floral soap. Unfolding it and inhaling the scent of rose water, she rushed to hug me exclaiming 'What a smell!', grateful for such a wonderful and 'very feminine' gift. Akim approached the gift matter in a simpler manner, giving her a few pennies.

'Pocket money. Maybe you want to buy something,' he said indifferently, kissing his sister dryly on the forehead. Miwa thanked him discreetly.

'And now for the main thing.' Slavik's eyes lit up. He ran into the chicken coop, where we had kept the gramophone all this time.

'Close your eyes,' he shouted. Miwa laughed happily, immediately following instructions. While she fidgeted in her chair, barely holding back so as not to run after Slavik, he returned with a suitcase in one hand and records in the other. Having put all this on the table, Slavik allowed his 'wife' to open her eyes. Words cannot express Miwa's delight. She bounced on the chair, jumped up, then sat down again and jumped up again. She clapped her hands, shook her head like her beloved Bagel, and laughed uncontrollably, throwing her head back. I could never have imagined that the appearance of an old musical apparatus would cause such a violent reaction. We put on one of the stolen records, 'Collezione' by Riccardo Fogli, started the gramophone, and carefully dropped the needle ... We heard a slight crackling, and then a melodic voice. This man who sang songs in a language we did not understand was so much to Miwa's liking that she began to dance, pulling Slavik along with her. Grasping his hips, Miwa pressed her slender waist against him and purred contentedly. I watched this couple with interest, wondering how they would turn out when they grew up. Would Miwa be as beautiful as she is now, or would she grow fat or wither, like many mature beautiful women? Would Slavik love her as much as he does now, and will they have children? Real, small children, whom Miwa will carry in her stomach ...

Akim interrupted my thoughts. 'Enough!' he shouted, rushing to the 'newly weds'. He pulled them apart roughly, pushing Miwa aside. The girl fell, hitting her stomach.

'Are you crazy?!' Slavik was about to grab Akim by the collar, but was distracted by Miwa, who was lying on the floor and groaning in pain.

'What? Where did you get hit?' he asked anxiously, sitting down beside her.

'My belly,' she moaned. 'Why, Akim?'

'Shame on you! You can't snuggle up to him like that!' shouted Akim, kicking the legs of the table. Obviously, a bottle of beer drunk in one gulp had gone to his head (especially the old yeast!), and now he was splashing out all his accumulated anger.

'I am his wife!' shouted Miwa in response.

'This is not real! This is a game!' Akim glared at the young 'newlyweds' with hatred in his eyes.

'Everything is real,' the girl answered firmly, 'and you could hurt the baby.' She pressed her palms to her stomach. There was a pause. We boys looked at each other in bewilderment.

'What child?' finally asked Slavik.

'The one which is in my belly,' Miwa smiled, stroking her stomach. 'There is a child in there.'

'But where did it come from?' asked Slavik, confused.

'From a kiss,' Miwa replied, embarrassed. And then it finally dawned on everyone what Miwa meant. A kiss! Of course. They had kissed with their tongues, and now there was a small worm inside Miwa.

'Miwa ...' began the discouraged Slavik, trying to smile, 'will we have a child?'

Miwa nodded.

'This ... This is wonderful,' he whispered, hugging his 'spouse'. Despite the inner horror that clearly filled the 'future father', Slavik tried to portray joy. Someone had once told him, he said to me later, that pregnant women should not be upset because they can get sick and something very bad will happen ... But what, Slavik did not remember exactly.

'We need to get rid of it,' Akim said, recovering from the shock. He stood in the middle of the room, examining his sister closely.

'Get rid of what?' Miwa asked warily.

'The child, of course. They say that when the doctors do not want the worm to grow, they cut it out,' Akim reasoned calmly. 'But the worm grows when you feed it ...' he continued after thinking, 'so you just need not eat for several days, and it will die of hunger.' Akim smiled, pleased with the decision.

'But I don't want it to die ...' Miwa was frightened.

'Look at that! Now you tell me that you will raise it?'

'Yes!' shouted Miwa, pursing her lips capriciously.

'You can't look after it. You are just a child yourself. If you don't want things to be in a good way, we will starve you to death so that this muck will come out of you.' Akim shivered in disgust. He wanted to say something else, but did not have time, as Slavik's heavy fist hit him in the jaw at full speed, throwing him to the other side of the room.

'Try touching her and I will knock out all your teeth and put you on a chain instead of Bagel. You will eat chicken droppings!' Slavik bent over Akim, squeezing his thin neck with his hand. 'It's up to us whether to feed the worm or not. Got it?'

Akim said nothing.

'I ask again, do you understand?' Slavik squeezed his throat tighter, after which he nodded.

'Now get out!' Having thrown Akim out over the threshold, Slavik turned to Miwa. She was still sitting on the floor, sobbing bitterly, upset by her brother's words.

'Don't cry, my dear.' Lifting Miwa, he pressed her to his chest. 'Everything will be fine. Now you will eat twice as much so that the child grows healthy,' he said, covering with kisses the girl's cheeks smeared with beets.

'And you will love me?' sobbed Miwa.

'Always, always,' Slavik smiled. He carried Miwa into the bedroom, closing the door behind him. For a long time I could hear them whispering about something, and then the voices died down. Soon Slavik came out of the room on tiptoe.

'She fell asleep,' he said, sitting down at the table.

'We didn't start on the cake,' I drawled in annoyance. Slavik smiled.

'Do you only care about that?'

'If I worried about everything that happens here, then I don't even know ... It's better worrying about the cake. At least this is a kind of worry that you can get rid of by taking a bite ...' I explained, reaching for the cake. Having cut it into several pieces, I put one on my plate, and moved the other one to Slavik.

'Vitka, what to do now?' Slavik sighed heavily.

I didn't answer, because I didn't really know what to do now. Miwa was pregnant, Akim had finally fallen out with Slavik, and my older friend himself was so depressed that he was already asking me for advice. Before, he had known the answers to all questions. But not now.

'I think everything will turn out fine somehow. Right?' I began uncertainly.

Slavik smiled, pouring some wine into his glass. 'It definitely will,' he replied thoughtfully.

9.

Autumn came. It tentatively knocked on our hearts with a gentle breeze which carried the scent of fallen leaves, and just as tentatively it crossed the threshold of Grad. The yard was covered with a carpet of rustling leaves and small twigs, which had been torn off by sharp gusts of the night wind. I never had a chance to clean them up. I was spending all my time in the garden, which produced a small harvest of beets and onions. Nothing else came up, even though I had planted it all with so much love and labor. It upset me enormously, but Slavik was looking for the best in the worst.

'Beets and onions are what we need. They are healthy and can be stored for a long time,' he said, comforting me. Even though I was disappointed with my agrarian talents, this did not diminish my will, and I drew up a seeding plan for next year. Tomatoes were by far the most important item. In the meantime, I cleaned up the yard as much as I could. Miwa ran the household, and Slavik continued to patch up the house, filling up slots and cracks, since cold weather was coming up. After the incident with Akim, a lot had changed in our relationship with him. Akim started coming home less and less often, disappearing into the forest. When he did return, he was either drunk or had a bad hangover. Our living together under one roof became so difficult that I even went to sleep in the kitchen, away from the odour of beer. It came as no surprise that by the end of September Akim wanted to move out.

'Two more houses nearby are empty, I'd better move out,' he said at breakfast.

'As you wish,' Slavik answered indifferently.

'I think you will be better off here without me,' continued Akim. After getting no requests or persuasions to stay, he kept talking: 'I will only be coming here to eat. Hopefully I can count on that?'

Slavik grunted assent.

'I'll take the mattress,' Akim decided. 'I'm sorry, Vitka, but you have all the walls in place here. In the other houses the walls are falling down, so sleeping on the floor is not an option.'

I did not mind, especially since I had already slept on the kitchen floor for a couple of weeks, using a thin woolen blanket instead of a mattress. When we were packing Akim's things, Miwa tried to stop her brother. Despite how he had offended her, she still loved him.

'Maybe you will change your mind?'

'No,' Akim snapped.

'Akim, but we all dreamed about it so much. About Grad and a free life ... And now when everything is so good, you want to leave,' she said through her tears.

'This is not what I dreamed about,' Akim dismissed, pointing to his sister's belly. 'I don't want to see it grow – it's disgusting.'

After her brother left, Miwa cried for a long time. Now I understand that her heart was torn between her love for her brother and 'husband.' She hardly realized that she would become a mother, although she was happy about it. For Miwa, what was happening was a game in which everything would end well. Therefore, Akim's decision was difficult for her.

'He'll be back,' assured Slavik, wiping her tear-stained cheeks. Nevertheless, time passed, but Akim never returned, settling in a neighbouring house, which was so ruinous the wind filled the room in which he slept with balls of withered foliage.

I had a classmate in the boarding school, Fima Vodovoz, whom I have already mentioned. I always knew that he was born under a lucky star. In spite of his repulsive appearance (hooked nose, crooked teeth and huge ears) and girly character, at the beginning of the third grade, a charming middle-aged couple adopted Fima. I remember a woman patting him on the head, and a man kindly clapping him on the shoulder when they were taking him away. And Fimka smiled happily. In parting, he glanced triumphantly at those who were seeing him off: teachers and us, his classmates. One could read in his eyes something like 'look, you losers, they chose me.' Later Klara Fyodorovna told us that Fima's parents took him to America and there he lived a happy life under the new name Efim Vysotsky. There were rumours that his parents arranged straightening his teeth and an operation on his ears, so Fima acquired a foreign polish, and with age, at least I think so, he graduated from a prestigious university, became a writer and now writes clever books, signing them E. Vysotsky. Well, I hope that this is how his future turned out.

Unlike Fima, I was not born under a lucky star; rather, on the contrary: on my birthday, Fate was in an extremely depressive mood, which is why She landed a lot of problems and hardships on my parents' shoulders and put me behind the thick walls of the 'Old Lady Willow'. Again, I never blamed my parents for this. Even more, starting an independent life in Grad, I was filled with sympathy for them, realizing how difficult adult life is. You have a lot to think about, a lot to plan; you must arrange your everyday life, get food, prepare yourself for the cold weather, take care of the garden ... It all is depressing.

When autumn arrived, I often remembered our boarding school, and thought that it was not such a terrible place. Yes, we were offended and sometimes beaten. The grey corridors of the 'Old Lady Willow' cast a gloom over us, and some of the teachers were downright cruel. But, probably, they were not that way from a good life, since there was nothing good in adult reality. I realized this by the end of October, when Miwa got sick.

As was typical for October weather, the air was damp, and the rains did not stop all day long, flooding my vegetable garden, which now looked like a fetid swamp. It's no wonder that each of us caught a cold, but Miwa, who was already prone to getting ill, fell sick more than the rest of us. As always, at first she coughed a lot, then turned pale, and after a few days she came down altogether, complaining of malaise and weakness. We decided collectively that she should have a good rest and sleep. Sleep heals, we thought. The days passed, however, and Miwa's condition only worsened. She became noticeably thinner. We cooked her soups from onions and beets, and made tea from dried herbs, which stank terribly. Nothing helped. Miwa was slipping away in front of our eyes.

'It hurts so much,' she moaned, turning from back to side with difficulty. 'Is the baby also hurt?' Most of all she was worried about how the child was feeling. Slavik assured her that everything was fine.

'I think that the child died long ago,' he said one day, taking me aside.

'Why?'

'She is burning from the inside, she has fever. I think the child just burned out there,' argued Slavik. 'It is, of course, for the best. We don't need a child now,' he switched to a whisper, casting anxious glances at the sleeping Miwa.

This news horrified me. I felt sorry for the baby, like any creature with the right to life, but half an hour after talking with Slavik, I forgot about the 'child.'

'Miwa needs medicine,' Akim said when the three of us were having dinner. Miwa ate in bed. She had no strength to get up.

'We will cure her with herbs,' snapped Slavik.

‘Your herbs will not help. We need a doctor. Let’s take her to the village. There is definitely a doctor there,’ continued Akim. Upon learning of the news of the child’s death, he had become noticeably kinder.

‘So that they can find us later, right?’ Slavik scoffed.

‘We won’t tell anyone. Let’s just leave her at the door of the hospital.’

‘Then how will we get her back? They will take her to the boarding school,’ Slavik said.

‘So let it be, she only causes problems!’ Akim blurted out.

‘If they take her away, they will start asking questions, she will tell about Grad ...’ I suggested.

‘And our life will be over,’ summed up Slavik.

‘Well, yes ...’ Akim pondered. He had no choice but to agree that herbs were an excellent medicine.

While Miwa was sick, Bagel did not leave her side. He licked her thin fingers, and when she fell asleep, he guarded her sleep for a long, long time, resting his head on the bed soaked in sweat. The room was filled with the sour smell of sickness, damp linen and dog hair. We did not like to go in there, as we ourselves were afraid to catch the infection that had fallen on our girlfriend. Slavik visited his ‘spouse’ several times a day, bringing tea or a plate of beetroot. Miwa struggled to take a few sips of the purple stew and most of the time returned it back to the kitchen. The floor near her bed was stained with vomit, which Bagel carefully licked, because he himself lived from hand to mouth. There was little food, and it was almost impossible to get to the village because of the rains. Therefore, beets with onions and crackers were our only food. We ate only when we felt dizzy from hunger. Because of the weather conditions, Akim had to temporarily forget about beer, which made him annoyed and willing to take it out on anyone for any reason. He tortured Bagel the worst because the dog annoyed him with howling.

On October 15, 1995, around lunchtime, Slavik and Akim decided to try their luck and get to the village. Food supplies were running low – we had eaten all the crackers and onions. The rains finally stopped, so there was hope that the road had dried out a little. I was supposed to stay and look after the patient. When the others left, I went out into the courtyard to get my head above water in the garden a bit, but after a while I gave up on this lost cause. My vegetable garden had turned into a swamp, and only fat frogs were missing to complete the picture. Back in the house, I brewed tea for Miwa (if an incomprehensible collection of dry herbs and roots could be called that!).

'Vitenka, come to me,' moaned Miwa when I went into her room. She was lying on her back, her messy dirty hair strewn across the pillow. Her pale forehead was sweaty, and her skinny arms quivered.

'Vitya ...' she repeated.

'I'm here.' Overcoming disgust, I sat down on the edge of the bed.

'I want to ask you ...' Miwa spoke with difficulty, gasping for the stale air. 'I want to ask when I die ... and you bury me ...' her eyes filled with tears, 'bring flowers to my grave. Those that have a very strong smell ... You know ... Do you know what my name means?' Overcoming the pain, she raised herself on her elbows. Her eyes glittered feverishly.

'What?'

'Fragrant ...' Miwa smiled tightly.

'And what does that mean?' I did not know the meaning of the word I heard.

'It means "this is the one who smells amazing" ...'

'I promise,' I answered. 'Only you will not die, you're still very young. Young people rarely die.' Miwa said nothing. She took a couple of sips of tea with my help, then she turned on her side with difficulty and dozed off. I left the cup with the 'aromatic' potion on the floor near the sleeping Bagel and went outside to get some fresh air.

It brightened up that day. As I said, it had not rained for several days and the wind had softened so much that there was no need to fear catching a cold in the throat. Bare trees pulled their hooked arms to our house like monsters from terrible fairy tales, and somewhere beyond the horizon, winter was already in a hurry. From day to day, the first snow should have fallen: fine snow which would melt quickly but foreshadowed the cold. We waited for it with anxiety and apprehension, not sure if our house would handle such an attack. Slavik assured us that Grad would withstand the winter, but I was getting worried. I went to sit on the steps and thought about Miwa. I didn't believe she would die. I did not believe at all that it was possible to die from cold, just like that. Old people die from it, because they are weak, or maybe stray animals, but not children. Then I remembered the meaning of the name Miwa, fragrant, and decided that when my comrades returned, we would need to fill a bucket with water from the lake, heat it and wash Miwa, because her room stank with the unbearable stench exuded by a sick body. She was too pretty to smell bad.

I sat outside until evening and returned to the house. My stomach rumbled unpleasantly, so I boiled finely chopped beets. After eating a couple of pieces, I put the rest on a plate, cooled it down and carried it to Miwa. She was lying on the bed in the same position in which I had left her. Her face breathed with serenity, and her pale lips were slightly open. Despite her illness and unkempt appearance, Miwa was still pretty.

'Miwa,' I called softly, bending over her, 'I brought some food.'

She did not wake up, so I lightly touched her on the shoulder. 'Miwa?' Bagel, who had been dozing before, roused himself. He sniffed Miwa, ran around the bed several times, and, sitting down in the middle of the room, uttered a long howl.

'Bagel, what are you doing?' I was surprised. The dog pressed itself to the floor, crawled to the bed and whined.

'Miwa?' I anxiously shook the girl by the shoulders. Only then did I notice that she was breathless, and the once porcelain face had acquired a deathly pallor.

Miwa had died.

I did not know how to deal with the dead body nor how to behave in general in such a situation. Terrified, recoiling to the door, I dropped the boiled beets from my hands, which Bagel immediately swallowed. Then I ran out into the street, where I sat until Slavik and Akim arrived.

Tired but joyful, they returned close to nightfall, each carrying a large bag of provisions on their backs. I called them.

'Hey there, Vitka!' Slavik waved, peering into the darkness.

'Why are you sitting here?' Akim was surprised.

'Miwa ...' I could only say, and while Akim was thinking, Slavik jumped into the house in two leaps, and Grad was filled with a heartbreaking cry.

10.

We buried Miwa not far from the house, in a place that she loved very much and often went to play with Bagel. The small hill which became her grave was blown by the winds from all sides, and at dawn and dusk an amazing view opened up from its summit. We washed Miwa before the burial, as I insisted, using almost all the flower soap. Slavik changed her into clean clothes and wrapped her in the lace curtains that served instead of a coffin. I read a prayer, Akim sang something sad in his own language, and Slavik covered the body with earth. We didn't have beautiful fragrant flowers to put on the grave, so we left a can of condensed milk, black bread and a red shawl that Slavik had stolen on the day of Miwa's death. It was supposed to cheer her up.

Surprisingly, none of us cried. We were just silent, watching the red shawl play in the wind, billowing over the fresh grave of someone's sister, someone's wife and someone's girlfriend. I thought that Miwa, although she left us too early, managed in her short life to learn something which is not given to many for years. She was a beloved wife, she carried the fruit of love, she was happy. There were adventures in her life, and a real adult life, without stupid rules and responsibilities. I sincerely grieved for her, but I was glad for her. There was everything and even more in her life. Of course, Slavik would not have shared my thoughts, and I did not dare to voice them. With Miwa's death, everything changed for him. Something died inside of Slavik with her. His usual enthusiasm vanished. Now I understand that Miwa was my friend's only love, the only person whom he adored, and who loved him back.

In the evening after the funeral, we sat at the table sipping red wine from dirty glasses. The table was set for four, but Miwa's glass was covered with a piece of black bread, and a thin church candle was burning in place of the plate. Akim said that the candle was like his sister, just as thin and fragile. We just nodded silently, each thinking his own thoughts. I don't know what Slavik was thinking, but for some reason I remembered my friend Sashka from the boarding school, who had silently looked at me from a photograph for forty-five minutes during Russian lessons. I was sorry that boys like Sashka did not know the happiness of life in Grad. They had never drunk beer, never looked after their own garden. I was twelve, and I had done this. Then, suddenly, for some reason, with all my heart, with every part of my body, I felt the pain of my friend, his fear. I knew how much he was afraid and how much he wanted to be with his mother.

That evening, for the first time in a very long time, I also wanted to see my mother. I wanted to crawl on her knees, bury my face in her chest and cry bitterly, while she stroked my head and whispered: 'Easy, easy, my dear'. I would continue crying until I finally fell asleep, and then she would carry me to the sofa, cover me with a woolen blanket, and lie down beside me, pressing my tear-stained face to her shoulder ... And in the morning! In the morning, I would wake up and the first thing I would see would be her eyes, tender and loving. And then ...

I glanced around our memorial supper and smiled sadly. I knew it would never happen.

Never.

Part IV

New Life

Prologue

December arrived in Grad with a heavy, squeaky step, sprinkling the rotten roofs of the houses with prickly white flakes. Most often, winter bursts inside in a mad whirlwind, sweeping and howling, but that winter was quiet. Like a hunchbacked old woman, it slowly stepped onto the threshold, cleared its throat, tapped a stick free of snow, and was now warming itself by the stove. Sometimes the old woman would sigh dramatically, furrowing her eyebrows, and then the howl of the wind could be heard outside the window. Winter rustled with branches, creaked and moaned, as if it wasn't winter at all, but some early spring, by God! A lop-eared boy with a long neck, whom an old caretaker once named 'Brave', left thc house to collect an impromptu bouquet every morning, while a pre-dawn haze hung on the still naked branches. In his hands, thin, tangled twigs, withered leaves and bird feathers turned into an intricate composition, exuding an amazing spicy aroma. Then he walked to a small hill, which was blown by winds from all sides (one could especially feel that in December!) and laid a bouquet on his girlfriend's grave. Although she was never his girlfriend, the memory of her would remain in his heart forever.

The 'Brave' got up just in time for dawn and could admire the view from the girl's grave. A snow-covered forest could be seen in the distance. It looked like the top of a cake sprinkled with powdered sugar, and the dirt road leading to it, which was rolled out by carts, resembled a strip of chocolate icing. Putting the bouquet on the grave, the boy always recited a prayer, and hurried back before his comrades woke up. He did not want them to know about his morning visits to the hill: they were between him and the girl, whom he had promised to bring flowers to her grave.

Meanwhile, for three friends, let's call them so, a new life began, in which at first glance there were fewer problems; but, on the other hand, the absence of these problems entailed a number of changes that touched everyone's heart. If 'Brave' found joy in his daily trips to the grave and reading prayers, the other two were mired in gloom. The Tatar orphan drank hard and fell asleep only to get drunk the next day after having sobered up a little. His swarthy face was now sallow, and dark circles loomed under his eyes, which conveyed perfectly the style of his life. When it came to the boy with a star-shaped birthmark, not a trace of his former talkativeness remained. He was painfully silent for days, and to his friends' questions, he either answered a monosyllabic 'yes', or simply avoided replying. Unlike 'Brave', he did not visit the grave, preferring to drown his outbursts of melancholy with the strong drinks that were present in abundance in the Tatar's house.

Together with the December snowfall, drafts came to Grad and new cracks appeared, treacherously scattering along the walls of the house. The roof of the Tatar's dwelling was completely rotten, so he returned to the house of his friends, where the ceiling, even though it leaked, still resisted the winter winds.

Grad fell into disrepair. Despite the friends' vain attempts to maintain its vital activity, time took its toll, and now any passer-by, noticing it, would have decided that the *khutor* was some kind of ruin or the scenery of a film about the hardships of the Second World War left behind by the filmmakers as no longer needed but too much trouble to dismantle. And if before Miwa's death, the tenants looked after their house, now the weekly clean, even washing the dishes, seemed to them a waste of time, a senseless burden.

That was how they met the old woman-winter. Having poured boiling water into a sticky cup, they sat down at the table, under which the wind drove clouds of dust. The old woman grunted disapprovingly, but without saying anything; she knocked with branches against the window, crackled with the first frosts and dozed off, her cloudy breath foreshadowing severe cold.

1.

With the arrival of winter, Akim came back to live in our house, as his house could not withstand the cold weather and the roof in one of the rooms collapsed. He returned silently, without asking Slavik's permission, but Slavik did not mind. We began to live a new, unfamiliar life, in which there were no more lace curtains or Miwa's laughter. Bagel, who spent several weeks at her grave, had now vanished. Every morning, when I visited our friend's grave, I had tried to bring him a crust of bread and boiled potato skins. The dog rarely took food from my hands, only looked into my eyes with longing. After patting his slender neck, I left the food at the grave, until Bagel disappeared at the end of December. If Slavik had known that the dog lived on the grave of his wife, he would have explained his disappearance with an ordinary reason: he was dead. Had become numb in the frost and now was just meat for the forest birds to feed on. I thought otherwise. I knew that Bagel had simply left. He left in search of a better life and better owners. He saw off the soul of Miwa, making sure that there was someone to take care of her there in heaven, and now he could leave Grad. How do I know this? Nikichna once told that animals are able to move between worlds, visiting the world of the dead if they wish. The old caretaker did not say why they needed to do this, but I thought maybe in order to see off their owners to heaven. I was glad that Bagel was there for Miwa, because she had loved him very much.

After Bagel disappeared, I began to remember often my little friend Lemon, who now lived in Fauna's study, delighting her with his amusing tweets. I really wanted him to be here, in the dilapidated house of our Grad. I think he would have revived us with his sonorous tweets. But when a strong wind burst outside the window and thrust through all the cracks, I imagined how warm and comfortable my friend was now. Dozing on his perch to the rustling of the pages of yet another clever book, which Fauna reads every night ... The room smells of marshmallows and hot tea, and a bulky oil radiator crackles against the wall. Imagining this picture, I could hardly restrain a smile, because what could be better than our friends' happiness? Especially if those friends, as my father used to say, 'can be counted on fingers'. Feathered

Lemon, Fauna and Nikichna, and the silent Sashka, forever frozen in a black and white photo. I didn't take Slavik and Akim into account, because my friendship with them aroused more melancholy than joy in my soul with every passing day.

Since we had buried Miwa, my thirst for information and new knowledge had not been fulfilled with the regularity to which I was accustomed, since Slavik spoke little, and told nothing. I re-read all the old issues of the *Murzilka* magazine and scraps of old newspapers from cover to cover. I learned by heart the story that in 1994 in the city of N., in the north of the country, a maniac strangler was caught, who had killed ten people. I could recreate in detail his portrait, printed on grey paper. Thin long nose, full lips, bangs over one eye ... Sometimes in my dreams I felt his sticky fingers on my neck and woke up in a cold sweat, and then I could not sleep until morning, and if I did, I still dreamed of his silhouette in the doorway. I also learned that in the village of T. a school burned down together with an elderly teacher who tried to heroically carry the complete collection of the *Library of World Literature for Children* out of the fire (and there were no less than twenty volumes!). As a result, she burned along with her precious books. As I pondered this woman's story, I often imagined how great it would be if Rusichka had been in her place. She would definitely carry something like *Das Kapital* or the complete collection of Lenin's works in thirty (no! better in fifty-five) volumes! I laughed, imagining with pleasure how she would writhe and puff, placing stacks of books on her chest ... They are falling, she bends down, gets angry, collects a new stack, and everything repeats ... then bright flames flare up on her clothes, she screams in pain and falls dead, surrounded by books dear to her heart ... Rusichka loved Lenin so devotedly and selflessly that after her death she would meet with him in hell (I was sure). I was just as sure about their meeting as about the fact that she would go to hell, where a little bald man was waiting for her, 'the tormentor of the entire Soviet people' (as Klara Fyodorovna would put it).

Thus, after rereading all the paper stored in our house, I began to look for something to do that would allow me to survive the cold. Alcohol didn't appeal to me as much as it did to Akim – it gave me a headache and a will to vomit. And yet, I couldn't sit all day, facing the wall, like Slavik did. I got the idea to clean up Miwa's grave. I decided to build a fence around the grave, erect a wooden cross and, if possible, scratch out and attach a sign to it, saying that here, on a hill, in the ground lies Miwa, an eleven-year-old Tatar orphan whose name means 'fragrant'. Fired up by this idea, first I began to make a cross. Having no experience in carpentry, after a couple of days of futile attempts, I turned to Slavik for assistance. To my surprise, he happily agreed to help.

'You've thought of a good thing, Vitka,' he said, taking up the tools he and Akim had stolen from the village. With Slavik's help, things went quickly, and the very next day we had a beautiful high cross. In the afternoon, we went to set it up on the grave. Having thrust it in as deeply as the frozen ground allowed, we tied a piece of linen tablecloth on top of it, which was previously used as a bedspread (we thought it was beautiful). I read a prayer, as befits such occasions, and then we stood silently on the hill for a long time, watching the faded winter sun slowly dozing off, immersing nature into frosty impenetrability.

My initiative gave Slavik strength, and now we thought together how to make a plaque and what to write on it.

'It is very important to choose the right words,' reasoned my friend. 'Miwa had a subtle soul, it would be important for her what we say ... Words that will remain in the memory,' Slavik said, remembering how his 'wife' was.

After a couple of days we made a wooden plaque and rubbed it carefully on the sides. Slavik burned the inscription for a long time. He heated his pocketknife until it was red-hot and traced letters. There were many mistakes in the text we wrote, because Akim, the only one who knew the rules of grammar, was drunk and didn't think much these days. He mumbled indistinctly instead of speaking and even pissed himself several times. Slavik suggested that Akim had already drunk his brains out. Although I could not figure out how it was possible to drink one's brains out, it sounded scary. Thus, we composed and wrote the text without Akim's help. After finishing the application, we nailed the plaque to the cross with thick nails. It turned out like this:

'Here lyes Miwa, dear waif and a gud frend. She loved singing and dogs, she was kind. We love you. Slavik and Vitya.'

It was decided not to put the name of Akim on the plate, since he did not like his sister, treated her really badly, and generally wanted to give her away to some other woman.

'Now it's better, humanly, like everyone else has it.' Slavik smiled contentedly. The grave really was beautiful. All that remained was to make a fence and plant flowers in the spring. I knew that Miwa was satisfied – she loved all that was beautiful.

Slavik said that Akim did not know how to drink, that was why he got drunk so quickly and became addicted so easily. Akim drank every day. During hard binges, he got up from the mattress only to relieve himself in a bucket that stood in the corner of the room (it was so cold outside that we organized a toilet right in the house), and then he fell back onto the mattress, pouring vodka diluted with beer down his throat.

'Sooner or later the booze will kill him,' reasoned Slavik. 'Everyone dies from drinking. For example, take my mother.' That was the first time in a long while Slavik had mentioned Auntie Alla. I felt sorry for Akim, so I decided to talk to him. After waiting for him to sober up a little, I brewed herbal tea and put some boiled carrots with dry bread on a plate. During a binge, Akim could spend days without eating; as a result, he was so thin that protruding bones could be seen even under his sweater.

'Where is this coming from?' Akim was surprised.

'You are very thin, you need to eat ...'

'Are you calling this food?' He grimaced, and for the first time I noticed that his front teeth were beginning to rot.

'Akim, why do you drink so much?' I asked, putting tea at his feet. Akim grinned.

'You know, my father drank deeply. He drank and beat my mother. And he beat me and Miwa when my mother ran away from home. She ran away because she couldn't bear it, and she didn't take us with her. Father kicked us out of anger. She never took us, although she knew that he would not stop ...'

'But you told us something else about your parents ...' I was surprised.

'Little did I tell!' Akim snapped. 'Not everyone has folks with money ... My father drank, drank, drank, drank ... and then bang, he fell off the bed dead. Mother was so happy that she went out for a few days. She was so happy that the police found her with a broken neck in a ditch. She was so happy.' Akim grinned, taking a sip of tea.

'This is swill.' He grimaced, tossing the cup, which shattered into small pieces. 'Therefore, Vitka, how can I not drink? You know how my dad answered the question "why do you drink?" He said: 'Because there is no one to sew on the button.' He always had the buttons torn off on the sleeves of his shirt. That's why he drank. Do you understand? Out of grief, that no one will sew a button.' Akim burst out laughing. 'Being here with you makes me sick, Vitka. Leave, out of harm's way,' he summed up, then reached for a bottle of beer and drained its contents in one fell swoop. His gaze dimmed, an unhealthy blush rose to his cheeks, and he fell into a troubled sleep.

I still did not understand why Akim was drinking, but Slavik explained it simply: 'From stupidity and cowardice.' I did not know the meaning of the word 'cowardice', but I understood that it was unlikely that it characterized a good side of Akim.

2.

We celebrated the New Year quietly and not festively at all. Akim got so drunk that he vomited for several hours, and Slavik spent the night at the foot of the bed on which Miwa had died. He stroked the dirty bed, which still smelled of her sweat, and kept repeating: 'This will be your best New Year ever, I promise'.

'I promised her that on New Year's Eve we would put toys on a Christmas tree and gorge ourselves on gingerbread,' Slavik explained, noticing the bewilderment in my eyes. 'I promised, you know?' He smiled, kissing the pillow, still exuding the scent of Miwa. 'She smelled so spicy ... As if someone had sprinkled spices on her head ... Cinnamon, cloves, dried parsley.'

Slavik recalled his wife on that New Year's Eve, and I listened attentively. We didn't have a Christmas tree, and the table was not laden with gingerbread. I cooked a plate of noodles, and for dessert we ate cherry jam with black bread. It was delicious. Really delicious. Despite the fact that the noodles stuck together and cooled down very quickly, and the jam gave off a smell of rust.

While Akim was rushing about in a drunken delirium, and Slavik remembered Miwa, I went out into the street, tightly buttoning my worn coat. Snowflakes sparkled in the yard. They covered the trees with white flakes and crackled under my feet. It was a beautiful winter. Calm, windless, a little mysterious ... That is how it should be on New Year's Eve. Because miracles always happen over the New Year. At least that's what Klara Fyodorovna used to say, who loved this holiday more than others. On that night she always created a fairytale for us, pupils of the 'Old Lady Willow', the best she could. And so we believed that the New Year was a magical holiday. But that year, the fairy tale bypassed Grad, apparently turning somewhere in the wrong direction. It was probably looking for us, and even asking winter whether it knew where the children of Grad lived. But winter, a decrepit old woman, weak in memory, could only shrug. Meaning, they are here somewhere, but I can't remember where, I'm sorry. The fairy tale wandered and wandered through the fields and forests, and finally waved her hand at us. She could not look for us for too long, others were also waiting for a fairy tale. And so she went on, and made others happy in another place. Thinking about where the fairy tale was wandering now, I celebrated the New Year. Mischievous snowflakes whirled in the wind, soaring to the clouds, as it seemed to me, to touch the very skies.

On Christmas Eve, when Akim and I were playing cards (he was surprisingly sober), Slavik brought in an unexpected guest. Before that day, he had begun to leave often, and when we asked where to, he always kept silent or answered something indistinct, like: 'Well, I just wander.'

'Hey, guys, meet Svetka,' he said at the doorway, pointing to a short blonde. She smiled, and I could see that she was missing a left fang, and had rolled pink lipstick on her lips. Sveta was thin, with a rounded belly. She had a lush chest and small piggy eyes. In short, not so beautiful.

'Who is she?' Akim tensed, putting aside the cards.

'My guest,' Slavik said abruptly. 'Better move your bum cheeks, give place to the lady.'

Akim obeyed reluctantly, giving Svetka a chair. She giggled ingratiatingly as she pulled a bottle of vodka from a shabby bag.

'I am not empty-handed here!' Seeing the bottle, Akim noticeably cheered up. 'Well, boys, let's celebrate?' Sveta sat down at the table with her legs crossed, and we began to celebrate. That evening, in spite of my dislike of alcohol, I drank a quarter of a glass of vodka and very soon felt noise and dimness in my head.

'Inexperienced kid!' Our new friend laughed, sniffing the sleeve of her jacket after drinking vodka. Although she called me a kid, she herself was barely a couple of years older. It's hard to say how the evening ended, as an hour after the start of the celebration, I fell asleep at the table. I only remember the loud hubbub and Sveta's rolling laughter ... I also remember the squabble. Then it became quiet, and a gloomy morning arrived.

During the night spent at the table, my legs had become so numb that it took a long time before I could move normally. I had a bad headache. Having warmed up a little and taken a couple of sips of cold water, I looked around. Akim was sleeping at the threshold in a pool of his own vomit. Slavik was not in the room. After several unsuccessful attempts to wake Akim, I threw over my shoulders a blanket, which we laid over the mattress on especially cold days, and went out into the street.

The wind was unpleasantly frosty. It dug into my skin like hundreds of tiny needles. I wrapped myself tighter in the blanket and walked to the place where a few months ago there was a vegetable garden. Now it was a frozen swamp. Having a sad look at the result of my agricultural labors, I kicked the dead wood sticking out from under the ice with the toe of my boot.

'Do you think you can restore it by spring?' I was distracted by Slavik's voice. Turning around, I saw my friend. He smoked a cigarette while hunkering down.

'Will there ever be spring?' I asked sadly.

'What are you saying? Stop this nonsense!' Slavik smiled. Then only I noticed that his face had scratches.

'What happened to you?'

'This? Oh! We got into it with our Muslim friend,' Slavik dismissed me. 'You haven't seen his face! I decorated it well.' He laughed, enjoying my bewilderment. He replied indifferently to all my questions about the reason for the fight, saying that it was all drunken showdowns, nothing serious. Having not achieved an intelligible answer, I decided to ask about my friend's new girlfriend.

'Is she your girlfriend?' I began uncertainly.

'Svetka? No. She is like, for a couple of times, and that's it. She is a street girl,' answered Slavik. I didn't know who a street girl was, but it sounded rude, so I decided that Sveta was from the category of people like the ones we had met on the train.

'Aren't you afraid that she will tell someone about Grad?'

'No. She herself ran away from the adults. She wanders from one village to another, selling embroidered handkerchiefs. And when nobody buys handkerchiefs, she sells herself. Such goods are in use today,' reasoned Slavik, and I nodded silently.

'Will she come again?'

'Who knows. If she liked me, maybe she will.'

Akim woke up in the late afternoon, and then I saw exactly how Slavik had 'decorated' him. Swollen red lips and a bluish swelling under the eye disfigured his face so much that it was unpleasant to look at him.

'What a face!' Slavik laughed. Akim answered nothing. He silently walked over to the large chest of drawers with which we were covering the largest crack in the wall, opened the bottom drawer and took out a bottle of wine. Opening it, he took three big sips, cleared his throat, blew his nose, and then rushed at Slavik, swinging the bottle at him. Probably our senior friend simply did not expect such insolence from a Tatar orphan, so he was not ready for an attack and the bottle hit him in the ear. It is difficult to convey my feelings – I was numb with fear, watching the furious fight of my friends. Although Akim was younger and smaller than Slavik, there was more strength in him. Who knows whether it was a hereditary feature or because of 'drunken fearlessness', but in that scuffle he was in no way inferior to our 'leader'. It is not necessary to describe in detail what happened; it was an ordinary fight with its characteristic abuse. It started quickly and ended just as quickly, leaving a scar behind Slavik's right ear as a souvenir. I did not know the cause of their conflict, but Akim never tired of repeating that Slavik had betrayed his sister.

3.

From that day on, the relationship between Slavik and Akim was worse than that of a cat and a dog. They quarreled constantly and small fights happened every other day. That is how bruises on the face and a bad mood became an integral part of the life of my friends. Now I existed on my own, like a brownie that no one sees, but everyone knows is there somewhere. If I happened to persuade them to sit down at the table together, we ate in silence, and all my attempts to strike up a conversation were met with sharp resistance. Slavik left home early in the morning, while Akim started drinking early in the morning (in fact, he also left), and I tried the best I could to manage the household. I cooked a watery soup out of beets and onions, and cleaned the steps of snow.

'Don't think that I got mad at him for no reason,' Akim once said, watching my futile attempts to wash the stubborn dirt off the table. As usual, he was lying on the floor with his head on his hand.

'He slept with that girl on their bed,' Akim continued.

'Who?' I did not understand.

'Slava. Slava slept with that blonde. Remember? The one that brought vodka?' I nodded affirmatively. 'Well, at night he took her to the bed where he slept with Miwa. And he took an oath, Vitya, he did! He said that Miwa would always be his wife. And the fact that she died did not change anything. Did not change it!' Akim's voice broke into a scream. He paid no attention either to me or to Slavik, who by that time had returned home and was witnessing the revelations of the Tatar.

'Shut up!' Slavik yelled, and everything repeated. Another fight and curses ensued. Unable to tolerate this relationship any longer, I ran out of the house and came to my senses only when Grad turned into a blurry silhouette somewhere in the distance.

With January, severe frosts had come to us, tightly shackling the earth. It had not snowed for some time, which made the trees look like emaciated ragamuffins begging for alms by the road. It was late afternoon, and I strode forward, leaving behind Grad and my scolding friends. My eyes were full of tears, and I tried to hold back my sobs. Nothing was what I had thought it would be. In my dreams, I had seen Grad differently, with an abundant vegetable garden, where branches bend under the weight of scarlet tomatoes; with a solid house, in which funny conversations and lively games never stop ... I imagined that I would read the *Murzilka* magazine and gorge myself on fruit marshmallows, but everything turned out to be wrong. We were slumming it in the cold. We were starving, choking on onion-flavored soup ... There was no vegetable garden, there was no cozy home. So I thought, wandering along the frozen ground road that twisted across the field and went deep into the forest.

At that moment, my soul felt very light, as if a heavy stone had fallen from my heart. I quickened my pace, ignoring the chill that pierced my bones. I wanted to break into a run and rush like hell until everything, everything would be hundreds of kilometers behind me, as if all this was not there: the boarding school, Miwa, Grad and our whole journey to find it. I cried. I cried like boarding school boys never cry, because for such tears you can get a full blow from older boys, and then the name 'crybaby' would be assigned to you and you would live with it forever. Involuntarily, I remembered Fima Vodovoz, whom Rusichka nicknamed Tanyusha for his gentle whiny character. If she could see me now, she would certainly have called me a girl's name – Svetochka or Katenka. One way or another, I cried hysterically, enjoying the loneliness and winter cold. The old woman winter pushed me in the back, urging me on with her battered stick. The stick groaned, trying to knock me off my feet, but the old woman would not be able to square off with me, Vitka the traveler, train tamer, amateur agrarian and honorable resident of Grad ...

I only slowed down when the evening loomed fearsomely over the forest. The cold tore through my lungs, and my legs ached from uncomfortable shoes that were not designed for running on an icy road. Having looked around, I realized that I had wandered very far – unfamiliar landscapes surrounded me. Squatting down, I thought a little and decided to move on. At least I'd end up somewhere. So it seemed to me.

I don't know how long passed before panic seized me. The frost became so intolerable that I literally no longer felt my legs, and my fingernails turned blue. It became more and more difficult to walk, as if an old woman winter had thrown a sack of potatoes over my shoulders and kept adding weight with each step.

Rusichka once told us about the Great October Revolution and those 'heroes' who took part in it. With tears in her eyes, she talked about how they, barefoot and half-naked, without feeling cold, advanced towards their goal ... She hated independence most of all – she simply did not know how to live in a new world in which everyone does not walk in formation and no one honors the beggars who 'created' the revolution. Democracy, freedom ... All these concepts seemed dangerous to Rusichka. Those were ideas that needed to be destroyed in the bud. I think that Fima Vodovoz described this syndrome in one of his clever books, which he signed beautifully, in a foreign way: E. Vysotsky. The syndrome of the 'Soviet man'; or even better, the syndrome of Rusichka.

When it got dark, I paused to reflect on my next steps. I didn't have the strength to go any further, so I sat down on a dead tree branch lying by the road, and hugged myself tightly in order to warm up somehow. I must say that the only clothes I was wearing were a sweater, trousers with holes on the knees and a pair of worn-out boots, also full of holes. I swayed from side to side, feeling how the cold fettered my whole body. My legs were numb to the very thighs, I could not feel the tip of my nose. It hurt a lot ... I cried. But not from pain, rather from a feeling of complete hopelessness. There was nowhere to go, I had no strength to run, the cold had penetrated every cell of my emaciated body, twisting my bones and pinching my skin, and I realized that any minute it would get to my heart, squeeze it with its icy hand, and, after making one last futile attempt to break free, my heart would stop forever. This is how I saw my end, something like that. Sad and very lonely.

'Oh, Vitka, you fool! You'd be lost without me, you so would!' Unable to believe my luck, I heard Slavik's voice, and a moment later he himself was hanging over me.

'Remember the golden rule: if you decide to get out of the house, don't forget to grab your hat and coat,' said my elder friend, shaking his head in displeasure. 'You're completely numb.' He handed me a padded jacket and a knitted hat.

'Put it on quickly and let's go make a fire, otherwise I'll kick the bucket here myself!' Slavik exclaimed, lifting me from my makeshift chair. Pulling on the clothes with difficulty (my body simply did not obey), I wandered off to collect brushwood, feeling the warmth slowly spreading through my body.

'Come on, come on, faster, you young fool,' urged Slavik, pulling the ear-flap hat more tightly over my ears. 'The wind is starting.'

I obediently picked thin twigs while Slavik looked for a place for a fire. After walking a dozen meters, he found a fallen tree, its trunk and branches forming a sheltered place, closed from the wind on three sides.

'Excellent!' I heard, and before I could blink an eye, a saving fire was already flaring up in front of me, warming my stiff hands. Soon my cheeks blushed, and my body went limp.

'There you go, eat.' Slavik handed me an open can of condensed milk and a piece of black bread. I silently took the food and emptied the can in an instant, soaking up the rest with bread. Now that my strength began to return to me, I was able to talk.

'How did you find me?' I began, admiringly hanging on every Slavik's word. Yes he was an extraordinary guy.

'There was nothing to look for! I just followed you.' He smiled. 'I kept a good distance so that you wouldn't notice ... And you, Vitek, were in such a condition that if I were two steps away from you, you wouldn't notice.'

'Why did you follow me?' I was surprised.

'What do you mean, why? Because you are a young fool, and you could get into trouble in such weather. And so it happened. You would have turned numb if it weren't for me. And you are my friend, and one doesn't abandon one's friends.' Slavik smiled again, and I could only blink silently.

'We'll spend the night here. The main thing is to keep a good fire. You sleep, and I'll sit here until morning. We'll pack up at dawn when the wind dies down.'

I didn't mind. Curling up on the crisp branches with which we laid the ground in our shelter, quickly I began to fall asleep.

'You are not to do this anymore.' Slavik interrupted my dreams.

In response, I just sobbed.

'Don't cry. Why run away at all?'

'I don't want you and Akim to fight and quarrel.' I muttered, burying my nose in my jacket.

'It's difficult ... But we'll try.' Slavik smiled.

'Just don't bring more girls so that Akim doesn't get upset.'

'Akim will get upset and drink without that. He is the kind of person who will always find a reason ...'

'But you slept with Svetka in your bed. You swore an oath ...' Despite Akim's frankly terrible behavior, in this situation I agreed with him. Slavik had sworn an oath of eternal love, and he had betrayed it so quickly.

'It doesn't matter who you sleep with. What matters is how you feel. Do you think I fell out of love with Miwa?'

I didn't know what to say, so I kept silent.

'You are not saying anything ... I haven't stopped loving her. You know, not a day goes by that I don't remember her voice, don't hear her ringing laughter. I dream about her. Dream of how she dances. I feel the touch of her palms on my face ... Svetka was just for a moment, just to forget. You know, Vitek,' he looked into the fire, 'my mother and I had a neighbour, Ivan Andreevich. He loved his wife, Vera Sergeevna, very much. And when she died, in her early fifties, Ivan Andreevich married again. Everyone just shrugged their shoulders, wondering how he could have done it like this, betray Vera Sergeevna. At that time I was just a kid and, having heard enough conversations, I decided to ask my neighbour directly why he did this. The man smiled kindly, sat me on his lap and said: "You know, Slava, there can be many women in life, but love is once only. You do not betray with your body, you can betray only with your heart. Verochka is always in my heart, I fall asleep and wake up with her name on my lips ... And the new wife, she is for the body." I poorly understood the meaning of what was said then, but now I understand that the death of a loved one is not a reason to condemn myself to loneliness. There will be others, many in my life, maybe I will even marry again. But Miwa is always in my heart. Here, deeply.'

Slavik put his hand to his heart. In the glow of the burning fire, I could see his eyes fill with tears, and I felt ashamed of my words. But he did not hold a grudge against me, I knew that. This is how Slavik was, easy-going and forgiving. A friend who did not leave me on a cold winter night.

4.

The morning was frosty and sunny. In spite of spending the night in the open air, I felt cheerful. Jumping up to my feet (I wonder where that burst of energy came from!), I did a few squats to warm up. Slavik was no longer asleep, and I did not know whether he had gone to bed at all. He was raking the smoldering ashes with a stick, the fire, which did not go out in the night wind, having resisted the bitter frost. Thanks to the warmth of this humble fire, we had survived through the night.

'I'm starving ...' Slavik smacked his lips.

'You have nothing left?' I asked.

'No, we ate everything yesterday. But that's okay, there is something at home. Let's move,' commanded my friend, and we hit the road. Slavik was silent the whole way, but I never stopped talking. My mood was upbeat.

'Do you think Klara Fyodorovna misses us?' I asked for some reason, suddenly remembering the old headmistress.

'Why did you remember her?' Slavik was surprised.

'It's just that she said once that she always feels sad at heart in winter. So I thought, what if she is sitting by the window in her office now, drinking tea and thinking about us. Missing us.'

'I don't know, Vitka. She has so many children that she would not be strong enough to think about all of them. Your head is going to burst if you keep thinking about everyone like that. No, she probably already forgot about us,' reasoned Slavik. But for some reason I believed that Klara Fyodorovna remembered us and even that she was looking for us. Probably not for much longer, but she was. Right now, she was sitting at the window feeling sad because her searching was unsuccessful. Eh, if she knew that Miwa was no longer in the world of the living ones, she would be grieving a lot. She loved the girl. Many people loved Miwa. Probably because she was beautiful. Beautiful children are more loved in general. I was sure of this after my years in the boarding school. They are more often forgiven for pranks and are not beaten when they cry for no reason, because their faces stay beautiful even with tears on them.

We walked in silence, each one deep in his own thoughts. I kept thinking about Miwa, Klara Fyodorovna and other inhabitants of the

'Old Lady Willow', especially about Fauna. She would not approve of the way we lived, because according to her understanding we were definitely living wrong. I was sure of that.

A couple of hours later we left the forest and found ourselves on a winding road that led towards Grad.

'We're almost there.' Slavik smiled. Out of sheer joy, we quickened our pace, anticipating a delicious breakfast, crackers with fried onions, but before we could walk a dozen meters, from behind another twist, a stranger's crumpled figure appeared. She was dressed in rags, and was pushing a rusty trolley, loaded with dirty bags. The woman blocked our way with the cart, straightened her back, and smiled maliciously, displaying her rotten teeth.

'Dear boys, do you know how far the nearest town or village is?' she began ingratiatingly.

'There is a village a couple of kilometers from here,' Slavik replied dryly, indicating the direction with his hand. 'Follow this road without turning, and it will lead you out,' he continued. By that time, we had lined up with the stranger, but she did not even think of stepping aside.

'And do you go there yourselves? Maybe you will show me the way?' She took a step in my direction, and I sensed the sharp stink of sweat coming from her clothes.

'We are not going that way,' Slavik snapped. We walked around the woman and quickened our pace again, when suddenly we heard behind us:

'There is a strange place out here. Orphan boys stagger in the mornings, someone lights a stove in an abandoned house ... Strange things are happening ...' She kept talking while we walked away, faster and faster, feeling alarmed, and soon her voice disappeared into the frosty air.

'Slavik, what do we do? This woman saw Grad. She will tell everything!' I lamented in the kitchen, barely holding back sobs.

'Do not whine, let me think.' Although Slavik tried to control himself, he was no less worried than I was. While we were discussing how we should proceed and how dangerous in fact this woman was, Akim, who had been sleeping on the floor, woke up.

'She's just crazy, nobody believes people like her,' said Slavik.

'Like who?' asked Akim, rubbing his swollen eyes. He had risen from the floor and was now sitting at the table, pouring red wine from a bottle into a glass with a trembling hand.

‘Where do you get this swill from?’ Slavik grimaced, spitting on the floor. I myself did not understand how Akim managed to get alcohol, being as he was in an extremely bad financial situation.

‘That is my little secret.’ Akim grinned, taking a savory sip of cheap liquor. He stretched with pleasure, coughing. ‘Well, now it’s good morning.’ His cheeks turned pink, and his eyes cleared. ‘So what kind of crazy woman are you talking about?’ he continued, putting his feet on the table.

‘Get your feet off the table!’ shouted Slavik. Akim obeyed reluctantly.

‘We just met a homeless person on the road ...’ I began, telling him about everything that had happened, and at the same time sharing my fears that a stranger might give us away. And although Slavik was able to instill confidence in my heart that no one would believe the tramp, Akim took the news extremely emotionally.

‘Are you out of your minds?!’ he shouted, jumping up from his chair. ‘You shouldn’t have let her go! She will spread the word!’ he yelled, running around the room.

‘What should we have done, strangle her?’ Slavik shouted.

‘Why not strangle her, what do I care!’ Akim shouted, kicking the leg of the table. It creaked treacherously.

‘Akim, you can’t do that,’ I began uncertainly.

‘What? What can’t I do?’

I did not have time to answer, as he jumped up at me and squeezed my throat with his hands. ‘Well, why aren’t you saying anything? What can’t I do?’ Akim shouted, squeezing my throat more tightly.

Now I understand that he did not intend to hurt me. It was alcohol talking in him, making his mood extremely changeable, and him even more hotheaded, with that already restless character. Still, I do not know how it would have ended if Slavik had not come to the rescue. In one fell swoop, he threw Akim aside.

‘Don’t you dare lay your hands on me’ my older friend hissed. But as expected, after getting to his feet and catching his breath, Akim rushed at Slavik. Another fight started. They beat each other mercilessly, cursed and insulted. Meanwhile, I huddled in the corner of the room, watching in horror. Distraught with anger and alcohol, Akim strove to bite Slavik’s ears, twisted his fingers and seemed not to feel the blows which Slava rained on him.

‘Stop it!’ I finally cried, but my scream faded into the squabble, hisses and growls spewed out by Akim’s bleeding throat. What happened next could be called an unfortunate accident, a terrible, tragic coincidence ...

In the hubbub, Slavik pushed Akim hard. He stumbled, staggered and, unable to maintain balance, fell, hitting his head on the corner of the table. Collapsing on the floor, he froze with an unnaturally arched neck.

We froze too. 'Akim?' Slavik whispered, bending over him. 'Hey, what are you doing? Stop fooling around!'

He pushed Akim in the ribs, but Akim didn't move. Slavik pushed harder, at which the body, frozen on its side, rolled onto its back, and we could see a thin trickle of blood running from Akim's temple.

I sat in the corner of the room until the late evening, swaying frantically from side to side. Meanwhile, Slavik was finishing Akim's wine, deeply concentrating on something. Akim's body was lying on the floor. We did not touch it. It is difficult to convey in words the feelings that overwhelmed me that day. Horror, fear, despair ... everything was tied up together, causing me terrible pain. The corpse of our friend caught my eye now and then, and a shiver ran through the body.

'We must take him out into the street, otherwise it will stink before morning,' Slavik hissed dryly, not turning his head in my direction.

'We should bury him ...' My voice trembled.

'Have you gone completely crazy?! How would we bury him in such a frost?' Slavik shrugged me off angrily. I tried again, but after getting a final refusal to bury Akim, I helped to pull him out into the street. Having laid the body on the threshold of the house, we folded his arms over his chest, and covered his face with a rag. At first, we wanted to cover the whole body with a blanket, but it was getting noticeably colder outside and we could use the blanket ourselves.

'He doesn't need it anymore.' Slavik sighed. So we left him on the doorstep, and lay down on the mattress. Covered up to our noses, we listened to the old woman winter moaning outside the window. She crunched her finger-branches, summoning a blizzard. I don't know for how long my friend didn't sleep, but I didn't close my eyes until morning. At the thought of the dead Akim, who was literally a few meters away from me, everything inside me was getting cold. I looked at Slavik cautiously, who had killed our friend, even though not on purpose. Killed. This word rang in my ears, rang out all the bells. He killed him. And I? And I saw it, I had nothing to stop it. I was paralyzed with horror, fear for my soul, which was now destined to burn in hell. At dawn, I fell into an anxious sleep, in which I saw the image of the exhausted Akim. He held out his hands to me and cried. Bloody tears flowed from his eyes. He asked me why I didn't help, didn't save him. 'Vitka,Vitka ... why?' he moaned, covering his bleeding temple with his hand. I could not answer anything, as if I was dumb.

My nightmare was interrupted by Slavik. 'Get up,' he grunted. It was early morning and the blurry silhouettes of trees were barely visible outside the window.

'Get all the essentials,' said Slavik, tearing off my blanket. My body instantly twisted from the cold.

'Are we leaving?' I asked.

'Yes, and very quickly.' Not daring to ask or argue again, I began to pack my backpack, stuffing the essentials inside. While I was gathering stuff, Slavik dragged Akim's body from the street – it now looked like a large icicle covered with a layer of snow.

'We must bury him next to Miwa ...' I began, but Slavik interrupted me.

'We don't have time. There is a possibility that the old woman has already told the village about us. They will come for us, and there will be a corpse. They won't take us to a boarding school, but to a penal colony. We must run, Vitka, burning a bridge over ...'

'We must bury him ...' I did not give up, but the cold disapproval in my friend's eyes interrupted me.

'Do you want to bury the one who offended you and even wanted to strangle you? This is a sign of weakness, Vitya.' Slavik grinned, and I had no choice but to agree. I continued to collect my belongings in silence. When we'd finished packing, we dressed warmly and went out into the street. Having gone to the chicken coop, Slavik returned with a can of kerosene, which we kept 'just in case' and 'for a rainy day.'

'What's that for?' I was surprised.

'I'll tell you this, Vitka: Grad was our dream, yours and mine, ours only. Everything went wrong from the start, when there became four of us. But now, we will start all over again. You will see, we will find our own, real Grad ...' So Slavik said, pouring kerosene on the threshold of the house, walls and door. I just watched in silence, unable to believe in what was happening. Then he struck a match. One, two, a whole box, and soon, too soon, the house was engulfed in flames. They slowly climbed the walls, then climbed through the windows and onto the roof, settling down in an owner-like way inside the house. Our house, our Grad burned, and my rainbow dreams of a free, adult life burned with it. If anyone ever says that their life has burned to the ground, they probably mean it symbolically. Life cannot burn down. But I really saw my life burning down. There were only two walls left ...

5.

I don't know whether the stranger from the road brought people to our Grad, or if the smoke from the fire attracted the attention of local residents. Whether anyone found Grad or not, remained a mystery forever. Early in the morning, when the dawn flared up with might and main, we were already far away, on our way to a new life and new Grad. The day turned out to be surprisingly fine, and while the frost was fierce at night, when the sun rose, nature transformed, hints of spring freshness flying out there in the air, although spring still was so far away.

Nature began to breathe with warmth during this time of the year, and the wind pleasantly caressed our skin, as if the old woman winter remembered her youth and now was sitting in her chair, her eyes closed, smiling, indulging in pleasant memories. Perhaps she was thinking about how wonderful it was to be a young fresh girl, running on tiptoe along the icy river with her snow-white hair down; how wonderful it was to shower the ground with snow-white flakes, collecting them heaped in the palm of her hand, and laughing loudly ... How wonderful, the old woman thought, it was to be young and carefree.

The weather became so good that Slavik unbuttoned his jacket, and I took off my scarf. I did not know where we were going. I just blindly followed my guide and only friend in this world. I wanted to start talking about Akim, discuss what happened. It hurt me that we had not buried him but burned the body instead, as our ancestors did, those who believed in plurality of gods. I can't remember what they were called, but Father Vladimir had spoken about them in his lessons. I felt sorry for the abandoned vegetable garden, although it had long turned into an icy swamp. But Slavik gave every appearance of not wanting to discuss what had happened. Therefore, we wandered, each deep in his own thoughts, until we stumbled upon a railway.

My heart started pounding! How long had I not heard the song of trains, had not inhaled their strong warm smell. That clickety-clackety ... My soul yearned for this music. 'Are we going by train?' I asked with hope. Slavik nodded. I was unable to contain my joy. Forgetting for a while about all the sorrows that had befallen us, and about the death of Akim, I admired the endless strip of rail that went far into the unknown, where our new life was.

Keeping our eye on the place where the train was supposed to slow down, we sat down to wait, and just ten minutes later, we saw its bulky outline. It slowed down as we expected, and we were able to jump inside easily, as we had done more than once in the past.

'We'll stay here until tomorrow morning or until the end, depending on how things turn out,' reasoned Slavik. For the first time, he did not know where we were going, that is how sullen he was. We had set off in search of a new Grad, but we did not know where to look for it. To tell the truth, at that moment the search for a new home was of little concern to me. I concentrated all my thoughts and feelings on the music of the railway, which greeted me in a friendly way: 'What took you so long, Vitka?!' And the only thing I could do was smile, justifying myself for leaving (not out loud though), saying that it had been a lot of work, taking care of the garden and keeping the promise given to one girl: to bring fragrant flowers to her grave. Nevertheless, the railway was not offended, it was too wise for this. Having seen a lot on its way, it was sympathetic to fools like me, because it knew that anyone who fell in love with the music of trains would suffer a life-long self-betrayal. Therefore, it was not angry with me, but tapped out its melody, clickety-clackety, and I slowly dozed off, lulled by the sound.

I woke up in the evening. It was difficult to say for sure, but the sun was already rapidly leaving the horizon. Winter, having regained its usual appearance of an old woman, enveloped the earth in frost. A prickly wind blew. It howled, seeping through the cracks of the freight train and painfully pinching my neck and arms.

'How did you sleep?' asked Slavik.

'Good,' I said, and I did not lie. After a hard night in the house, I had 'cleared' my head a little.

'I did not manage to.' Slavik sobbed, clasping his head in his hands. 'Vitka, what is going to happen now?' His voice trembled. 'You know that I did not want to. I did not mean it, you know. I did not like Akim, but I did not want to. Do you understand?' repeated Slavik, and even in the darkness I saw his face contorted with pain.

Of course, I knew that he had not done it on purpose. 'It happens ...' was the only thing that I could answer, because I did not know how to calm someone who has killed another person. Probably any words are powerless here, so I got up, went up to my friend and hugged him without uttering a word. At first, he jerked, even recoiled slightly, but then succumbed to my impulse, allowing me to pity him. I don't think that Slavik was often hugged in life, or maybe no one had ever hugged him at all (and this was possible!). Therefore, he felt awkward. Not because he was hugged, but because he was touched tenderly in general. It seems to me now that, apart from kicks and slaps, and the love he had experienced with Miwa, Slavik did not know he could get physical contact from another person. Bruises and abrasions had replaced kisses and hugs since he was a child. This is how his childhood was, not the worst, I tell you, but not one worth dreaming about.

The train was slowing down and regaining its speed, winter beat with its icy stick on the carriages with fierce force, and Slavik and I sat hugging and simply pitying each other. We pitied each other the only way we knew how, because no one had taught us how to do this.

6.

At dawn, we got off at an unknown station, so deserted that neither hucksters nor beggars were hanging around. Having exchanged our last flashlight for bread and water from the half-asleep watchman, we had a snack and went on. By that time, a plan had matured in Slavik's head. After a detailed study of the map of the area that hung at the entrance to the pharmacy (closed for renovation, as the announcement said), my friend suggested that we follow in the direction of the town of K., where we would be sure to find shelter for the rest of the winter. I did not contradict Slavik, as I completely trusted him. Thus, early in the morning, we set off in order to reach our destination by the evening, according to Slavik's calculations.

As we walked, I thought about my parents again. The crackle of snow underfoot evoked memories of the days when my father and I had walked in the courtyard of our small house. It was a joyous winter. I was no more than five, maybe even less, but I remember those days to the smallest detail. We played snowballs, Dad threw me in the air, and then Mum drew angels in the snow. I remember how my feet cramped from the cold, but it was a pleasant pain. I remember how my mother made hot chocolate afterwards, and we ate curd cake. There were so many feelings, so many good warm memories in the simple sound of the snow crackling under my feet, that I wanted to keep going without stopping to remember it longer.

'My grandmother told me that when the snow crackles under your feet, it means that spring will arrive early.' Slavik broke our silence. Slavik's grandmother was an amazing woman! She had a story for everything.

'How is that related?' I asked.

'Long-term observations,' my friend replied seriously, and we went on in silence again.

Despite all our efforts and only one halt, we did not reach the town of K. by evening, turning off the road into a thicket of evergreen bushes, which we decided to make our temporary refuge. The old woman winter took pity on us that night and calmed the wind, hiding it in her travel bag. She told the trees to stand still and take revenge on the snowflakes, keeping them away from our lodging. I was very grateful to her for this, because we did not manage to make a fire. We had to sleep on cold branches, wrapped in our outerwear. The night was quiet and unbelievably beautiful. Unable to fall asleep from the piercing cold, I admired the starry sky and the huge milky crescent silvering the treetops. It was so beautiful that I could not sleep until the morning. Only when the sun replaced the nightly beauty, did I doze off for a short while, until I felt the touch of Slavik's cold fingers on my wrist.

'Come on, let's go,' he said in a chilled hoarse voice, and we hit the road immediately. We walked quickly, trying to keep warm, until we noticed in the distance a thin line of smoke emerging from a chimney. A hundred meters from us there was a small house, sheltered from prying eyes by an even line of young birch trees, which watched the peace of the owners like guards. A little further off we noticed a barn, from where we could hear the grunting of pigs and the bellowing of a cow. There was a chicken coop close to the barn, and a stable near it.

'Rich household!' Slavik whistled. He paused, thinking of something. 'You stay here, and I'll check it out,' he finally said, leaving me to wait. He returned soon.

'There are old people living there, sort of like a husband and wife, and there is a woman with them. Maybe a daughter, or a hired worker. There is also a guy, but he is definitely a worker. You won't be able to get in there, the yard is full of dogs. And what kind of dogs! We are barely a mouthful to them.' Slavik shook his head, puzzled. 'We should think. And it's hard to think on an empty belly.' He sighed, squatting down.

'Why do we need to get there?' I did not understand.

'What do you mean why? We should have something to eat, and I would like to get some new clothes. Ours are not very suitable for such frosts.'

'Maybe we could ask?' I suggested hesitantly.

'Ask for what?'

'Well, knock on the door and ask for food ... What if there are good people living there?' I did not have time to finish, as Slavik's face beamed. He jumped to his feet and began to dance happily, waving his arms.

'Vitka, you're a damn genius!' he shouted, foolishly pushing my shoulder.

'Of course! We, or rather you, will ask. Your face is sweet and your eyes are sad. We'll tear your coat now, and who would resist? Especially when it comes to old people.'

I did not want to go and beg by myself, but Slavik convinced me that I alone had much bigger chance than the two of us did.

'I'm already an adult, and adult beggars are only ever sent packing. Children are rarely abused by anyone,' he explained. Thus, with a mournful face, a hungry gaze and a torn coat, I headed towards the unknown house where, I hoped, good people lived. Two huge shaggy shepherd dogs announced my approach. They jumped to the gate, poking their noses between the bars, and growled angrily.

'Naida! Shere Khan! What is it there?' A formidable bass thundered throughout the entire yard. Its owner, a tall grey-haired man, wearing high boots and a long sheepskin coat, appeared. He walked slowly towards the gate, limping slightly.

'What is it, my dear ones?' He turned to the dogs, who wagged their tails happily at the sight of the owner.

'Help the poor beggar, for God's sake,' I whined when the old man came very close. Having not noticed me at once, he started with surprise, and the dogs started howling.

'Quiet, I said!' Hearing the man's shouting, the animals quieted down at once. 'Who is wailing over there?' He bent down, squinting one eye.

'Just a poor orphan,' I answered in a trembling voice.

'For God's sake. Look at him.' The old man chuckled. He had an eagle profile and a lush mustache.

'Where did you come from, you sly one, eh?' he asked, opening the gate slightly. It was then that I was able to see how huge he was.

'Nowhere ...' I hesitated. 'Help the poor beggar, for God's sake ...'

'Why do you keep repeating "for God's sake", "for God's sake"? Ugh!' He spat on the ground. While we were talking, Naida and Shere Khan kept trying to squeeze between the owner's leg and the gate, not, seemingly, out of a desire to tear me apart, but simply with curiosity. But the man would not let them out, pushing them away with his hand.

'You sons of bitches! Go away!' he shouted, pushing one of the dogs to the side. It screamed pitifully as it ran away.

'Naida, do you want to get some too?' The old man turned to the second dog. It wasn't long before that one, in turn, followed its friend.

'So where are you from, little beggar?' The owner of the house took a step towards me. Luckily for me, a woman's voice interrupted our conversation.

'Khariton, you old grumbler, what's going on there?' The fragile figure of a grey-haired woman appeared on the threshold of the house. She was clearly younger than the giant Khariton, although it was also possible that she had aged well. After all, this happens.

‘A little scoundrel. He cries out for help for God’s sake, damn him!’

‘Who? The boy or God?’ The woman laughed loudly.

‘What an intolerable woman. God, of course! Why curse the boy? It’s not his fault that he has sawdust for brains!’ said Khariton loudly.

‘Let me pass, old man, I’ll see what’s going on here.’ The woman came up to us and, pushing the giant aside, looked out the gate.

‘Whom do we have here?’ she smiled, leaning towards me. She smelled like baking and flower soap.

‘Have you swallowed your tongue? Answer her!’ the old man barked. I cringed, frightened by his menacing look.

‘Why are you scaring the child?’ The woman frowned her thin eyebrows in displeasure and turned to me again ‘What’s your name?’

‘Vitka ...’ I whispered, swallowing.

‘So, Victor, do you like apple pies?’ she asked with a wink. I smiled in response.

‘What the hell are you thinking? Maybe also invite him to the house, sit down at the table?’ the old man became angry.

‘Close your mouth, Khariton, I’m sick of your lamenting.’ The woman waved him off, taking my hand. ‘My name is Ada, and this grumbler, as you yourself understood, is old Khariton. My husband. He is kind at heart, but terribly quarrelsome.’ She chuckled, casting a glance at her husband, who was locking the gate, muttering something under his breath.

I followed Ada into the house. The first thing I sensed as I crossed the threshold was the deep aroma of fresh pastries. The house was well heated, and on the dining table a ginger cat was dozing, stretched out at full length.

‘Meet Squirrel. Also called Lazy face.’ Ada patted the cat on the head, but it did not even move. The woman took me into the kitchen, sat me down, and began to set the table. Apple pie and sausage sandwiches, a bowl of chocolates and a huge cup of sweet tea – she put all this in front of me, saying that she would not let me leave the table until the plates were empty. There was no need to ask twice, and I pounced on the food like a wolf cub that had been starving for weeks. While I stuffed my belly, Ada watched in silence. When I finished eating, I wiped my lips with my sleeve and smiled contentedly. A pleasant warmth spread through my body, and my stomach rumbled happily.

‘Where did you come from, Vitya?’ she finally spoke up, sitting down beside me.

‘I suppose, he escaped from some boarding school ...’ Khariton muttered, going into the kitchen. He looked like a giant against the small room. After his words, I tensed, afraid that this elderly couple would recognize me as a fugitive. Apparently, Ada noticed my confusion, because she covered my palm with her hand.

‘You can tell the old woman what happened. I know how to keep secrets.’

‘Could you give me a jacket and some food?’ I asked, ‘I really need to go.’

‘No “thank you”! Not a “please”! You warmed up the snake, woman!’ Khariton started swearing. I felt ashamed of my behaviour and hastened to thank my hostess for her hospitality.

‘I’m not helping you for your gratitude, boy,’ she answered sadly, then stood up and left the kitchen. She returned with warm clothes in her hands: a down jacket and a fur-lined coat.

‘Our son wore them when he was little. I keep everything for future grandchildren, but you obviously need it more. So they’ve come in handy.’ She smiled, putting the warm imported clothes on my lap. At the sight of such beauty, I beamed.

‘Thank you. I’ve never seen such beautiful clothes,’ I said enthusiastically. She smiled again, and Khariton grunted with displeasure, meaning something like: ‘You are spending expensive things in vain.’ Ada packed a large bag of food, into which she put biscuits and bagels, several bags of cereals, jam, stew and crackers.

‘Can you carry it?’ asked Khariton, grinning at my attempts to throw the bag over my back.

‘Let me help you.’ He easily lifted it with one hand, hanging it on my shoulder. ‘Don’t drop it, there are glass jars in there,’ the old man said. Now he didn’t seem so angry to me.

They took me to the gate. Naida and Shere Khan walked at the old man’s leg, waving their thick tails.

‘Bloody clingies!’ smiled Khariton, first stroking the fluffy Naida, and then the long-legged Shere Khan. The dogs squealed contentedly.

‘Be careful.’ Ada stroked my head, crossing me goodbye.

‘If I find out that you cheated someone or stole anything from the neighbours, I will find you! I’ll box your ears!’ the old man snapped, showing his upper teeth after the example of his creatures.

‘Old fool!’ Ada exclaimed, laughing.

‘Farewell, Vitka.’ She waved her hand at me, and I left. After warming up and eating in their kitchen, my energy was renewed and I was able to hurry to Slavik.

My friend was amazed at the generosity of the owners of the house. I spoke in detail about my adventures, and only restrained myself in describing how well the hostess had treated me. While I was warming myself there and eating goodies, Slavik was freezing and starving. Wearing the new fur-lined coat – it was just a little short in the arms – he opened a can of stew, emptying it in the blink of an eye. The same fate befell the jar of jam and the packet of biscuits.

‘What generous people they are!’ he said. ‘You should have asked for more money or something valuable, Vitka ... To sell later,’ Slavik thought out loud.

‘They already gave me so much ...’ I replied.

‘For people like them, this is not much. Their closets are full!’ said Slavik, but I didn’t agree with him. He did not know Ada and Khariton, that is why he talked up a storm. Having smeared the last of the jam from the jar, Slavik stretched out contentedly and ordered me to get ready to go. It was almost impossible for me to leave this place, where a friendly house with wonderful old people stood just a few meters away. It seemed to me that if I came back now and knocked at the gate, they would shelter me ... Because they really wanted grandchildren, and I would have been a good grandson, that’s for sure. Instead, I trotted after Slavik, well-fed and satisfied with my new down jacket.

7.

At midday (or a little later) we arrived in the town of K. If we'd been the heroes of some nineteenth century novel, I would have written that before us stood the massive town gates, defended by sharp-eyed young warriors on piebald stallions. But in fact, the improvised entrance to the town was embellished by a line of rickety kiosks and a huge metallic plaque on which was inscribed in faded letters the name of the town, the population (no date given for when it was counted) and the distance to the church of St Barbara the Martyr. Covered with a thick layer of grimy snow, the town was grey and dreary and had a whiff about it of mould and old persons' wardrobes. Having taken a look around, we decided to set off for the church, where, as we well knew, it would be possible, not only to find out what was what, but also to spend the night. In small towns church officials had often let us in for the night. Ten minutes' unhurried walk brought us to the church, a rather elegant edifice for the town of K. Against a generally featureless background its gilded cupolas shone and its massive wooden door was embellished with elaborate carving, like that which topped the entrance gate of 'Old Lady Willow'. The elite among the local scroungers had gathered by the church steps: half-crazy old women, ragged urchins, gypsy children and a couple of alcoholics. All these gentlefolk were waiting for some resident of the town to wander in for midday prayers.

'Tell me, please, whose parish is this?' Slavik began, turning to a toothless old crone who was leaning against the church wall. She cast an appraising glance at him.

'And who might you be? I haven't seen you round here,' she said.

'We're not locals. That's why you haven't seen us,' replied Slavik haughtily, echoing her words.

'Look at Mr Important,' a second old crone chimed in. She was sitting on the steps by the church door, smoking a *papirosa*, her legs crossed. 'Did you hear that, you scruffbags. Hark at Mr Important!' She turned to a group of grubby gypsy children, the oldest of whom was about my age. They replied with an outburst of whooping. The scene was really depressing. I wanted to get away as soon as possible, so as not to look at these objectionable people one moment longer, but Slavik was in no hurry to withdraw.

'What's the matter with you, woman? We behaved nicely towards you, but you ... We would have thanked you properly, but seeing as you didn't ... With these words Slavik took a tin of stewed beef out of his bag, spun it round in his hands, and put it back. On seeing this treat, the old crone's eyes lit up.

'Wait a minute, boy, not so fast,' she gabbled. 'Has someone offended you? Well, kids, was it you?' The gypsy children shook their heads. Slavik, who had turned around as if to leave, stood still. 'We make friends with those who are kind to us,' she guffawed, licking her parched lips. 'The parish priest is Father Innokenty, a nice old man,' she began and soon, in exchange for a tin of meat and a packet of buckwheat, we had found out everything we needed to know. Slavik chucked a packet of biscuits to the gypsy children, who tore it open frenziedly. They began to fight over the biscuits, which had spilled out onto the ground, pulling each other's hair and shrieking like dervishes.

'Little devils,' laughed the old crone, flinging a fag end into the bushes. She carefully put the tin and the packet into a small bag which stood at her feet. When she walked past, I turned away in disgust, so repulsive was her appearance. This did not upset the old crone, however, who was clearly used to such treatment. Having collected the last crumbs, the gypsy children began to cadge a refill from Slavik, but instead received a goodly dose of abuse.

'Shove off, you scumbags.' He waved his hand at one of the boys, a green-eyed, swarthy youth, and the group broke up in all directions.

'You'll regret this,' said Green Eyes through gritted teeth. In reply Slavik merely guffawed. The gypsy children disappeared and now, apart from us, the only people remaining by the church were a drunken middle-aged woman and a couple of youths flogging junk of all sorts: damp matches, worn-out rubber sneakers and crows' feathers (I've no idea what they were used for). We went round to the back of the church, where we found a dilapidated extension, the house of Father Innokenty. The kind-hearted old man readily agreed to let us overnight there for a couple of days, and, after a symbolic sacrifice of two tins of strawberry jam, even assigned us some bed linen, a towel and a bar of soap. Next door to the extension was a barn, cobbled together with, as they say, whatever came to hand. This was the bath house. Father Innokenty stoked up the stove, heated up some water in an iron bucket and left us to get washed. After our ablutions he would be waiting for us in the church.

The interior of the church was not as impressive as the outside.

The frozen end wall, riddled with black mould, was embellished with an icon of the Virgin Mary and Child, and a few more images of saints unfamiliar to me. Father Innokenty was writing something in the church register and did not immediately see us come in.

'Say a prayer while I sort out these entries.' He smiled, turning the page of the stout tome. Slavik had no intention of praying and instead started to examine the candles burning on a brass candelabra in front of a Crucifixion. I fell to my knees before the icon of the Virgin and quickly gabbled, one after the other, all the prayers that Father Vladimir had taught us. Maria regarded me graciously, touched by my efforts to appease her. And I really did try to appease her. After all the sin of murder was lying heavy on my heart. And, although I did not have blood on my hands, my soul was bleeding; after all I had done nothing to prevent what happened. A treacherous tear welled up in the corner of my eye and slowly rolled down to my chin.

'Why are you blubbing?' Slavik sneered, sitting down beside me. 'Get a grip.'

'Slava, don't you want to pray? After all you ... You've a sin on your soul,' I whispered, touching him on the shoulder.

'Don't touch!' said Slavik with a yell that even startled Father Innokenty.

'Quiet, boys. You're stopping the saints praying for our souls.' And again he bent down over his book.

'Don't ever say it's my sin. There was no sin on my part; it all happened accidentally,' he hissed. His angry tone deprived me of the strength to hold back the tears; they spurted from my eyes, distorting my face with grief.

'Vitka, stop it!' He seized me by the elbows and shook me.

'Stop this! This is a House of God!' Father Innokenty angrily pulled us up short, but we didn't listen to him. Slavik bawled at me, slapped my cheeks, but I went on howling heartrendingly, in floods of tears. All Father Innokenty's attempts to separate us ended in failure. In the end, he was forced to throw us out. We fell into a grimy snowdrift and continued to bawl and brawl. This went on until I managed to break out of my companion's grasp and take to my heels, Continuing to hurl curses at him, I ran off in no particular direction, merely putting distance between myself and my erstwhile best friend. I was seething inside; my heart was beating wildly and I wanted just one thing – to disappear and never again see his superior smirk. But Slavik did not lag behind me. He caught me up and shouted something at my back, but I wasn't listening; my temples were throbbing, but pain and hurt drove me forward. By now, though, Slavik was not hitting me but trying to restore peace between us.

'Vitka! Calm down! I didn't do it deliberately!'

Gradually I did calm down. We were lying on the pavement, at the corner of the local grocery store, behind some dustbins.

'Okay then! Forgotten!' snapped Slavik, getting to his feet. He brushed the dirt from his trousers and helped me to my feet.

'Why did you do that to me, eh?' Slavik asked as we went back to the church. I walked with bowed head and cast-down gaze, like a guilty small boy who would soon be punished by his parents. But I wasn't guilty of anything.

'What do you mean? I didn't say anything bad.' I was offended and clenched my lips. Slavik smiled kindly, casting a conciliatory look at me.

'You're still young, Vitka. You don't understand a lot. Just swear that you won't blab to anyone. Ever.' His face tensed up and his look became hard. There was nothing for it but to pronounce a solemn oath, in which I said that in the event of my beginning to blab, my tongue would shrivel, I would go blind and my legs would stop functioning. Satisfied with what he'd heard, Slavik shook me firmly by the hand. Being in an elated frame of mind, he was ill-prepared for what, or rather, who, lay round the bend ahead of us.

'You again!' Before us rose the slight figure of the green-eyed youth with whom Slavik had clashed earlier in the day.

'Get lost!' barked Slavik, pushing him away. The boy emitted a piercing shriek, more like a war cry, and in a moment we were surrounded by a crowd of lads, twenty at least of them. They were of various ages and builds, to suit all tastes, as they say. Some were my age and younger, some, to all appearances, even older than Slavik. Not all were gypsies, it seemed: pale skin could be glimpsed beneath the dirt on some faces, and fair hair protruded from under some caps.

'What's all this, lads?' Slavik began calmly. Not a trace of his former aggression remained. Now his movements were supple and his voice soft. As he had considerable experience of street fights, Slavik knew it was stupid to play the hero in the situation that was developing.

'You're not so brave now, eh,' laughed Green Eyes.

'Well, how can you be brave when you're surrounded by such a fearsome lot,' my companion went on in a wheedling tone. The boys were pleased that Slavik considered them fearsome; actually they looked rather wretched and were fearsome only by dint of their number. They whooped loudly.

‘You don’t know the half of what we are. We can stab you!’ The gang leader squared his shoulders as he pulled a penknife out of his pocket. ‘See that?’ He waved it in front of our noses.

‘You’ve probably stabbed lots of people,’ said Slavik fawningly, examining the blade.

‘Lots,’ growled Green Eyes. ‘But don’t mess with me. You’ll take me now to your grub.’

‘What grub?’ said Slavik, his eyes round with astonishment.

‘Don’t give me that. Cut the chat-up stuff. I saw myself you’ve got a load of goodies there.’

Slavik bit his tongue.

‘So, you’ll take us now to your grub and then we’ll decide what to do with you. Visiting hooligans!’ He again roared with laughter and the others happily joined in. Having had their fill of laughing, two of the older boys took me and Slavik by the arms and pushed us roughly, telling us to go forward. We didn’t argue and obeyed in silence.

I was terribly scared and imagined vividly what these underage bandits, after sniffing paint, would do to us. What’s more, it was a crying shame to hand over our supply of food, especially when I thought of Ada and Khariton who had gone to such lengths to prepare it. All so that these miserable brats could scoff it. I despised them, despised them with all my heart. My blood boiled and it seemed that with every step my bodily strength was increasing and, if only the opportunity arose, I would wring the necks of all of them with my bare hands. As if aware of my attitude, Slavik gave a quick look in my direction and winked conspiratorially. We approached some lopsided iron gates which masked the ruins of a yellow three-storey block. It was then that Slavik thumped one of our escort as hard as he could on the ear, yelling to me: ‘Bend down!’

I bent double and Slavik took a second boy out. The whole action took a couple of seconds, and meanwhile, the rest (the majority of whom were a few steps ahead of us) tried to grasp what had happened. We did not hang around and took to our heels.

Followed by shouted threats from the gypsy boys, we ran at breakneck speed towards the forest. Slavik hurried me along, dragging me by my coat and shrieking that if I did not get a move on he would personally finish me off. I ran without feeling in my legs. My lungs were bursting from the frosty air and the same thought hammered away at my temples: 'Let them stay well behind. Lord help me!' I don't know – perhaps He heard my prayers or maybe we were simply running fast, but soon I could no longer make out the voices of our pursuers, who were falling further behind.

'Stop!' Slavik commanded at last. We stopped abruptly and I at once collapsed into a snowdrift, exhausted by the unplanned cross-country run.

'Looks like they're well behind,' said my companion, listening intently. The forest exuded silence; even the wind had dropped temporarily, as if astonished by what it had seen. Slavik sat down on the snowdrift in which I was lying, flung his arms wide and convulsively took in gulps of air.

'Not a bad training run!' Slavik laughed. 'But you did well. You didn't lose it.' He clapped me on the shoulder approvingly. Despite awful weariness and a pain in my chest, I was happy with myself.

'When will we go back?' I asked, gradually getting my breath back. Slavik's answer horrified me.

'We won't be going back.'

'What! All our stuff is at Father Innokenty's place. And our food.'

'To hell with it. That rabble is waiting for us at the church. If we ... they'd have our guts for garters, believe me.' Slavik swore roundly and kicked at a frozen lump of earth. I hastily crawled out of the drift, having felt the damp reach my back. If we were to spend the night in the forest, it was best to stay dry.'

'How will we get a fire going?' I buttoned up my overcoat and pulled my hat down more firmly.

'Rejoice in the fact that your rarely smoking friend has a lighter in his pocket. So saying, he pulled a piece of battered plastic out of his pocket – our guarantee that we would survive the night.

8.

We spent the night listening to the moaning of the wind, which launched furious attacks on our refuge, trying to annihilate it. Slavik did not close his eyes but kept the fire going, sitting with his knees drawn up to his chest. It was agonizingly cold and even the first rays of the morning sun did not warm us up. All they did was cast reflections of the snow onto our skin. My lips turned blue and it was so difficult to speak that Slavik and I confined ourselves to nods and gestures. When it was completely light, he suggested we should go. But where to? He did not know but said again we had to go. The wind got up; it kicked me in the side, blew me off my feet and tore the hoods off our heads, as if laughing at our helplessness. The thought flashed through my mind that the Lord was punishing us for the death of the Tatar and his sister. The wind was so cruel – it seemed to want to tear to pieces two boys making their way through the undergrowth. Slavik sank his neck into the collar of his jacket, creating the impression that his head came straight out of his shoulders. He cursed the bad weather roundly, declaring that when he was rich, he would go away to warm countries like Tahiti or the Bahamas. Wherever those places were, they were bound to be nice.

The further we went, the more blustery and cutting was the wind. Now and then I lost my footing, stumbled, and fell to my knees. Sometimes Slavik didn't even notice this and carried on forwards, battling the icy blasts. At such moments I would shout and call to him, but he couldn't hear, so loud was the howling wind. After a couple of dozen paces he would turn round to see how I was and, if he didn't see me, would come hurrying back. Slavik would pull me out of snowdrifts by the scruff of the neck, shake me down, and on we would go. This went on until we reached a ravine. A deep hollow, from which tree roots protruded in all directions, blocked our way.

'What now?' I asked fearfully.

'We keep straight on,' replied Slavik determinedly, and moved forward. I followed his example, stepping gingerly over the steep slope. We began to descend slowly. The wind got up, buffeting our backs. When we had got down as far as the middle, Slavik, who was two paces ahead of me, unexpectedly turned round, winked, and yelled:

'Don't funk it! Just a bit to go!' His voice sounded confident and I at once felt better, as if I'd gained additional strength. I smiled in reply, at which my companion pulled a funny face and raised his leg as if about to take a giant step down the slope – but just as he began to clown around the wind howled deafeningly and spun Slavik full circle. He staggered, threw out his arms and the next moment was somersaulting downhill. I was petrified, unable even to utter an audible gasp. There, at the foot of the ravine, Slavik lay, and did not move.

However hard I tried, I was not able to get down quickly. I groaned and gradually crawled down until, finally, I found myself (so it seemed to me) by Slavik's lifeless body. I touched it gently, then began to shake it vigorously. Soon Slavik began to groan faintly.

'Vitka, what've I done to it?' He nodded towards his leg. 'I can't feel the bastard.'

'Oh, Slavik!' I whistled, looking at my companion's right leg. Below the knee something sharp, like a broken tree branch, was protruding. I staggered back in horror.

'Oh!' I repeated and fell to the ground. I felt I would lose consciousness there and then.

'Blast you!' was Slavik's only response after he'd looked at his leg. Blood was streaming from an open wound.

'What shall we do?' I asked. Slavik said nothing for a minute or two, then suggested bandaging the wound. We didn't know how to do that properly, so we put tourniquets, improvised from scarves, above and below the wound as best we could.

Slavik's lips had turned white. 'We ought to free the leg from where that branch thing is,' he said, his voice sounding unusually quiet. But however hard we tried, we achieved nothing. At every attempt to reset the leg Slavik gave a piercing shriek. At one of the attempts I lost consciousness completely and only came round when Slavik rubbed snow over my face.

'It's no good.' He grinned sadly. I sat beside him, swaying from side to side, a cry of horror stuck in my throat. I wanted to run for help but Slavik begged me not to leave him.

'Let's give it one more try. Let me have a breather,' he said through gritted teeth, closing his eyes. In spite of the bandages, blood was seeping from the wound. I didn't tell Slavik about this, so as not to upset him. After all, we still didn't know how to put on bandages.

Slavik, it seemed, lost consciousness for some time, then, abruptly raising himself on his elbows, he shrieked with pain. He tried to stand up, but his protruding bones prevented him. Now not only his lips but his whole face and hands had lost their vital colours. He was lying on the ground, saying nothing and staring into space.

'How do you feel?' I asked hesitantly. It was agonizingly cold and the wind had still not abated.

'It hurts a lot,' replied my companion, and passed out again. When he came round, he opened his eyes and looked about himself fearfully.

'Are you still there?' he asked. I hastened to reassure him that I wouldn't budge an inch.

'We'll get you out of this. I don't know how, but we will,' I said, but Slavik merely smiled. His smile was strange and therefore not pleasant. For a time we stopped talking. Slavik was groaning. From time to time I turned him over to try to ease the pain, but then he would quickly lose consciousness and lie very still. I myself was gradually dozing off, but then he suddenly called to me: 'Vitka, do you remember how we watched *Crime and Punishment*?'

I nodded.

Slavik swallowed hard. 'Do you remember I said afterwards that punishment would certainly be yours if one did anything bad?'

'I remember.'

'Do you know, it's come.' He shuddered and gave a hoarse laugh. I knitted my brows in incomprehension.

'If you're talking about Akim, I take back what I said! No blame attaches to you!' I forced myself to say, stifling my sobs. I didn't want him to think I thought him guilty of the Tatar's death.

'No-o-o-o,' drawled Slavik with a grin. 'That was an accident with Akim. I had something else in mind.'

And with that, he began his confession. He recounted how, in the summer, when we were living with Grandma Marusya, he'd had a spat with her about Miwa (I knew about this anyway) and then, on one of the nights, as the rain was easing off (those days were infernally rainy), he had crept into the old woman's room and smothered her. He had pressed a pillow so hard onto her face that she had not been able to move at all and had given up the ghost very quickly.

'I did everything so quickly that Miwa didn't even wake up,' he said, and, to my horror, I heard how simple and easy it had been to take a life. It was as if he were talking about something completely commonplace.

'I'm like Raskolnikov, Vitka. Killing is simple. Especially a feeble old woman.'

'But why?' I forced the words out with difficulty.

'She wanted to report on us, to take Miwa away. I couldn't hand the little girl over to her. It was stupid, very stupid of me. Maybe if Miwa had stayed with her things would have turned out differently. But I ... Vitka, I'm not sorry about anything. I have no regrets. No!' Slavik forced himself to shout. It seems to me now that he showed such simulated lack of concern, such cold-bloodedness in order to provoke hatred and contempt in me.

'You go and live, Vitka.' A bitter smile twisted his lips.

'What do you mean by that?' My hands trembled.

'Leave me. Just leave me. My punishment has come, only I didn't think it would come so quickly.' He coughed.

'I can't.'

'Yes, you can. If you stay, we've both had it. That's too soon for you – you're still young.' Slavik smiled. His expression was now peaceful, as if the pain had eased. I stood up and, hesitating only for a second, began to scramble up the slope. I turned round several times to look at my former companion. He was lying motionless in the snow. At that moment I did not feel guilty for abandoning Slavik. Just as perhaps he intended – I hated him.

9.

I walked through the forest, stifling my sobs. In my time at the 'Old Lady Willow' I had learned to cry without tears. A howl of despair rose inside me and my heart contracted, suffocating it in my chest. It had been like that whenever Rusichka insulted me or one of the older children pulled me by the ears. And now this repeated itself. I set off at a run, but my legs would not obey me. I kept stumbling and getting caught up in branches. It seemed to me that Slavik was calling me, begging me to return, but my legs carried me onwards. The face of Sashka from the black-and-white photograph stood before my eyes. He was looking reproachfully at me and asking: 'Vitka, what have you done? Have you left your friend to die?' But I couldn't have acted differently. My conscience called on me to stop, to go back, to summon aid, but my heart was thumping. I could not entirely grasp what Slavik had done. I found it repellent that everything good between us had died instantly, as if I no longer had, and never had had, an older friend.

I ran further and further until finally I was exhausted. Walking quickly now, I noticed a path, sprinkled with snow and concealed behind a high hill. I followed it and came to a riverbank. The river was narrow. Not far from me was a wooden landing stage which extended practically to the middle of the river. Around it, the ice had been shattered, most likely by local fishermen. I sat down on the bank, my head in my hands. My brain was scrambled. I thought about my life, short, but so grown-up, which, so it seemed to me, had had everything: adventure, dangers, friendship, betrayal, humiliation and joy. Some people don't go through in years what I'd been through. Once again I recalled my silent friend Sashka. How I wanted to console him, to share his pain. I regretted that boys like him had not experienced such happy moments as I had. Then a surprising calm came over me, a calm such as made me fearful.

It was usually like this before a death, so Granny Marusya used to say. When death creeps steadily up on you, puts its hand on your shoulder, things became very, very calm. Death brings tranquility; nothing else worries you. You are ready to step boldly into its kingdom, side by side with it, as its equal. I stood up, collected some stones lying by the river and stuffed them into my coat pockets. They bulged under the weight. I was calm. As I approached the landing stage, I felt my heart give a leap, but this feeling quickly passed. Once, Fauna had told me about an unusual foreign writer, a woman, whose name, of course, eludes me. All I remember is that her surname was something like 'Wolf'. This woman had drowned herself. And, in order not to float, she had filled the pockets of her dress with stones, which she had gathered on a riverbank, as I had. How good her books were was difficult to judge. I hadn't read them, but her method was sound. I don't know whether she could swim, but I certainly couldn't. In my hometown there were no reservoirs, and we'd never heard of swimming pools, so I never got to learn. And even if there had been a river or a lake, there would have been few people to assume the role of teacher. Maybe just Slavik. He would certainly have taught me to swim. But that was then ...

When we set off in search of Grad, my heart had rejoiced at the mere thought that ahead of us lay unforgettable adventures. I aspired to a new free life. But everything turned out differently from what I had imagined in my dreams. And now here I was standing on the edge of a landing stage, my pockets stuffed with stones. At last I gave vent to tears. I didn't sob, but simply wept 'like a girl', as Rusichka would have said. Tears ran down my cheeks and I gradually began to feel better. I regretted one thing – that no one would now bring flowers to Miwa's grave. And I was still thinking about Slavik. My pangs of conscience gave me no peace and, in my mind, I begged forgiveness of him for having abandoned him. But I could not have done otherwise. My heart did not forgive me. The children of Grad were no more.

'What are you doing lad?' The unexpected sound made me shudder. I turned round and saw, three yards away, a stocky man with a big round face and a luxuriant moustache. He was looking at me in alarm.

'You ... that ... don't fool about.' The man threatened me with a fist that Slavik might have termed a fat bunch of fives. He was so big that even at a distance he seemed to tower over me, so help me.

'Don't come near me,' I yelled, gripping the railing, which I had previously scaled. I was now standing on a small projection. The man relaxed his fist.

'What are you doing, lad? Has something happened? I'll help you. Just tell me the problem!' His voice was low and hoarse, but there was something immensely prepossessing about it.

'You won't be able to help me,' I gulped, smearing tears over my cheeks.

'There, there. Tell Uncle Misha what's what,' he said, advancing a pace towards me.

‘Don’t come near me!’ I shouted, taking a pace forward, but when I was already knee-deep in cold water, I felt a searing pain. The stranger’s hand, like an iron vice, had gripped my neck and a moment later I was standing on the landing stage,

‘Aha! I’ve got you now,’ said the man and, instead of trying to squirm away or cry, I looked him in the eye. I don’t know what he saw in my look, but his grip slackened.

‘Where are your parents?’ he asked.

‘They’re dead,’ I said, untruthfully.

‘Are you doing this because of them?’ He nodded towards the river. I shook my head.

‘But do you have relatives? Where do you live?’ He got no answer to these questions. I lowered my eyes and did not myself understand how it was that my mind was a complete blank, but my body relaxed.

I came round in Misha’s hands. We were still on the landing stage. He was sitting with his legs tucked up, had sat me on his knee and covered me with his peacoat. He smelled of cigarettes and eau de cologne.

‘What’s your name?’

‘Vitka,’ I sniffled.

‘Do you want me to be your dad, Vitka? I’ll keep an eye on you to make sure you don’t accidentally drown, you silly ass.’ Misha laughed, his bottom row of iron teeth gleaming.

10.

The train wheels pounded; the engine puffed and revved, carrying us at full speed into the beautiful unknown. And this unknown really was beautiful, I could feel it. Me and my Daddy Misha were sitting on the lower shelf of a passenger compartment. There were two men sitting with us, one reading a newspaper, and the other sleeping. My Daddy Misha put boiled eggs and brown bread with butter on a newspaper. Our lunch. Before we got into the carriage, he had bought me a packet of popcorn, but made me promise that I won't touch it until I'd had lunch. I was going to keep my promise. I liked our compartment and the smell of it. I have never travelled on a train in such style.

Daddy Misha was a retired officer, a veteran of the Afghan war, where he'd lost his bottom row of teeth. He was concussed so heavily that he had to relearn how to speak. This was a solidly built, broad-shouldered man of forty-three years of age. He had a kind heart, despite the menacing look from under the black shaggy eyebrows. His wife had left him; she wanted to have children and Daddy Misha was not able to make her happy this way. Himself, he also wanted to have a horde of kids, more than anything, but no luck. His wife left, married someone else and with him she gave birth to strong boys and charming girls. Misha was able to forgive her and even blessed her new marriage, truly wishing her happiness because he did have a kind heart.

Misha lived in isolation; he was moonlighting as a night watchman and helped people when they needed something fixed (he had truly golden hands). And he also liked ice fishing. With him, I ate all the possible kinds of fish that could be found in local waters. When he went on a fishing trip on a cold January afternoon, he could never have guessed what kind of 'catch' he would be coming back with.

For the whole of the first month with my new father I said nothing. At that time communication between us was more like the taming of a wild animal. For hours on end I sat on a small round stool in a corner of the kitchen and could only be tempted off it with sweets and marshmallows. Whenever Misha tried to hug me, I would break out of his arms. In bed, I would groan all night and wake up in a cold sweat. Misha's rosy-cheeked sister Lyudka dubbed me 'the little wolf'.

Every day she brought us fresh bread and, for me, a bun with apple, blackcurrant or cinnamon spread. The abundance of fillings were just what my stomach wanted. Every day I grew to like the lady more and more.

When the first breath of spring could already be felt in the air, I began to speak. I went up to Daddy Misha, hugged his strong neck and whispered: 'Daddy, you won't put me in the boarding school, will you?'

'Of course not!'

'Even if you haven't got any money?' I said, pressing my whole body against him.

'I haven't got any anyway!' He laughed loudly and took me in his arms. From that moment onwards, he became my Dad.

Daddy Misha never asked about my past, never asked who I was or where I came from. 'Making conversation is women's work. The more reason to listen to them,' he said. In January 1996 my life began with a clean slate. In September that year, just after the monetary reform, he sold his two-room flat in the town of T. and, through friends, got documents for me which stated that retired officer Mikhail so-and-so was the father of Viktor so-and-so. Everything official. We got our things together, caught a train and went to meet our new life.

Di-Di-Dah – the train wheels rumbled as if overjoyed at our meeting. The train tried to go faster and faster, as if showing off to me, while I scoffed hard-boiled eggs and bread and butter, and listened to Daddy Misha's stories about the war in Afghanistan. And it seemed there'd been nothing before that, as if I'd just come into the world in Autumn 1996.

Epilogue

For many years I dreamed at night of Grad and of laughing Miwa. In my dreams there would come to me Akim who, without fail, would propose having a glass each, and Bagel, who was chasing crows in the yard. Only Slavik was not among them. As I woke up I often thought that perhaps he'd been able to escape or maybe his own Misha had come to his rescue. I don't know. Now that I'm over thirty and Daddy Misha is practically unable to see without glasses, I have been able to tell him my story, but I'll faithfully keep my pledge never to tell anyone about Grad, or about what happened there. For Daddy Misha I was a gift from God, a consolation sent from Heaven, and where my sinful soul had actually come from was a matter of indifference to him. Having left the town of T., we settled in a cosy little village in the North, where Misha bought a nice three-room house. In view of the fact that I was well behind my contemporaries, I was placed in Class Three of the local school. This did not stop me from making friends there, however, or even from being in the good books of my class teacher. Then came technical college and the army, after which I left the countryside to enter an institute (to the delight of Daddy Misha), but after a couple of years I went back as I was homesick. I occupied myself with household affairs and was happy. All the locals envied my and Daddy Misha's kitchen garden, and the fame of our apple orchard extended well beyond the confines of the village: none was more fruitful or produced such tasty apples, so it was said. But dreams of Grad did not leave me and I decided to visit the places of my childhood nightmares, in order to effect a once-and-for-all cure.

A year ago, citing urgent business, I caught a train, and in twenty-four hours I found myself in the town of M. It was the middle of October, the warmest October I remember in my whole life. The trees had begun to turn golden and a rich aroma hung in the air. A gentle breeze held me in its embrace, as if it recognized in this lantern-jawed man the same 'brave' Vitka who, in former years had the run of every street and gateway. But it was not part of my plans to stay long. I knew that Grey Willow Boarding School had been closed ten years earlier and the building was semi-derelict now. Nikichna had died at the end of the 1990s (and fearsome Licorice rather earlier, I imagine) and the

Director, Klara Fyodorovna, had long since retired. I knew nothing of the fate of Fauna, Rusichka or other heroes of my childhood years. I wanted to believe that Fauna had met a bold and handsome officer, had married him and now lived happily with him. As regards Rusichka, I was sure that her life had not gone well. It never does for people like that. I wished her a long, lonely life ...

Likewise, I knew nothing of my parents. When I visited our old house. I questioned the neighbours, but only got one, barely audible, answer from an old man. They had apparently gone abroad, with a child. That was all I knew. They had had a new baby and gone away. Was I sad about this? No. In fact I felt nothing. I even thought I would not recognise them. Their features had been erased from my memory. Only their outline remained ...

From M., by reliving our journey bit by bit, I moved heaven and earth to find the approximate location of Grad on the map. I was amazed that we four children had covered so many miles of road. After having a coffee and a cigarette at the railway station, I hired a driver with an old *Niva*. He took me to the neighbouring town, where I spent the night. In the morning I caught a bus and by that evening I arrived in the next little town, from where I again took a train. Three days of travelling took me to the village named after a celebrated Soviet general where, many years before, we had stolen confectionery and bought chickens. And, after a few hours spent wandering in the vicinity, I came across the ruins of Grad.

Two houses had been completely destroyed and of the house where we had lived, only the side wall remained, wreathed in wild vines. Whatever fire had not devoured, Time had annihilated. Inside, everything had contracted, as if the shapes of the past had sprung up before our eyes, and shrunk with our departure. I stepped across a mound of charred bricks and went up to the wall which, miraculously, was still intact. Placing my hand on it, I smiled sadly. More than twenty years earlier a crumpled sheet of paper in a frame had hung there: 'Pledged by the children of Grad', and alongside this the words 'Wishes of the children of Grad', on which each of us had included three wishes relating to our life in Grad. Miwa wanted to have a dog, as I remember, and Akim wanted to drink beer on Sundays ... And Slavik wrote that Miwa would always be his wife. I sat down, clasped my knees and closed my eyes. Scenes came to life in my memory. Beneath my feet a wooden floor was laid out and the walls were growing up out of the ground. A gramophone was playing Riccardo Fogli love songs. Miwa was dancing and teasing Bagel. Then there was Slavik, making something out of wood and casting patronizing looks at me and the other children.

I opened my eyes, picked up a pebble and scratched something on the wall. I had just one more wish ...

Before I left I decided to visit Miwa. I collected a handful of leaves and mixed them with dry stalks. The result was surprisingly attractive. I took the bouquet to the small hill I remembered so well, exposed to the wind on all sides, from which at sunrise and sunset there was an amazing view. To my surprise I found that my young friend's grave, although neglected, was untouched. Of course, the grave marker Slavik and I had once fashioned had gone, the wind having torn it to bits long ago, thus destroying all evidence that here, in the damp earth, lay Miwa 'a deer waif and gud frend'. But I could still make out the mound beneath which her body lay.

I apologised to the girl that I'd been so long in coming. 'Forgive me, but I won't be coming back again,' I said with a sad smile. I knew she would forgive me. Miwa was too kind to hold a grudge against anybody.

I lit a cigarette and contemplated a young ash tree which was growing near the girl's grave. The trunk of the tree was still slender, but the roots had already sunk deep into the ground and the gusty wind did not affect it at all. I remembered Slavik's grandmother who thought that all unhappy people became trees when they died. Young, beautiful trees. Their roots cling together and in spring comes tender bud-burst. I gazed at the young tree as it swayed in the wind and believed it was Slavik.

The nightmares of childhood left me forever.

Afterword

Not far from the village named after a famous Soviet general who, according to the villagers, lived here for several years, behind the woodland, beyond the lake, there was, in former times a *khutor*. The *khutor* burned down in 1996 and all that remains of it now is the tumbledown wall of one of the houses, and, covering a huge burnt patch, bindweed and ragweed, running wild. The apple trees have completely withered and the kitchen garden has become a quagmire. The local inhabitants find it difficult to say to whom the *khutor* had last belonged and why exactly it had burned down. The place has an evil reputation. Some people maintain that the sound of an old gramophone can be heard at night coming from the ruins, and it is well known that one might hear girlish laughter there, especially on fine spring days. On one occasion, a drunken peasant swore blind that he'd seen with his own eyes a tall, thin boy, with a birthmark like an exploding star under his right eye, carrying a huge sack towards the ruins and then simply dissolving into thin air. Old women say that if you come to the ruins on August 29th you can witness a strange sight: at a poorly furnished table sit three children – a pretty little girl, a swarthy boy and a lad of about fourteen. They are celebrating something and chatting animatedly, while a smoke-grey dog is running round the table. The table is laid for four and every year the children wait for this fourth guest. Sooner or later their guest will come. But when – is a matter of time.

Local young people merely laugh at the tales of the old women, but all the same they give the ruins a wide berth. And the few who do stumble across them, whether through ignorance or curiosity, can see a strange inscription scratched on the corner of a half-ruined wall: 'I want to go back home.'

Translator's Afterword

The Children of Grad is Maria Miniailo's fourth book and was published in 2019. The author was born in 1988, some three years before Ukraine achieved independence from the Soviet Union. Before that it was one of the fifteen constituent republics of the USSR and, although nominally independent and even having, theoretically, the right to secede, was firmly under the control of Moscow, with the Russian language and Russian culture predominant.

Most of the action of the novel takes place between 1994 and 1996. When it begins, in the Grey Willow Boarding School in the sleepy Ukrainian provincial town of M., the country had been independent for some three years. Some things had changed – the church, for instance had reopened – but the shadow of the Soviet years still loomed large.

The most unpopular teacher in the school is the teacher of Russian language, nicknamed Rusichka, who, for instance, always marks the anniversary of what she calls the Great October Revolution with enthusiasm. On the other hand, the most popular teacher is the teacher of Ukrainian language and literature, who is known as Fauna because of her love of wildlife and who, out of the classroom, speaks only Ukrainian to Viktor and his friends.

The relationship between the two cultures, Ukrainian and Russian, forms an important layer in what is a multi-layered novel. It takes on a darker tone when Slavik, who has been impressed by a Russian film version of Dostoevsky's *Crime and Punishment*, decides he is justified in emulating Rodion Raskolnikov's violation of the commandment 'Thou shall not kill'.

The main action of the novel – the escape from the school and the search for Grad and happiness – is instigated by Slavik, together with Viktor. They are joined, unexpectedly, by Akim and his sister Miwa who, symbolically perhaps, are described as Tatars. Grey Willow school has a multi-ethnic population; in addition to Russians and Ukrainians professing Orthodoxy, there are Jews, Moslems and Buddhists. Akim and his sister are Crimean Tatars, a people who were the original inhabitants of the Crimea and who were decimated by Stalin for alleged collaboration with the Nazis during World War Two. Crimea was part of Ukraine between 1954 and 2014, when it was forcibly annexed by Russia.

Slavik's vision of a land run by children, without any adult constraints, has echoes of J.M. Barrie's *Peter Pan* and Alain Fournier's *Le Grand Meaulnes*, although, as it turns out, suffering, violence and death are far from absent in Grad. The four children themselves have literary ancestors in the 'homeless' (*besprizornye*) children, orphaned by wars and famine, who fended for themselves on the streets of Soviet cities and featured in works by such writers as Esenin and Platonov. Like the *besprizornye*, the children of Grad are brave, resourceful and old beyond their years. They are unlike some of the children at Grey Willow or the gang of street toughs encountered by Slavik and Viktor in the town of K., who are nearer in character to those children portrayed by William Golding in *Lord of the Flies*, displaying the same propensity for casual, primitive violence.

By contrast, most of the older people encountered by the children are sympathetic and kindly: the head teacher of Grey Willow, Father Vladimir, the caretaker, Marusya, Ada and her husband Khariton, Lacho the gypsy, Father Innokenty and even Slavik's alcoholic mother "Auntie" Alla.

This novel can also be seen as a Bildungsroman – the journey from childhood, at the age of seven, to adulthood, at the age of thirty, of the narrator, Viktor. That he reaches that age is due to the kindly intervention of another older person, 'Daddy Misha', a veteran of the Afghan war, which ended with the withdrawal of Soviet forces from Afghanistan in 1989.

The Afterword of the novel returns the reader to another of its major themes; the relationship between human beings and the non-human living world of plants and animals. At Grey Willow school, for instance, Viktor acquires the ironic nickname 'Brave' because of his initial fear of the caretaker's ancient cat, Licorice. 'Fauna' acquires her nickname because of her love of Nature and gives Slavik a budgerigar. Slavik himself has tales of a 'tiger-wolf' found dead near Kherson and explains to Viktor what tigers are. Ada and Khariton, the old couple who befriend the children, own a cat and two formidable dogs, while Miwa dreams of also owning a dog, and eventually becomes the doting owner of Bagel. Her 'pregnancy' is explained by Slavik in terms of a worm in the stomach (Miwa thinks it has something to do with peas). Even the dead dog found in the grounds of Grey Willow becomes an object of some importance to Slavik and Viktor, who give it a reverential burial and the ghost of the long-dead Bagel seems to haunt the ruins of the *khutor* in the Afterword.

The plant kingdom too plays an important part in the novel, from Slavik's belief that dead human beings become trees to the crops carefully planted and harvested by Viktor at Grad. Almost the last image of the Epilogue is an image of trees. In the Afterword we reach the present day and see that Grad itself – in reality an abandoned and ruined farmhouse – has reverted to Nature. Just as vines are said to climb up the walls of Grey Willow, so a ruined wall wreathed in wild vines is all that remains of the *khutor*. To revert to Nature – ashes to ashes, dust to dust, is, of course, the fate of all living things. Childish dreams of happiness, on the other hand, simply come to an end. Viktor does find happiness, but not in Grad.

Maria Miniailo's novel is unmistakeably Ukrainian and is redolent of the post-independence era, but, like all important novels, it has relevance for the whole of humanity.

Michael Pursglove
2021